12
BLISS
STREET

12
BLISS
STREET

Martha Conway

 St. Martin's Minotaur ≈ New York

www.minotaurbooks.com

Library of Congress Cataloging-in-Publication Data

Conway, Martha.
    12 Bliss Street / Martha Conway.—1st ed.
      p. cm.
    ISBN 0-312-31543-0
    1. San Francisco (Calif.)—Fiction.   2. Kidnapping victims—Fiction.
I. Title: Twelve Bliss Street.   II. Title.

PS3603.O67A613   2003
813'.6—dc21

                                          2002191954

First Edition: June 2003

10 9 8 7 6 5 4 3 2 1

For Richard, John Henry, and Lily,
and for my mom, in memory

Acknowledgments

My grateful thanks to Alice Boatwright, Richard Conway, Christian Crumlish, Maggie Gifford, Jim Henry, Sonia Lagan, Katie McGlade, Carol Manning, Briggs Nisbet, Kelley Ragland, Miriam Gamoran Sherin, Bill Spieth, the Spiethsteins, Matt Williams, and, especially, Richard Frankel.

One

After her divorce Nicola began buying lingerie: dark blue contour bras, demi bras in little-girl white, embroidered bustiers, stretch mesh chemises, and a red girdle with removable garters that the catalog listed as a Jolly Susan. She wore silk panties to work and at night bathed in almond oil baths, the scent of which reminded her of the young boy in Istanbul who sold her husband a wallet. That had been their last trip together as a couple, a belated sort of honeymoon. But it was just another mistake, along with the home haircare pyramid scheme, the water bed, and Scooter's office fling (if you could call a video-delivery van an office), all of which led to Nicola's increasing awareness that her husband was unstable and not in the fun way.

They were together for four years and the no-fault was final four years ago. Nicola married Scooter (Scott, as she tried calling him in the last months) straight out of college, confusing his exuberance for joie de vivre, but as it turned out it was more like the excess of someone in panic. They moved to San Francisco with a group of friends who once a year rented a Winnebago and drove to Tahoe naked, for fun. Nicola was now thirty-one, still living in San Francisco, and had fantasies of sitting in a bar wearing a bustier under her business suit. And where were her friends? Back in New York, back in Michigan, back in Louisville, back with their families or doing time in obscure cities for career reasons, all respectable, all buying, she supposed, one hundred percent cotton underwear.

Sometimes when her boss corrected her in a meeting (usually erroneously), Nicola shifted just a little to feel the silk of her panties slide over her skin. The feeling was better than chocolate.

The morning Nicola saw or thought she saw Scooter again after almost three years she was sitting on a San Francisco muni train wearing a new chocolate-colored silk bra with a matching teddy under her work blouse. In her purse was a notice of eviction. Nicola kept taking the paper out and looking at it, then putting it back in its envelope thinking, I can't think about this now, and then taking it out again. She worried by nature; this was one of the things she disliked about herself. Also her need to plan, weak arms, and a tendency to be polite rather than truthful. She had dark shoulder-length hair, very straight, and straight dark eyebrows. There was something Asian about her appearance, an illusion, though she liked to wear short flared trousers when she could find them.

Nicola looked at the letter again. It seemed so final, so here it is and there is nothing more to say. Frustration clutched her stomach like hunger. She loved her home; she did not want to move. She did not want anything to change. After she left Scooter stability seemed much more appealing, and Nicola had become very habitual over the last few years. Every morning she power-walked on the raised bicycle path along the beach, visited her dog Lester, who lived with her friend Audrey (Nicola's landlord wouldn't let Lester in the house), then rode the muni train to work. It was an easy commute, only fifteen minutes, even in traffic. The train went straight up Taraval Street, leaving the ocean behind for coin laundries and manicure shops, copy shops, liquor stores, Chinese herbalists, an Italian restaurant that served Hawaiian entrees on the first Monday of the month. Nicola looked out the window while soft beautiful women waited on the corner like Chinese angels with their hands on their hips. Why should she give any of this up? When she lived downtown it took her fifty-five minutes door to door by the express.

At West Portal the train entered a closed station that led to a tunnel; this was her stop. As she waited for the doors to open, she noticed a smallish man on the opposite platform wearing a large brown overcoat. He was in profile, and it took a moment to register. Then all at once she turned to fully face him, willing him to turn too. He didn't turn; he stood still, facing the mouth of the tunnel. Nicola climbed off her train just as another train came in—"Scooter?" she called, but the noise level was too high. She turned and went for the escalator, hoping to get a closer look, but the train just in from the tunnel opened its doors and the man got on and sat in a seat facing away from her. Nicola rode up the gritty escalator anyway, crossing over to the next platform and coming back down to see if she could get a better look from this side? But his train was pulling away.

"Scooter? Scott?" she called again thinking some of the windows might be cracked open, but the man did not move his head and although she began to run she couldn't catch up with him.

Nicola worked as a design engineer at an Internet design company called Slash Dezine with offices just three blocks away from the West Portal station. Most of her coworkers were under twenty-five, addicted to sugar and caffeine, and could sleep four hours a night and yet still wake up with great-looking skin. Today was Friday, which meant a

CPR meeting—customer project review—at ten A.M. sharp. This was actually difficult to get going since most of the staff straggled in around noon, then worked until one or two in the morning. The exception was her boss, Guy, who was almost for sure at least forty and who had dark, curly hair only slightly too long and long sideburns and was altogether very seventies looking. Nicola had been slightly attracted to him before she realized he was an asshole.

"Head count," said Guy. "Where's Rick?"

Nicola sat down across from Audrey, her closest friend and the one who had basically gotten her this job two years ago. Eleven of them—everyone but Rick and Alia, the CEO, who was at a Death by Yoga retreat—were sitting around a table in the small conference room overlooking another building's exhaust system. Alia's father owned the building and let them use the third floor almost for free. A group of dental offices took up the second floor and, at street level, there was a beloved coffee shop, which paid an enormous rent to make up for the third-floor write-off.

"Okay, Rick is off the team," Guy said. "Just kidding. Okay, who's coffee girl? Laney, are you coffee girl?"

"How 'bout a coffee boy, ever hear of one of those?"

"You are so retro," Guy told her. He sneezed. "Just bring in the whole pot and everything."

He was the only one who drank office coffee; the others sat around the conference table holding oversized cardboard cups from the cafe downstairs. Laney came back in with a glass coffeepot and one mug and set them down in front of Guy, who sneezed again. He had some kind of nasal-sinus-histamine problem and some days sneezed almost continuously, often violently enough to leave the room, yet he never carried a tissue. There were times when Nicola thought, if he sprays my keyboard one more time. . . . Recently she began keeping hygienic baby wipes on her desk.

"Ah, God," Guy said. He unscrewed the top to his prescription nasal spray with hydrocortisone (or was it something silicon based?) which acted as a protective buffer between his sinuses and the outside world of pollen, dust mites, and airborne dander by thoroughly coating his nasal passages with something or other—"like hair implants," as Nicola's coworker, Audrey, explained.

"Ah, God, okay," Guy said again. He took another shot of his inhaler and shook his head a few times—maybe to distribute the spray more evenly?—then turned stiffly toward Nicola.

"Nicola," he said. "What's the word on Concentric Circles? Figure out the confetti problem?"

She put down her coffee. "Well, as I explained in my memo—"

"What memo?"

"Yesterday's memo. In your box."

"Okay, I didn't get it, but go on."

Nicola paused. If she was too technical, Guy would have to pretend to understand and that pissed him off.

"We basically have to do a goNetURI and call in an outside program." She listed a couple of animation programs that Guy always blocked.

"Why can't the browser handle it?"

"There's a bug and almost half the time it crashes."

Guy wrote something down.

"Go Net whatever is not right," he said. "You should use a mouseover command, but in any case, you can figure the specifics out later."

She had figured it out, it was goNetURI. Nicola felt a familiar wave of frustration and she moved herself slightly on the seat to feel her silk panties while Guy listed his usual technical grievances and why her solution might not work. He really was awful. His wife had been in a girl band in the eighties and now sold facial treatments over the Internet, and they had one little boy who also had some serious allergy problems—or was it a learning disability, or that problem where every so often you forget to breathe? Nicola couldn't remember exactly, but she tried to keep little Guy, Jr., or whatever his name was in her mind while Guy was sneezing on her and explaining how she was, once again, wrong. But it was hard. Her friend Audrey was too afraid of him to roll her eyes, but you could see that she wanted to. Only Laney provoked him openly, and they were probably having an affair.

Rick came in at last and Guy treated him to a paragraph of friendly abuse and then began to question him about college basketball and they laughed about some coach for ten seconds or so at which point Nicola shifted her attention back to herself. She thought about Scooter, then the eviction notice, then Scooter again. The man in the overcoat could not have been him. When had she ever seen Scooter out of his jean jacket? Though it *was* pretty cold out. The conference room window was decorated with a string of red chili pepper lights— it was Christmastime, which meant rain. Her eviction notice, served to her that morning by an overweight man with a ponytail, had come in a red envelope. A malicious joke, or did they always come that way?

Nicola took a sip of her coffee. There was one thing she did know: she would never find a house as good as the one she had now. A workman's cottage they called it, ninety years old and hidden from the street behind a larger family house. She had lived there for four years and the rent, which was absurdly low to begin with, had never gone up. A similar place could go for over three times as much in this market. Maybe more.

"So we set on that, Nicola?" Guy was saying. "Hello?"

"What?" Nicola looked up—she had missed the segue back.

Guy snapped his fingers. "Come on, come on."

"Yeah, okay, I'm set," Nicola said. She picked up her pen. "Test a mouseover command? I'm set."

"Jesus, I was talking about Fred," Guy said. He looked at Laney and rolled his eyes. Nicola felt her face grow warm.

"He called me this morning," Guy said again. "He wants me to sit in on your next meeting."

"He wants *you* to sit in?"

"That's what he said."

"But you haven't even seen the latest milestone!"

"Well, Fred tells me you're hard to work with."

Nicola stared at him. "What?"

"I know, I know." Guy laughed, and Nicola felt her face get even redder. "But I was thinking about it and I thought, maybe you just need to smile more."

"Excuse me?"

"You know, smile, be nice. He's a good client. I'm just saying."

"You think if I smile that will solve all of Fred's problems?" Nicola asked.

"I'm just saying."

"And yet I've never seen you smile in my life," Nicola said.

Guy raised his eyebrows. "You can be a little sharp," he said. "People don't like that."

"I just . . . I want to get the job done. I want it to be good. Fred and I are actually on the same side on this."

"No, Fred is on the paying side."

"He wants certain features and when we deliver he decides he wants something else," Nicola told him. "He's like a man who keeps arguing with his architect: take down this wall. It doesn't matter how often we explain that then the whole structure will collapse."

"Why are you fighting me?" Guy asked.

Because I'm right, Nicola thought.

"Just, be nice when you tell him something won't work," he said, and he brought out his inhaler. "Smile, flirt with him a little if you have to."

I can't believe this, Nicola thought.

"Otherwise," Guy said, "I'll have to sit in, and you know how I hate to sit in. I remember all the times I'm forced to sit in when I'm cutting the bonuses."

Was that a threat? I practically run this whole business, Nicola thought, and she looked across the table at Audrey, who raised a pierced eyebrow back. Nicola fought the temptation to say what she felt, a familiar feeling. She was from a hardworking family, a family of professionals, all of them smart and patient and willing to try difficult tasks. Her father ran his own cement business; her mother was a speech therapist who specialized in children with head traumas. Nicola grew up in a large stone house in Cleveland Heights, Ohio, and although they had plenty of money she and her brothers went to neighborhood schools—or, as her mother put it, they supported the public school system. Nicola was the middle child, the neat one, the only girl. At seven she was reading to blind children on Saturday afternoons while across the hall her mother fund-raised for upgraded equipment for them. She was raised to be productive, useful, helpful, organized—in short, valued for her abilities.

And now she was being asked to, what, smile?

"So, before we move on," Guy continued, holding his inhaler out like a pipe, "let's go over Nicola's tasks. One, test browser solutions before you go all geeky on me. And two, smile. Simple, right? I'm sure you have a lovely smile."

Nicola looked at Audrey again then looked back at Guy.

"Don't you have a lovely smile?" Guy asked her.

She smiled.

"Lovely," Guy said. "Let's move on."

He turned to Rick again and Nicola felt her face stiffen with embarrassment. What an unbelievable asshole. And he was so wrong about the browser solution. He was just so consistently wrong. She would have to do what she usually did: fix the problem and show Guy the result and then listen to Guy tell her that since it was fixed, okay, but really she could have saved a lot of time by doing something or other else. Mostly she tried not to think too much about it, but the day was fairly crappy already at only ten twenty-five A.M. and she felt annoyed and sick of the whole game. Nicola looked around the stainless-steel table at everyone waiting for their share of abuse, while Guy sneezed again violently (his bowed head praying over his coffee cup) and she thought if I were his son I'd hold my breath too.

Two

The morning did not get any better. When she got back to her desk Nicola found e-mail messages from three customers: one had a crashed disk and asked if she could send thirty-five pieces of artwork all over again; one hadn't paid for their last job and wanted Nicola to "rethink the billing"; and one who called her incompetent.

Nicola stared at the word on the screen. He actually wrote the word incompetent. How could he say that when last month she customized a java program that solved a problem no one at his company had been able to solve?

She looked up at the whiteboards above her desk, where part of the code she had written for him was still visible. Nicola shared a room with five other people: Audrey, the Web master; Christian, Andrew, and Louise, the other designers; and Carlos, an artist. Their desks, wooden tables with two or sometimes three computers on each, were divided from each other by industrial metal shelving. Aside from the computer equipment everything in the room was fairly low end—Christian's desk, for instance, was held together by a bungee cord.

Still, it was a beautiful space: high ceilings, a skylight, and along one entire wall a stained oak bookshelf that Audrey made when the company was first getting started, five years ago. Guy had his own office, Alia and her assistant, Laney, sat in the large front room looking out over the street, and the rest of them shared two rooms in the back. Everyone had their own plastic toys and water pistols and user manuals and extra cables or modems, everyone had the same trouble finding the perfect pencil or an empty storyboard page, but they all shared whatever they had. There was a lovely green velvet recliner in the corner where you could sit, flip through a magazine, take a break. Next to it stood a fan that ran without a knocking sound unless it was really, really hot.

Bastard. That code was beautiful, so simple and useful. Nicola made herself compose a polite reply back, answering his charges one by one, but as the morning wore on she became hungry and less and less patient. Her head felt like a heavy, porous rock steeped in toxic thoughts and even coffee didn't help, though she tried it many times.

Where can I go? she kept thinking. It was a bad time for renters and she did not have enough money to buy. As she stood up from her chair she kicked an empty box into the wall with more passion than she had intended.

"*What* is up?" Audrey asked. "Is it diet day or something?"

Nicola sat back down and looked at her monitor. She really didn't feel like going into the whole eviction thing with everyone right there.

"Oh, I thought I saw Scooter on the muni."

"He's back from L.A.?" Audrey asked. She had gone to college with Nicola and Scooter, and had even lived with them for a while before she married a pierced, red-headed surfer named Declan.

"Just someone who looks like him."

"Doesn't he still owe you money?"

"And I'm sure that's why he's here," Nicola said. Why *was* he here? Or whoever it was. Another customer called her, got snippy over the phone, and this time Nicola was actually rude.

"Nicola," Audrey warned when Nicola hung up.

"I know, but you know I get like this when I'm hungry."

"So get some food," Audrey said.

Nicola looked at her watch. There was a man who often ate lunch at a nearby café and they had begun to say hello to each other; he had dark skin and almond-shaped eyes and he usually ordered chorizo pizzeta, a specialty there. She didn't know his name but she thought of him as Chorizo. In her purse was a small vial of angel water— orange flowers mixed with myrtle and rose—which she planned to sprinkle on her neck and behind her ears and maybe a little bit under her teddy before lunch. He didn't usually get there until one, but she was so hungry.

"Do a cookie run while you're out," Carlos said.

"Chocolate ones," Louise said.

"No, the ones with sprinkles."

"Those are carcinogenic," Nicola told him.

"How can sprinkles be carcinogenic? They're made for like three-year-olds."

"Survival of the fittest," said Christian, a vegetarian who maintained a very active Web site on meat production in America.

"You're maxed on sugar anyway," Audrey told Carlos. "Look, you've lost control of your line."

"It's supposed to look that way."

Nicola walked over to his desk to look at his drawings.

"Christ, Carlos!" she said. "Are these Fred's? These are supposed to be in the computer by Monday! You're going to have to call Fred and ask him if we can reschedule the meeting because I am not talking to him one more time today, and then you better dose up on caffeine or something, because if we don't show him something soon he's going to walk, and I wouldn't blame him. Put your dart gun down, I'm not kidding. You need to organize yourself; this table is a mess."

"Whoa," Carlos said. "Mommy's back."

"Oh, all right, but you know how I am; you're cutting it too close for me."

"Go get some food," Audrey said. "Carlos will work on it over lunch, right, Carlos?"

"It will be fine, Nicola," Carlos told her. "I have something in mind that's absolutely bulletproof."

"Bulletproof?"

"Don't get hung up on the negative vibes," he said.

Nicola stared at him. "I'm going to lunch," she decided. She picked up her purse and tried to normalize by telling herself they were a good team and they always came through, but meanwhile she could feel Carlos watching her with that little grin on his face which at times like this she hated.

"But you've absolutely got to work on this while I'm gone," she couldn't help adding.

Carlos said he would and then watched her, still smiling, as she closed the office door behind her. A few seconds later when the elevator dinged he looked over at Audrey.

"She needs a lot more than food," he announced.

Outside it was windy and cold and the man Nicola thought of as Chorizo was already sitting at the West Portal Café reading an article about pigeons poisoned near City Hall. It was a bit soon for lunch, but his mid-morning massage had ended earlier than usual and he decided to sit and look over the afternoon paper, which had just come out.

The front page featured a grainy black-and-white photograph of a policeman touching a dead bird with his foot, and as he looked at it he found himself thinking about his wife, who was currently imprisoned in Cyprus. His common-law wife. But is it still common law if you haven't seen each other for over five years, he wondered? He read the first paragraph of the article again. No one had seen anything. The police claimed the act was deliberate, done at night, chicken feed dipped in poison then scattered on the curb. He thought how his wife would enjoy this sort of thing. Did she ever get newspapers, he wondered? There was so little he knew. Did she read? Exercise? Did they even have pigeons flying around where she was? The article, he noticed, did not say what kind of poison was used.

He put the paper down for a moment to examine one of his fingernails. He had not exactly been physically faithful, but then again neither of them had ever been physically faithful even when they lived together. What they had was different. More. Americans could never understand this. He thought of a television talk show host he had recently seen, who called people like him spiritually defunct. She understood nothing. The first principle of Shambhala is to be unafraid of who you are.

Turning his left hand toward the light, he noticed the thumbnail could use some shaping, and he rubbed it gently with his forefinger. It had been five years, almost six, since he had seen his wife, but he would not give up on her. He would not give up, but in the meantime he knew she would forgive him his needs. It didn't mean he wouldn't wait for her. He would wait. He would wait, save money for the legal expenses, for the bribes, for whatever it took to get her out. All the money he earned was for her. He would never tell her about the girls, there was no need, but if she knew she would understand. They were all dead anyway.

Chorizo picked up the newspaper, folded the page back, then began to read the article about the pigeons once again. And he thought: Well, and perhaps she has girls herself, there in the jail on Cyprus.

———————

Nicola left the building without her jacket and immediately regretted it but didn't go back. A man reduced to selling flowers from the back of a Volvo station wagon was cleaning the sidewalk with an industrial hose, and a spray of water caught her arm as she passed. West Portal was dry and flat, once an arroyo, and it was said that its winds would drive you to sex or suicide. Someone was always spraying the sidewalk and the wind carried droplets up onto passersby, mostly women with strollers and men begging change wearing army jackets and unusual headgear.

What is the point, Nicola was thinking as she gave one man some change. Usually she enjoyed doing all the little tasks that spelled survival—mailing her tax returns or buying stamps or scheduling dental appointments—but on days like this she could imagine letting everything go until she was one of those people with unpaid bills in a shoebox under her bed and an eviction notice served—the last of which, of course, had already happened. And then what? The man begging change could imagine what; at some point he could see himself here on the street. Or at least, Nicola thought, he could not *not* see himself here on the street. Well, thank God, she wasn't that far gone. Or was this the beginning of that kind of nightmare? It seemed unlikely, given her job and her taste for trendy shoes.

The café was only a block away and as Nicola pushed open the heavy glass door she was surprised to see Chorizo already sitting at a far table. The café was small and narrow with white plastic chairs and red-and-white-checked plastic tablecloths that wrinkled in hard little waves.

There was an open table near Chorizo and Nicola took it, smiling when he looked up, since they were at that point. He was older than she was, in his late forties probably. She liked that. Maybe he was even older.

He dressed well and was tall, or medium tall, with thick dark hair like the feathery waves of a raven—or did she mean vulture? A black-

bird, that was it. Today he was wearing a button-down shirt in an
unusual shade of blue, and dark pants. As she looked at the laminated
menu Nicola stopped thinking about Guy and Scooter and her landlord, and she began to alternate instead between fantasies of a short
passionate affair with Chorizo—food in the bed sheets, et cetera—
and a milder, long-lasting relationship as she saw him through his
later years, listening to his stories about dinners with Noam Chomsky
or Butros Butros Ghali and helping him step into the tub.

Her waiter resembled a goat, with glasses so small they looked
like eyelids. "I'll have the chorizo pizzeta," Nicola told him.

Chorizo looked up briefly at that. "They do those so well," he said
to her, then returned to his paper.

She turned to see what he was reading—another article about the
dead pigeons, she saw—but although she had a comment ready he
didn't look up again. Nicola pulled out her *SF Weekly* and opened
it, angling the paper so Chorizo could see she was reading the Per-
sonals if he happened to look. This she had planned in advance. All
around her people were dressed casually but well, typical San Francisco. The café was cold, also typical, and Nicola found herself craving
hot chocolate. It was said Montezuma drank fifty cups a day on the
days he visited his harem, and she thought about the plumbing system
in Mexico, then lifted her hand to her nose to smell the angel water
on her fingertips and glanced at Chorizo.

Was he Russian? Mexican? There was definitely something Asian
or Indian or Slavic about his wide, flat cheekbones and almond eyes.

The goat served him his pizzeta and a small side salad with feta
cheese and lime, then brought a basket of mini corn muffins to Nicola's table. The food here was unusually good. Chorizo ate the Eu-
ropean way, keeping his fork in his left hand. Turkish, Nicola
decided. His fingers were thin and long and there was something a
little wolfish about him, but in a sexy way. Looking down at the
stained tablecloth she let herself imagine his fingers unbuttoning her

blouse slowly, and the feel of the shirt over her shoulder blades as he drew it off.

When her own pizzeta came, she plucked three paper napkins from the metal dispenser, then ate the American way: with her hands. The sauce ran over her lips and she wiped her mouth and imagined how his hands would trail from her neck to her shoulders to her spine, his thumbs on the small of her back, his mouth on her throat. She imagined him lifting her chocolate-colored teddy over her head. If she turned slightly Nicola could see his dark hair in the corner of her eye, and she liked this, a little frisson of reality in playland.

"Did you enjoy the pizzeta?" Chorizo asked softly.

She could feel him unfasten her bra. She could feel his warm breath on her back.

"Lost in your own world?" he said.

At that Nicola looked up. He was watching her. His slanted dark eyes made him seem worldly, knowing, as if her mind were an un-rolled map before him. Was he wolfish, or more like a fox? All at once Nicola felt both caught and excited—he knows exactly what I was doing, she thought. There was a sign she had often noticed down the street: "Suspicious activities are recorded and forwarded to the appropriate authorities"—a titillating idea. A wave of power rushed through her.

"Exactly," she said, looking him in the eye.

Did his expression change? He looked at her more closely.

"I've seen you here a few times," he said. "You must work nearby."

"Very close."

"What do you do?"

"I'm a dental hygienist," she said.

The lie—where did that come from? As soon as she said it Nicola felt another electrical charge, and the thought came to her that she could do anything, it didn't matter, what did it matter? The morning

was a waste; the whole year, let's face it, was not so great, but forget
it; here she was now, here she was, and she was ready for something
unplanned and unordinary.

"You must like mouths," Chorizo was saying, then smiled, showing his teeth.

And she thought: they have their uses.

Chorizo looked Nicola over. She surprised him, she really did, and he
liked that in a woman. He put away his paper, then moved his chair
slightly closer to her table, turning so she could see the birthmark on
his neck, which other women said was sexy. Not his wife, never his
wife, but some of the others. A vampire's kiss, one called it. He liked
that.

She was bolder than he had imagined. He saw it in her eyes:
something pleased her. A woman who likes pleasure; well, well. In
the last few weeks he had pegged her as the administrative type—
one who pays an unhealthy attention to details. The nurse with pursed
lips. But here she is, smiling and showing her palms, which everyone
knows is a sign of flirtation.

And then, when she bent down to pick her napkin up from the
floor, he saw the shiny chocolate-colored strap under her blouse.

Well, well, he thought again.

Lingerie.

She's wearing lingerie. And all at once he could picture how she
might look without the business suit. Wearing just—was it a camisole? And perhaps matching panties? He could see her on the bed
he used, her skin going cold. The peculiar shininess that comes at
death. She could be the next one. He definitely saw it. She could be
next.

He moved his chair closer.

"**And what do** you do?" Nicola asked, picking up her napkin.

"Oh, like everyone else I'm in computers," Chorizo told her. On the wall behind him stood a picture of a spiky asparagus, and Nicola strained to listen as Chorizo spoke about high-potency something or other. The truth was she didn't really care about his job. On his wrist he wore a thin silver bracelet and he had a birthmark like a dark fingerprint on the side of his neck.

He had very good manners, she could see that. His eyes never left her face. She wiped pizzeta sauce from her hands and considered. He was kind of a smooth guy. Too smooth? To be honest he wasn't really her type, but she was feeling good now for the first time all day, possibly all week. And maybe the whole point was that he wasn't her type.

Plus the mark on his neck was kind of sexy.

"Are you from California?" Chorizo was asking.

The café's fluorescent lights blinked for a moment, a line of long, sharp clouds overhead, and Nicola hesitated then told the truth. "I was born in Ohio."

"Ohio. I've always liked the sound of that name."

"But I grew up all over," she lied, twisting her napkin. She told him her parents were in the foreign service and her first memory was when she lived in Nigeria and a chicken attacked her—a story her college roommate once told.

"I'm from Turkey," Chorizo told her. Nicola nodded, she'd guessed that, and looked down at his loafers—polished brown affairs that seemed to be woven from thin strips of bark and then glazed.

"A little town you've probably never heard of called Kas."

That surprised her. "Kas!" she said, looking up at him again. "I've been to Kas! I bought a rug in Kas! I loved that town. I ate fresh calamari for breakfast there every day, just caught that morning."

This was the truth, though on the last day there she felt too sick to go out afterwards, and later Scooter wouldn't let her buy a lobster-in-a-box in the Boston airport while they waited for their connection home. Chorizo asked her where she had bought her rug and when she described the store he said, oh yes, the owner was married to the Australian who worked in a jewelry store next door. They spoke about the cafés along the harbor and the underwater excavation led by a professor from Massachusetts, which Nicola and Scooter (she didn't mention Scooter) had seen from a tour boat.

"Kas is a beautiful town," Chorizo said, picking up his water glass. "It's unfortunate that it has no beach."

"The ports aren't deep enough for the cruise boats. You're lucky in that."

Chorizo pulled in even closer and put his water glass down on her table—a gesture Nicola found oddly intimate. His hand so nearly brushed hers that she could feel, for a moment, a sudden warmth. "Ah, but they bring in money," he said. "Now, Egypt. Have you ever been to Egypt?"

"I've always wanted to see the Temple of Isis," she told him.

"An interesting cult. There's a legend that she preferred eels for her breakfast. She sent her best fishermen to catch them and they always went in the dark, when there was no moon."

"Because eels come out at night," Nicola said. "To feed."

"That's right." He nodded. "The ancient priests who took care of her temple bathed five times a day."

"After visiting the purgatorium," Nicola said.

Chorizo said, "So you know about this too?"

He smiled then, and Nicola, placing her twisted-up napkin on the table like some kind of offering, smiled back. Her heart was racing. She didn't just feel good, she felt great. She felt as though she were flying, or might fly, or at least knew what it felt like to fly—the sensation of strength in her arms (or wings or whatever), and the lift and the power and the speed.

Chorizo watched her listening to him and he couldn't help smiling, she seemed so young and so genuine, and she smiled back not knowing that he had his plans and they might include her.

The waiter came to take away the spidery nest of food left on her plate, and while she was looking away he calculated quickly: about five feet five, say a size eight. Many things were in his favor. They were in a corner, no one was looking at them. A chance meeting, that was good too.

What comes is meant to come, he thought.

The waiter stepped away with the plates. Nicola looked back at Chorizo.

He understood the signal. It was his move.

"I have an idea," he said. He looked at her steadily. If all went well he would never be able to return to the café—he couldn't risk it. A pity. He did so enjoy their pizzeta, but that was—what was the phrase?—the downside of the trade.

He smiled again.

"Let's do something foolish," he said.

Three

fter lunch Nicola went up the side staircase of her building and in through the fire door—which claimed to be alarmed but wasn't—so she would not have to see anyone right away. The hallway was empty; the whole floor seemed empty. Group lunch, she guessed. She hated the smell of this side of the building, which had recently been recarpeted, and went straight to the bathroom, which was large and cold with exposed pipes and a cement floor and a large poster of Audrey Hepburn in tights.

The door closed behind her. No one was here, thank goodness. Nicola went over to the mirror and looked at herself. Oh, my God, her hair looked just terrible. She touched it, trying to rearrange it back into something more reasonably called hair, then started to cry.

Oh Christ, oh God, she was thinking. What was wrong with her? Things had been going so well with Chorizo. Outside it looked like rain, but it had looked like rain for days without anything and newscasters were beginning to throw around the word drought. Nicola was just looking for a tissue in her purse when she heard a movement in one of the stalls and someone said, "I'll be gone in a minute." She stopped crying. "Who is that?" she asked.

"Nicola?"

"Audrey?"

"What's going on?" Audrey asked from inside the stall. Her voice sounded faint, as if passing through a sieve.

"Oh nothing," Nicola said. She thought she might start crying again. "It's just, you would not believe what a bad day I've had and how awful my hair looks," she said.

Audrey came out and washed her hands and looked at Nicola, then she soaked some paper towels in cold water.

"Your hair doesn't look so bad," she said. She gave Nicola a wet paper towel. "Here, put this on your eyes."

"Thanks."

"What is it, Scooter?"

"Scooter?" Nicola had forgotten about him. "No. God, no. No, it's just, there was this man at lunch today. At the café. I've seen him there for the past couple of weeks, actually, but today for the first time we began to talk and it was amazing because I was, to tell you the truth, I was fantasizing about him while I was eating and I don't know, I was into it, and then out of nowhere he began to talk to me. It was like he knew what I was doing, that's what it felt like at least, and I found that very exciting, it was very exciting, and our conversation was . . . it had a rhythm, you know? When things are, I don't know, *going*. And then we got to the part where he asked me out. And you know what I did? I said no."

"Why did you say no?"

"I don't know! He said he was taking the afternoon off to see the Picasso exhibit, and did I want to come? And although I was expecting something—well, really I thought he was just going to ask me for my phone number and maybe that was what freaked me, this immediate decision. I got all timid and I did what I always do, I said no."

"You don't always say no."

"I always say no, my first response is always to say no."

"What about that other guy, the C.P.A.?" Audrey asked. "What happened to him?"

"Oh, he had really chubby fingers, which was especially apparent when he wore his wedding ring." Nicola took the paper towels off her eyes and looked in the mirror.

"No way!"

"Yeah I ran into him at the Safeway last weekend and he was wearing this wedding ring."

"Okay, so he's not a good example," Audrey conceded.

"I feel like I've flunked math class *again*," Nicola said.

"You've never flunked a math class in your life."

"But I know what it feels like."

Audrey laughed and gave Nicola new wet towels and took the old ones and resoaked them.

"To say I'm disappointed in myself just doesn't begin to cover it," Nicola said. She adjusted the silk teddy inside her shirt. "There's something very fraudulent about me, you have no idea. I like to pretend I'm something I'm not."

"Welcome to adulthood," Audrey said.

"I'm not kidding."

"Neither am I."

They laughed, looking at each other through the mirror. Audrey had a round face and dimples and she could be incredibly feisty. The first time they met Nicola thought, Well, I won't be friends with *her*. But it didn't turn out that way. Audrey worked out every morning before work and her arms were incredibly strong and Declan, her husband, could lift his own weight. He was from San Diego, where they sold surfboards at yard sales, and he got his first boogie board at something like age three, then moved on to skateboards in kindergarten. Every Saturday he and Audrey either drove three hours north to ski board or three hours south to surf, and in addition they were building a house in Marin by themselves. Nicola usually went over to their place after work to drink beers and complain about Guy and to see her dog Lester, who lived with them since her own landlord wouldn't allow pets.

Nicola lifted the wet paper towel to check the puffiness of her eyes. She thought of Chorizo's fingers, the silver bracelet on his dark wrist. Even his awful shoes were somehow endearing.

"I wish I could just say yes," she told Audrey. "For once in my life I would like to say yes."

"I think you do okay."

"Do you remember Francis? From our freshman year? Maybe this was before I met you. He was a senior and premed and he was really funny. There were always old dirty clothes all over my room and he made up this game called sockball that he used to play with my dirty socks."

"Anyway," Audrey said.

"Anyway," Nicola said. She touched her eyelid. "One night he came over and he said he had something to say to me but that he was embarrassed and he thought he would be more comfortable if I had a bag or something that he could put over his head while he was saying it. But I didn't have a bag. So he said, what about a towel? So I gave him a towel and he put it over his head and then he told me he liked me and would I go out with him some time."

"That's very funny," Audrey said, looking at herself in the mirror.

"But guess what I said."

"Well, but he had a *towel* over his head."

"Why can't I just say yes? Francis was a really nice guy! He was funny! He was premed!"

"I'm sure he'll end up forty years old and channel-flipping like everyone else," Audrey told her.

"My point is that there is something seriously wrong with me."

"You're having a bad day," Audrey said. "Have you spoken to Lester today? Why don't you call her? Declan is probably home."

"That's a good idea. You know, I was thinking yesterday that maybe I should give Lester a girlie middle name. To avoid all the gender confusion."

"What, like Lester Anna?"

"Or Lester Louisa."

"Or Lester Pearl."

Nicola laughed. "Lester Pearl," she repeated, and reapplied the paper towel to her eyelids. "I like that," she said.

She called Lester when she got back to her desk; Declan, who was in fact home, switched to speaker phone so Nicola could hear Lester's paws click over the hardwood floors. Then Louise brought back some chocolate cookies and after two of those Nicola did feel better.

What it was, she decided, was an episode day. This was a technique she had learned from Scooter; once when he was watching some science fiction show and the characters were even more than normally stupid he said, Don't they realize this is one of those episode days? And it was true, Nicola thought—there are days that are simply uncontrollably unavoidably bad and you better just expect more of the same and not try to fight it.

That was today.

She looked at her watch; her cardio-kickboxing class was at six. Then it was the weekend and she would relax, go to a movie, or do something fun. What? In any case she would *not* look at the rentals in the classifieds, not this weekend. And she would not drive up and down streets looking for for-rent signs in windows. Well, maybe just the street along the beach, the Great Highway, a street named in the old Scots tradition of long high narrow roads and not in the modern tradition of on-ramps. But, on second thought, apartments along there would be so expensive. No, she would not drive down any streets. Maybe she would just peek at the classifieds.

"Do you want to go out with Declan and me tonight?" Audrey asked her.

"I have my kickboxing class," Nicola said.

"Well, call us later if you want."

Her class was held at a Karate Academy down the street and Nicola considered not going. The truth was she didn't like jumping, which almost all sports, she found, required. Also exercise clothes depressed her. Also she disliked locker rooms, all that gray expanse of gray with identical locks on the lockers, which was ludicrous when you thought about it because who would ever want whatever was inside? The chocolate cookies were definitely wearing off. At the gym Nicola changed her clothes, then took her place in the line of women, most of whom had clenched jaws and were already kicking the air and punching.

"And jab! Jab! Jab!" her instructor Alicia shouted. "Get that leg up, Nicola!"

One hour, she told herself, then pizza with anchovies and a corn-meal crust. She fell down twice during the matches trying to kick her opponent, an apologetic lesbian who never even made contact. After the second fall Alicia told Nicola she wasn't trying. Wasn't trying! She had been the kickball champion of her third grade, but everything had fallen apart since then. Alicia, meanwhile, was slim with the whitest teeth Nicola had ever seen.

"Nicola, raise your leg!"

"Nicola, your leg!"

"Nicola, leg!"

I'm getting worse with each class, Nicola thought. Worse. How could that be? A gritty sweat was trickling down her temples and her arms felt only loosely connected to her body, as if stuck on with paper fasteners.

Afterwards Nicola showered then tried to do something with her hair, which looked even worse than before. It was dark when she finally left. The sidewalk was crowded with people walking their dogs or reading posted restaurant menus and, down the street, some kids were selling chocolate or something for their school. Nicola walked in their direction, heading for the gourmet pizza place on the corner. Although she tried to remind herself it was just an episode day, she couldn't help feeling disheartened.

She was hungry and tired and her arm felt bruised where she had fallen on it. The sidewalk was sloppy with worms of wet paper and bird poop, and Nicola caught herself going over the bad points of the day from the top. If I see Chorizo on Monday, she told herself, and if he asks me out again, I'll say yes. Or maybe I'll ask *him* out. Or maybe I'll ask if I can share his table, and then I'll eat lunch with him and then ask him out.

Probably she would think up various responses for various circumstances over the entire weekend, and this sort of depressed her. Yes, she practiced. Yes, yes. Yes. She never noticed before how much it sounded like sex.

"Help our school, buy a candy bar?" the high school girl asked as Nicola approached. She was tall with inky black hair and bangs that seemed to have been cut with pinking shears. Her long arms held the chocolate protectively against her chest—or was she just cold? Next to her a boy in combat pants was leaning against the low brick wall that separated the sidewalk from a small parking lot. They were young, maybe sixteen. Nicola didn't catch the name of their school.

"No thanks," she said. Then she stopped. What had she just been telling herself? "Wait. Actually, why not."

"Chocolate, milk chocolate, dark chocolate, or something with nougat?" the girl asked.

"What's the difference between chocolate and milk chocolate or dark chocolate?"

"I don't know," said the girl. She wore black jeans and a big puffy black coat and she pursed her lips into an uncertain smile.

"I'll take the milk chocolate," Nicola told her.

"A bunch of these got stolen," the girl said, "from some seventh graders. Can you believe that? Stealing candy from kids?"

"From babies," Nicola said, looking in her wallet. "Like the saying."

"Hunh?"

"Stealing candy from babies."

"I know, I can't believe it," the girl said. "Do you believe in karma?"

"I only have a twenty," Nicola said.

The girl and the boy exchanged a look.

"You go," the girl said.

The boy pulled himself away from the wall, and Nicola noticed some duct tape stuck on his jeans. Was this what they used as patches these days? "We keep the money in my mom's minivan," he explained. "Over here."

He headed toward a caramel-colored minivan in the corner and Nicola followed him. The lot was just a few feet from the street but it was quiet here and dark and felt weirdly empty after the sidewalk scene and Nicola thought under the right circumstances this would seem creepy.

"Did you know that people who eat chocolate live longer?" the boy asked her. He had a raspy voice, maybe a shade too high, and his hair was buzzed short, army-style. "Studies show," he said.

He took Nicola's twenty, then went around to the other side of

the van and pulled open the door. For a second he disappeared.
When he came back his hand was closed, but when he opened it
there was no money inside. Instead he suddenly grabbed her wrist.

"What?" Nicola said, as if he had said something she hadn't quite
heard.

"Come here," he said, and his expression tightened.

All at once she understood and a cold flush went through her. He
pulled her toward him and put something—the duct tape—on her
mouth with one hard push so that it wrinkled and didn't adhere very
well. Instinctively she pulled at it with her free hand and thought:
The girl will help. Then she remembered the girl was with him.

"Hey," the boy said as she tugged at the tape, and he pushed her
hand from her face. "Dave!" he called.

The girl came up from behind Nicola and took her other hand.

"Quickly," she said.

They were standing in the dark shadows of cars. The boy pulled
off another strip of duct tape from his jeans and Nicola felt her arms
being pulled behind her from two directions, the boy's and the girl's,
and she realized they were trying to get her hands behind her so they
could tape them up. She struggled and then let her legs collapse so
she was kneeling on the parking lot, her head bowed in front of her
execution style. Mainly she was just trying to keep her left arm—the
arm the girl called Dave was holding—in her lap or in front of her
chest so they could not tape her up, and she found herself staring
hard at the blacktop: a dark, almost glittering surface.

"Stop!" the boy said in his raspy voice.

Why was no one coming into the parking lot?

"Come on, Dave, you have to be quick," the girl said to him.

Wait, Nicola thought, which one is named Dave? And as if they
sensed her distraction, they both pulled on her arms hard at the same
time and got them behind her, and the boy quickly taped her two
wrists together. Nicola's mouth went dry and she curled to the ground

feeling altogether submissive without the use of her hands. Her mind seemed to have shrunk to a pinpoint which could understand almost nothing of what was happening.

The boy and the girl pulled her into the back row of the minivan, then the girl, who may or may not be the one called Dave, wound some dark cloth around her eyes. She said, "You know, you won't be hurt."

Her arms hurt, her face hurt, and she had skinned at least one knee falling down on the blacktop. The girl tightened Nicola's seat belt, then climbed into the front seat.

She said, "You did it."

"Yeah," said the boy. "Do you have the candy?"

"How did you do it? I don't think I coulda."

"Visualization. The whole time we were at it I saw her taped up in the back."

And here I am, Nicola thought. Although she wanted to believe the girl when she said she wouldn't be hurt, her mouth was still dry and her heart was still racing. From the front seat she heard the click of seat belts connecting. Then the boy started the engine, and the doors locked in unison.

Four

At the first stoplight the van turned left, then left again, heading downtown. Overhead wires crisscrossed like shattered glass and behind them the ocean glittered darkly, blowing off foam. It was cold in the van. The boy, who was driving, put his palm to the instrument panel, then adjusted the airflow through the vents. He was smaller than the girl and had a thin, strained face. The girl stared straight ahead with the candy in her lap.

"We should do a circle when we get there," she said.

The boy didn't answer. The van swerved a little and Nicola righted herself awkwardly, her hands taped behind her. What did that mean, a circle? Were they witches or warlocks or what do you call them, wicca?

Light came up from beneath her blindfold, and when she looked down Nicola could see a pinkish blur which was the tip of her nose. She didn't think witches called themselves Dave. Or was this a new gang thing, the Dave gang? Nicola almost laughed at that and realized she was still in shock.

She tested the strength of the duct tape on her hands and tried to think if she'd seen any weapons, any bulges that might have been weapons. When she first saw the boy, didn't he have his hand in his pocket? Like he was holding onto something there?

Boy Dave and Girl Dave. Dave and Davette. Maybe they're trying to get *into* a gang. Maybe this is some kind of Dave wicca gang *initiation* thing.

It was quiet in the van. Nicola figured they were on Portola Street now, winding their way past Twin Peaks. For a while she was able to mentally follow their progress. At the top of the hill Portola became Market Street and the van lurched down, beginning its descent. A picture of the area formed in her mind as if she were touch typing: the cars and lit cafés, the people walking slowly as if they were blind. For a moment she felt as if she was floating helplessly among them.

No one knew she was here.

After a while Davette opened the box of candy bars and broke off a square for Dave, then took one for herself. The smell of nougat wafted back. Still no one spoke. Where were they taking her? Their silence was beginning to feel menacing.

At last they turned off Market Street and into a small alley. As the van slowed to a stop Nicola's heart began to beat fast again.

Davette swallowed. "Do the wallet first," she said.

They were going through her purse. Dave counted out the bills then he examined Nicola's plastic cards: VISA, VISA Gold, YMCA ID and towel card. Her library card. Her driver's license which expired last birthday and the renewal sticker behind it. Everything that listed who she was: Nicola Elizabeth Swain, thirty-one years old, divorced, no children, residence 3584A Santiago Street. Born in Cleveland, Ohio, allergic to codeine and hazelnuts. Five foot five, black hair, green eyes, good skin.

How much did they want to know? How much was documented?

"Here's the ATM card," Davette was saying. "Under 'A.' "

"What kind of person keeps their plastic ordered alphabetically?"

"Look at all this. Pills in the pill case. Sunglasses in the sunglasses case. Pens in the pen holders. And all the pens have their original caps. It's so, like, yin."

They talked as if she wasn't there. That annoyed her. Her stomach clenched with hunger and Nicola remembered again that she hadn't had dinner.

"Life according to plan," Dave said, zipping up his jacket.

He jumped out of the van. As he slid open the back door a rush of foggy cold air blew in at her.

"I'm going to take you out on the street and unblindfold you," he told her. "Don't do anything since I have a knife."

On the street he ripped the tape off her hands in a way that was really painful and Nicola found herself again the stereotype: rubbing her freed wrists. When he took off her blindfold she saw they were in an alley behind a small fenced lot. Several rent-a-Dumpsters stood between here and the next busy street—Seventh?—and there were other signs of recent construction.

"This way," Dave said.

They walked behind her, each one holding one arm. What did they look like? She tried to calm herself by concentrating on what she would tell the police. They were heading for the ATM on the corner and when they got there the boy pushed Nicola toward it and told her to take out her maximum. As she punched in her secret code the girl repeated it, "four-nine-two-one," the first line of a math puzzle Nicola had enjoyed as a child.

She glanced over at them.

"Don't look at us!" Davette hissed. But Nicola couldn't see anything—somewhere between the van and here the Daves had pulled cut-up watch caps over their faces, and for a second that freaked her.

When she was done, Davette pocketed Nicola's money while Dave retaped her hands, then they led her, again from behind, back to the van. No one came into the alley.

I've got to do something, Nicola told herself. As she listened for the sound that meant car she found herself thinking of the summer she spent in Saudi Arabia, when she'd felt something similar to this: trapped and invisible. Her father went there to negotiate a deal which took longer than anyone expected. After a month he rented an apartment in Riyadh and brought his family over; after two months he hired a tutor in Arabic.

Nicola, who was fourteen at the time, mostly sat outside by the apartment pool reading Harlequin romances whose covers had been ripped off by customs officials. The pool was usually empty, though sometimes sand cats with ears like pygmy elephants wandered in from the street and Abdul, the pool cleaner, chased them off with a plastic leaf net. Abdul would not look Nicola in the eye and when she came near him he muttered a curious phrase which the apartment manager once translated for her: it has been this way since the time of the Prophet.

She learned to keep her shoulders covered and to receive change with her right hand. On the weekends her father took them to the desert for wadi bashing—a drive and a picnic—where they would see Bedouins driving small Isuzu pickup trucks with camels in the back. Everywhere she went old women in long black abayyas glared at her, reminding her of her lowly status, Nicola supposed. No one spoke to her. Plenty of Saudis spoke to Mark, her older brother, and even to her little brother, Eric, but never to her. It was as if they didn't see her. Like she didn't exist.

When Nicola got back to the States things were different. She was in high school now for one thing, and here it seemed no one raised their hands in class anymore and the girls sat slumped at their desks with their legs stretched out in front of them looking like beautiful caged felines. Nicola was used to being the one who knew all the answers, but now this was uncool. At first she felt grateful to the Saudis for teaching her how to keep quiet until suddenly years later she realized she had gotten into the habit of not saying what she thought.

And here she was, still not speaking. Well, there was the duct tape, of course. But why didn't she shout when the boy first took hold of her wrist? Why didn't she scream?

They got back to the minivan and Dave began to fumble with the lock. Nicola steadied and centered herself. When he dropped his keys she thought, Okay. Quickly she turned to face the girl and brought her leg up heel first in a solid thrust-kick.

"Whoa," Davette said as she fell.

"Hey, hey," said Dave. He was still wearing his mask.

Nicola turned and kicked out, but she missed his chest and got his arm instead. Her hands were still taped behind her. She kicked again and missed. The darkness was like rain; it got in the way. Also garbage bins, the Dumpsters, the sense of narrowness in the alley. She heard people laughing on another street and Dave made a grab for her. She kicked again but her footing was off. She kicked again. Dave's fingers pinched her arms like an old woman and Davette got up and took hold of her other arm. They got the van's back door open and together they pushed her onto the floor.

"Shit," Dave said. "What the fuck? Don't you have a brain?" His voice ended with a squeak like a bath toy.

"We're not supposed to talk to her," Davette reminded him.

"We said we wouldn't hurt you," he went on. "I think I'm getting a bruise on my arm. What if I was a hemophiliac or something?"

"You're not a hemophiliac."

"If I was, I'd be dying right now."

When they spoke they seemed almost harmless. Just teenagers,

Nicola thought. Davette helped Nicola up and got her back in the seat. She had pretty brown eyes behind her mask.

"Hemophiliacs don't bruise," she said. "They bleed."

"They can bruise."

"Bleeding is the problem."

"I'm making a point." He sounded annoyed.

"Stop looking at your arm."

"Why the fuck did she do that?"

Davette tied the silk scarf around Nicola's eyes, but she made it a little looser this time. "Quit complaining. I was the one she knocked to the ground." To Nicola she said, "Don't do that anymore." But she didn't sound angry.

Dave clapped his hands on his jeans and climbed into the driver's seat. "To my mind, being tied up and all is a good reason *not* to start kicking around and hurting someone who could, you know, obviously hurt you more."

"She's not as tame as she looks," Davette said shrewdly.

The minivan's ignition bells rang. Dave backed the van up into a driveway and turned it around.

Davette held onto the dashboard. "You're going the wrong way," she told him.

"We need to get to, you know, the place."

"What I mean is, this is a one-way street."

Nicola, blindfolded again, her hands taped, strapped in by the seat belt, was annoyed with herself. She was sore and tired and hungry. Her purse, the template of her existence, was in the hands of teenagers. It was after eight, she guessed, the time of video previews. No one would miss her until Monday. Her mind was like a truck backing up in the street. She should have centered herself more between kicks. She should have run.

Five

Chorizo sat in the darkening room and waited for the girl to come to him. The shades were open—soon he would have to do something about that—but for now he was enjoying the haze from the streetlights, which lit the room to a perfect, soft degree. His rattan chair was uncomfortable. The bed would be even more so. He thought he could smell the faint rubbery smell of cast-off condoms and he willed his mind to narrow to the task at hand.

She was standing next to the cheap wooden dresser, holding onto the edge.

He said, "Did you know that if you meet a whore in the morning this brings good luck?"

His father once told him this, or was it his uncle? The girl was blindfolded but smiling and he knew she was just feeling the high. It was a game to her, still a game. He had given her one pill after dinner and then, when she was in the bathroom, he broke up a second pill into her drink. They were Marlina's pills, but Marlina wouldn't talk;

she needed the money he gave her and she needed that boyfriend of hers and she knew very well that Chorizo could get rid of both if he wanted to. Marlina was a prostitute and a former heroin addict. But these days due to circumstances—meaning Chorizo—she was willing to watch her boyfriend Ricky do the shooting up with junk bought with her money while she concocted little plans about how she was going to get some training in a hair salon or maybe go back to school, do the GED, and then go from there. Next month maybe, or the month after that. Every time she brought Chorizo the pills she had a different story. Tonight Chorizo had let Marlina use a first-floor room for her business, and so here he was now in her room, a prostitute's room, though the girl didn't know this.

"Where are you?" the girl asked. She let go of the dresser and ran her foot across the ragged, run-down carpet.

She was pretty, but thin. As Chorizo watched her, he twisted the chains of his bracelet and thought, Two pills, that would do it. Two pills would kill anyone but the most hardened addict, and she claimed she almost never did drugs. She was a liar, though, probably. And a slut. He himself took nothing, only sipped a little wine and pretended to take a pill when he offered her one, calling it Ecstasy. In a way he was right.

A liar, a slut, a fool. What time was it now? He stretched his arms above his head, then went to the window, which was cracked in one corner, and looked down to the street. The motel was near the water, not too far from Fisherman's Wharf, and outside it was gray and foggy and windy. Even from here he could hear tourists laughing as they ate their soft-shelled crabs, and the obese seals on the pier barking for food. He ran his fingers along the shade. He had to admit that he liked the motel's seedy location—he loved San Francisco at night. He loved the transvestites, the junkies, the runaway trust-fund babies on speed. He loved how they could mix with rich corporate lesbians and tech support managers and everyone else who came to California looking for something. Everyone mixed with everyone, on this street at least. Everyone mixed with everyone else.

The fog was like the lightest of snowfalls; it made the street cozy. And for a moment looking down Chorizo felt something in him relax; he felt almost at peace. He could do what was needed. He could do whatever was needed. Chorizo pulled down the fraying shade and went back to his low uncomfortable chair and held the rope in his lap. He was ready. Trained. Focused. The mind of a warrior.

Two pills, he was thinking. It had worked before.

"Come here," he said to the girl.

She was still standing on the thin carpet holding her own hands in front of her, blindfolded, stuck, not moving. She laughed again. It was only a game.

"I'm trying," she told him.

Six

I t was after nine when the Daves drove into the garage of a narrow,
two-story structure and parked. They got the candy and the
purse, then led Nicola up a flight of uncovered steps to a room
that was essentially a platform built above the garage.

They were near the industrial part of the bay, one street over from
train tracks. Upstairs it was cold and damp and smelled like plywood.
Heavy sheet plastic divided the room in half. Dave went around the
room pulling down blinds while Davette steered Nicola: "Stop. Now
back a step. That's it, okay, sit."

It was like a game Nicola played in grade school. Afterwards they
would attempt to raise her prone body by chanting light as a feather,
stiff as a board.

Davette said, "I'm just going to tie you in."

Nicola tried to adjust her balance—she was sitting in an armless
desk chair with wheels—while Davette wrapped a bungee cord
around her waist, then hooked it to the back rest. Nicola's hands,
still taped, were pressed between the chair and the small of her back,

which she thought was probably good for her sciatica.

She was wondering, what now? It had not been difficult to follow their route here since Dave kept saying things like "We're looking for Berry Street now." Plus Nicola knew the area—the year she left Scooter she was working in an office south of Market, though not quite as south as they were now. On Fridays after work she and the receptionist visited all the nearby bars in search of the perfect Tom Collins. Leslie, the receptionist, was blonde and had the energy of a Mouseketeer, and she attracted a lot of attention. They met men and learned how to play pool passably, but even so the nights just got longer and longer.

"There's like one working light bulb," Davette said after a minute.

"I thought I checked those."

"And what's that in the corner, a tarp?"

"It's for water," Dave told her. He shook out a plastic sheet. "Holds thirty gallons. The spigot goes here."

Davette knelt down and began rummaging around in her backpack. "Here, hold out your arm."

"For what?"

"The circle. Like I said. I need to get back some positive energy."

She struck a match. The air smelled of sulfur and dirt and Nicola could no longer smell the angel water she had put on that morning for Chorizo. She closed her eyes under the blindfold and found she was more comfortable this way.

"I need a bowl, or even a mug would work. I wish there was some running water nearby."

"We could stand by the toilet," Dave said.

"Was that a joke?"

They pushed some furniture around, then Nicola listened to them argue: Do you want this stone, no the white one, no that white one, okay get the book, no east is that way, no because the bay is over there. She began to seriously wonder about these two. They had stopped speaking to her again and it seemed like now they were just carrying on with their usual Friday night lives. The heat came on and Nicola counted how long it lasted, two minutes, but when it stopped she felt no warmer.

"With this stone," Davette chanted, "anger be gone. Water bind it, no one find it."

Her voice had dropped an octave and Nicola could imagine her standing there with sacred objects (the nougaty candy?) in her hands. She began to count the seconds until the heat started again, and found in this way she could keep track of the time.

Focus on the details, she thought. What to tell the police.

"Here we're supposed to think about what we did wrong. You know like those kids, with the candy we stole. And then her."

Dave put his hands in his pockets. "JTRY, she did knock you down," he reminded her.

From the other side of the wall came a low muffled voice, or maybe it was more than one, and something else which took Nicola a long time to identify—a baby? a cat?—until she finally thought, birds. Green parrots, macaws, something large and tropical. She heard screeches and calls, another low voice, maybe the sound of a radio. The walls were so thin. Temporary housing, she wondered?

"Okay, now, put all your emotional energy into the cup," Davette told Dave.

"Like, think about it going in there?"

"All your anger and stuff."

"I'm not really angry," Dave said. "I'm more like on edge, or I don't know what exactly."

"Well just put it in."

Slowly the smell of incense worked the room.

"Take a sip from the cup."

"What's in there again?"

"Mine the cup, and mine the wine of life," Davette chanted. "Drink deep!"

They were quiet for a moment. The circle was done. Nicola pulled at the tape on her hands again, mostly just out of habit. Then she heard Dave say, "Now."

Still, it took her a second to realize they were looking at her. Dave came over to the desk chair and knelt down. For a moment he said nothing. Nicola could hear him breathing beside her.

She sat very still. He touched the duct tape over her mouth then traced his fingers along her face, feeling the soft down on her cheek. His hand was cool and firm.

"So," he said to her. "You know this game, right?"

The girl was lying on the bed wearing a dark red nylon camisole that Chorizo had given her. He had taken off her blindfold. Her wrist was tied by a rope to the bed frame.

"I feel funny," she said.

"You feel good," he told her.

He was sitting on the side of the bed, stroking her hair. She was very pretty and feminine lying there all tied up. Getting her to agree to the rope was easy. He knew it would be. All he did was tell her the first principle of Shambhala: Don't be afraid of who you are. Then he held up the rope.

It's a game, he had said. The rope is a game in a night in a thrill with a stranger. Don't be afraid of the thrill, he had said. Don't be afraid of who you are.

And she wasn't. Chorizo touched her bangs. Frankly it was astonishing to him how unresisting they were, these women. How trusting. Of course, the drugs helped.

"So what's Shambhala anyway, a religion?" she asked now. She yawned, then giggled. "Maybe you can convert me."

Chorizo smiled. "Maybe I can."

"What do I have to do?"

He stroked her hair and she stretched a little, a slight arching of the back, then a smile. A cat, he thought.

"It's all about waking up," he said.

The girl yawned again. "Then you won't convert me."

Chorizo stopped touching her hair. That annoyed him—why? It was a game to her, just a game. It was supposed to be a game. But his beliefs, what he believed—well that was important, that wasn't part of the game. Maybe it was his fault for mentioning Shambhala in the first place. Chorizo looked at his watch, then turned and lifted the video camera out from under the bed.

"What's that?" she asked.

"I'm just going to take a few pictures," he told her.

Game, Nicola wondered? She opened her eyes under the blindfold and thought, Stay calm. The smell of sulfur was still in the room.

"We're not supposed to talk to her," Davette told him again. She was standing with her legs spread, still holding the cup.

"You know this game," Dave said again, ignoring her. "You had your turn. And now it's his."

His? What is this? Oh my God, Nicola thought. They think I'm someone else.

"Oh whatever, it's your own sick game," Dave went on. "But just so you know I think it stinks. Because some kids tied *me* up once. And let me tell you when it happens for real it's not a game."

Nicola thought: But they looked at my wallet, my IDs. They know my name. They should know it's not me that they want.

Davette put the cup on the floor. "I didn't know this," she said.

"It was like seventh grade. They roped me into a chair in the science lab and then just left me. At first I was all, what'd I do? I was nice enough to those guys, I don't know. But they were just mean, I guess; it wasn't like you and me where we needed the money. They were just mean."

So they're doing this for money? Nicola needed to scratch her face but settled for rubbing her cheek with her shoulder.

"Here," Dave said. His raspy voice was brittle, kind of mean. He scratched Nicola's face roughly, and Nicola pulled her head back.

"Hey, I'm trying to be nice," he said in the same voice.

"Dave," Davette said.

"Okay, okay. Well anyway, after that experience I went out and bought an Israeli M-15 gas mask. And then, boom, full-on survivalist mode. Food purification and storage. Scavenging techniques. And water, there's a lot to that subject alone. Like, for instance, if you get really desperate you can break the water heater and drink out of that."

"What about the toilet tank?" Davette asked.

"The tank is okay. The tank, the heater, any self-contained unit. What you don't want to do is drink out of the toilet bowl. But back to my point, which is that even though this is just a game to you, it can actually hurt someone. Like us. Remember we're just the what, the referees or whatever, me and Dave."

"More like the lackeys. The hired help."

"The hired help, okay. So no more karate or whatever it was you did back there on the street. So he's getting you back; too bad, but don't take it out on us. Accept the situation, this is like what Buddha teaches, right?"

Nicola moved her head to the side, noncommittal. She had no idea what he was talking about. She was really very hungry now, and the phrase *chocolate milkshake* kept coming into her mind.

"We set on that?" Dave asked. "We friendly again?"

What is this, is he trying to bond with me now? This is the worst kind of torture, Nicola thought.

"That's good," Davette said. She came over to where Dave was kneeling. Nicola rubbed her cheek again with her shoulder and Davette touched Nicola's face gently, scratching the itch. "So maybe now we should untape her for a minute."

"What?" Dave asked. "What are you talking about?"

"Untape her mouth."

"Are you kidding?"

"Just the mouth."

"We can't do that."

"Why not just her mouth?"

"So she can what? Talk?"

"It just seems like we should do something positive," Davette said. "One positive thing. Otherwise what was the point of the circle?"

"Forget it. We stick to the script."

"Well, then, what were you just doing now? The little lecture there?"

"It's called setting the rules."

"Let's just untape her mouth, that's all," Davette said. "For just like a minute. For like five minutes. Just the mouth."

"Christ," Dave said.

"Otherwise the circle was pretty much pointless."

"But I mean, how stupid can you get?"

"WWJD."

"DBAL!"

"WWJD."

"Oh Christ," Dave said. "Listen. If this fucks us up I'll blame you."

Davette knelt down in front of the desk chair. Her long spiky hair fell into her face.

"You okay?" she asked Nicola. "This'll hurt," she told her.

Nicola nodded.

"Let me do it," Dave said.

He worked his fingers under the tape and when he loosened the edge and pulled away the feeling was, in fact, very painful. Nicola opened her mouth and closed it. The hairs above her lip felt as though they were standing straight up.

"That better?" Davette asked.

Nicola had to clear her throat to speak. Then she said, "You have the wrong person."

"Yeah, he said you would say that," Davette said.

"What? Hold on," Dave said. "I thought he said not to talk to her?"

Nicola tried to face Davette. Where was she exactly? Her blindfold was beginning to get damp from sweat. "I don't know who *he* is," she told her. "I don't know about a game. I didn't take a turn with *any*one. You have the wrong person."

"I can check the script, but this is pretty much like what he said."

Dave opened his mouth. "There's an actual script?"

"But it's true," Nicola said. "I'm in the dark here."

"Hey, you're funny," Davette told her. She stood up and looked around for her backpack. "You're like punning, right?"

Nicola closed her mouth. This was getting nowhere.

"I need some food," she tried.

"This was a total mistake," Dave said.

Davette had begun putting her circle supplies away. "What, so she's talking, that's all right. You can't have any food," Davette told Nicola. "Not until after."

"After what?"

"Okay, I'm putting the tape back on," Dave said.

"Chill out. Christ," Davette said. "She can ask whatever she wants; that doesn't mean we tell her."

"This is nuts. We should stick to the script. Where *is* the script?"

"Dave. Settle. And, you, never mind after what," Davette said, zipping her backpack.

"I need to go to the bathroom," Nicola told them.

She could feel them looking at her and she waited out the silence feeling like a starchy English actress.

"Well, we can't have her peeing on the floor," Davette finally said. Nicola felt a small sense of victory, the first of the day. Davette came over and began to unwind the bungee cord. "Can I have my blindfold off?" Nicola asked.

"Negatory," Davette said.

They led her to a small, cold bathroom where she was directed around a freestanding shower stall to the toilet. Nicola could smell something moldy and damp and she thought of her mother: bath towels and guests only keep for three days.

"You can do your skirt, right?" Davette asked.

"Not without hands."

"Oh, right."

"Wait," Dave said. "You're untying her hands now?"

"Well, I'm not going to, you know, and all. She's okay as long as she doesn't have her eyes."

A breeze came in from somewhere and Nicola felt her skin pinch and resist like the rough hide of an animal. She leaned off-balance slightly while Dave knelt behind her. "And so," he said as he ripped the tape off her hands again.

"I think you're enjoying that," Davette said.

"I feel there's a technique to be learned."

Nicola lifted her hands to her blindfold.

"Ah-ah," Davette said. "None of that. Hands at your sides. Stand here. Okay, okay, now do your skirt."

"What about him?" Nicola asked.

Dave said, "I'm staying."

She maneuvered her underwear under her skirt. When she was done Nicola held out her hand. Dave opened the cupboard door under the sink then pushed something aside.

"Huh," he said. "Looks like we're out of t.p."

"You were supposed to go through the place!"

"I guess I didn't have to go then."

Nicola could not believe it. Who were these kids? How could they possibly be the ones in control? They were too stupid to check out this place (should she call it a hideout?) and too stupid to hide the fact that someone else was involved, someone who called this a game. Earlier, at the ATM, they had to stand out of camera range and worry about someone seeing them because they didn't think to buy wigs and sunglasses beforehand. They were young, nearly half her age. She would have planned this much better.

She tried to be patient while the Daves looked at each other uncertainly, hoping something would come to them. The heat came on but again it did no good—probably they had forgotten to open the wall vents.

This was ridiculous.

"There's some Kleenex in my purse," Nicola finally said.

Seven

Downstairs Chorizo could hear Marlina shriek and laugh. She was always so loud with her customers. He sat on the bed and willed himself to focus, to let go of the irritation, and found himself rubbing the tip of his thumbnail.

The girl opened her eyes for a moment. She was even sleepier now, and wasn't talking so much—he was glad of that, actually. She didn't bring up Shambhala again.

She pulled her leg out from under the thin bedspread. "I feel so warm," she said. "Kind of mushy."

Chorizo nodded. "That's right." Marlina shrieked again and he adjusted the bedspread over the girl's exposed leg, then took hold of her hand. Inhaled to a count of four. There is no good and bad, he told himself; free yourself from judgment. He wasn't sure if he was thinking about the girl or Marlina. Or himself.

He touched the bangs on the girl's forehead, which were wet with sweat. He stood up, pulled a handkerchief from his pants pocket, and wiped his fingers. Was the camera in focus? He checked it again, carefully bending over the table where it was propped and aimed.

Good. She looked good.

He adjusted the window shade again, then walked back to the foot of the bed and sat down by her feet, careful to stay out of the camera's range. The girl closed her eyes, but he noticed the color of her face had not yet changed. Marlina shrieked again.

He had some time. He looked at his thumbnail again, which still needed shaping, but he didn't have anything with him.

So he said, "I'm going to tell you a story."

The Daves spent the next hour playing two-handed spades while Nicola counted off the minutes by keeping track of the heat. Neither Dave nor Davette took off their jackets, and Nicola could tell whenever Davette moved by the soft puffy sound of her coat.

She was so hungry now she could hardly stand it. And with her hunger came a percolating annoyance. Her feet were cold, her hands were cold. The skin underneath the blindfold felt clammy, and possibly she was developing a headache.

But when a noise rang out Nicola was momentarily so startled that she did not at first recognize it. It was a phone.

Dave fumbled around in his coat pocket. "Yeah?" he answered. He paused. "Yeah we did. Yeah. Okay. Cool."

He hung up. Now what, Nicola wondered.

"It's midnight," Dave said.

This was his favorite story, the one about the crocodile and the monkey.

"Once upon a time a mother crocodile lived with her son on a great, wide river," Chorizo began. He adjusted the girl's blanket again and paused for effect. He loved the sound of his voice.

"One day," he continued, "the mother crocodile told her son that she wanted the heart of a monkey for supper. 'But how will I get one?' asked the son. 'Monkeys don't go into the water, and crocodiles don't climb trees.' The mother said, 'Use your wits.'

"So the crocodile came up with a plan. He swam out to the tallest tree on the riverbank and looked up to where a large, fat monkey was playing in its branches.

" 'Oh monkey,' sang the crocodile. 'The fruit on the tree on the island behind me is perfectly ripe and ready to eat. I'm going there myself. Climb on my back and I'll take you, too.' Now the monkey had always wanted to taste the fruit on this particular tree, and when the crocodile offered him a ride he didn't think twice, but just jumped on the crocodile's back and off they went.

"When they were in the middle of the river the crocodile suddenly dived under the water and nearly drowned the monkey. As he came up sputtering and coughing the monkey cried, 'Why did you do that?' 'To kill you,' replied the crocodile. 'My mother wants monkey heart to eat.' 'Well, I wish I had known,' said the monkey, 'because then I would have brought it with me.' 'What?' cried the crocodile. 'You left your heart back in the tree? We must go straight back to get it.' And at that he turned around and swam back to the riverbank.

" 'Now go get your heart and bring it back to me,' the crocodile told the monkey. 'Then perhaps we'll visit the island.'

" 'All right,' said the monkey, and he scampered up the tree.

"The crocodile waited a long time but the monkey did not come back down.

" 'Oh monkey, where is your heart?' he called out at last.

" 'It's up here!' the monkey replied. 'And if you want it, you must climb up and get it. Then perhaps we'll visit your mother!'

"And," Chorizo said, "the little monkey laughed and laughed and laughed, and the crocodile had nothing to do but swim away."

The girl's eyes were still closed. The color of her skin was beginning to change. Chorizo ran his hand up her arm to the rope. He touched each of her fingers then ran his hand back down to her shoulder.

"I like that story," he told her. "Because it shows what you need to succeed. You need heart—courage. It was courageous of that little monkey to climb on the crocodile's back." He was still stroking the girl's hair. "Now you have courage, I can tell. You came with me here, you took a chance. But heart is not all. You also need strength and cunning. The monkey had all three. He clung to the crocodile when they were underwater and did not drown. And he used his wits to save his skin."

The girl struggled for a moment. "I like it . . ." she said.

"You liked the story?"

She plucked at the nylon camisole. "I like this thing I'm wearing."

Chorizo smiled. She was not paying attention. Well, she was not that bright; he knew this even before. As he sat on the bed, touching the girl's forehead, the door opened slowly and he saw Ricky peek in. He signaled to him: yes. Ricky stepped all the way into the room, then closed the door softly behind him.

"But what you are lacking," he told the girl, "is cunning. A woman especially needs cunning. She needs cunning and courage and strength." He thought about his wife. "Mostly strength."

"It's a good color for me," said the girl, and she closed her eyes again. Her forehead was pale gray, a bit grainy. She was fading away.

"You're not listening. All right. That's all right." Chorizo looked at his watch. "Why don't you turn your head this way. I have someone I'd like you to meet."

Dave reached into his pants pocket and took out a miniature steel multitool—twelve components for cutting, turning, gripping, holding, twisting, measuring, opening, pulling, slicing, filing, cleaning, and scraping. For a few minutes he opened and closed this or that tool, testing the sharpness of one, the grasp of another.

"This is something I always keep with me," he was saying. "Ever since I got tied up that time. In addition to tweezers and a pager, it also has a lock pick. See that? But right now I'm looking for a weapon."

"Aggressive," said Davette. She was beginning to sound tired and cranky.

"My cousin gave it to me. His stepdad's in the CIA. And look what I have here, your twin companion." He threw her an identical tool and Davette looked at it with the expression of someone who had never seen a toilet before—my what goes *where?*

"In case she gets all feisty again. See?"

He pulled out a knife blade the size of a thumbnail.

"Well that will be useful for picking your teeth," Davette snapped. She turned the gizmo around in her hands. "What's the monitor for?"

"That's the coolest part; it has a built-in GPS thing. A global positioning system. Like, you know, what they have in rental cars? The map things that show you where you are all the time? And here, you can use this button to signal me, and my tool will act as a receiver. You don't even have to know where you are, the satellites will pick up your location and signal my map. You can be anywhere on earth and I'll find you."

"I can be anywhere?"

"Mine has parallel multichannels," Dave said. He put the tool back in his pocket. "I have no idea what that means."

"So have you tried it?"

"Um, I still don't get the whole longitude thing," he admitted.

They decided to give Nicola some water before they left. Dave untaped her mouth then held the cup to her lips. The cup was cold, and the water tasted slightly metallic. Nicola swallowed, then said, "You can't be in a building."

"What?"

"If you're using a GPS tool. You can't be in a building, in a cave,

or underwater. You said you can be anywhere on earth, but that's
not true. The receivers need clear air space to receive the satellite
signal."

"God, where's the duct tape?" Dave said.

"The signals travel on a super low frequency," Nicola continued.
She was a little surprised at herself. Maybe this was the effect of being
gagged so long? She was irritated and wanted to irritate back.

"They can go through clouds or glass or plastic, but nothing solid.
Did you know that radio waves travel at the speed of light? I learned
that just the other day."

"Oh shit," Dave said.

Davette looked up. "What now?"

"There's only, like, this much tape left."

Unreal. Could they do anything right?

"Where's the tape you just took off?" Davette asked.

"Squished."

They decided not to worry about taping her mouth. Together they
took Nicola down to the van, but this time Davette got into the
driver's seat.

"Is there any more of that chocolate?" Nicola asked.

"Our plan is to pretend you're still gagged," Dave said.

"Because I did pay for it, you know."

Davette started up the van and immediately began quarreling with
Dave about the best way to go.

"You know the new stadium? It's like a block away," he said.

Nicola guessed they were taking her to India Basin. For a while
Davette drove south alongside the CalTrain tracks, but she kept
having to back up when the roads ended in water. She was young,
Nicola thought; she should not be driving, she should be lying in bed
staring at a rock poster taped to the ceiling. It was hard to understand
how the world could be so heavily populated by creatures such as
the Daves with their grand ideas and their total lack of sense. Scooter,

her ex-husband, included. And Guy. And half of her clients, middle-aged guys with lofty technical agendas who couldn't program their way out of a speed-dial menu. Meanwhile, Nicola thought, where were the women like me? Tied up in a minivan no doubt, or roped to a desk chair.

But at last they got to wherever it was they were trying to go, and Davette cut the engine. It was windy and dark out and they were only a block or two from the water. The Daves took Nicola out of the van. Just like before they removed her blindfold and took up their places behind her and like before they pulled down their cut-up watch caps even though there wasn't a body in sight. But when Nicola saw that they were walking her to another ATM machine, she just could not believe it.

"This is it?" she said. "This is your big crime?" She didn't mean to say anything, but she was so hungry and annoyed and she so didn't think the Daves could do anything meaningfully bad to her that she just couldn't keep caring.

"What do you mean?" Dave asked.

"I mean, you're doing all this for my daily limit? You're going to starve me before you can get very much out," Nicola told him.

"Starve you how?"

"The way you usually starve someone—lack of food."

She could not believe how insanely stupid they were, what a huge risk they were taking for this petty amount. Her fingers were cold. She blew on them, then punched in her code furiously.

"I don't know why you need me out here anyway," she said. "You could have come alone; you have my code."

"Oh, yeah, I forgot; we were going to do that," Dave said.

Nicola gave him the money and curled her fingers into her closed hands. She was beginning to feel as though nothing would surprise her. "Here you are, go wild," she told them.

Dave became peevish. "You know, you're really testing our limits," he said in his high, raspy voice.

"Oh, just take me back to the van. Let me guess, you're supposed to keep me for another day, get out another wad, then tie me up somewhere on the beach just before dawn."

Dave and Dave looked at each other through their cut-up watch caps. This is absurd, Nicola thought.

"So you do know the script," Davette said. But her voice sounded a little uncertain.

"I *don't* know any script, Dave," Nicola said. "I haven't been playing any kind of game with anyone. Whoever told you that was lying in order to get you to . . ." Nicola paused for effect.

"To get us to what?"

"Commit a serious felony."

The Daves looked at each other again. Dave said, "Is she like improvising?"

Davette laughed a short laugh in relief. "That's it."

"Where's the guy behind all this?" Nicola asked.

"You mean the guy you work with?" Dave asked.

"He told you I work with him?" A sudden gust whipped her hair into her face.

"Come on. You all play this game together. Your company. Building trust or whatever." He squinted his eyes at her now, but he was looking a little uncertain. It was really cold out, and he put his hands under his armpits.

Nicola said, "This is what he told you?"

"It . . . isn't it true?"

"No, it isn't true. But let me guess: you're giving him the money you get from me. Then he's supposed to pay you, right? Well, I guarantee it he'll disappear before you see a cent. Listen, use your heads; he's using you to steal from me. You have kidnapped me and you have stolen my money and I *will* go to the police. But I'm guessing he plans to be gone before then. If anyone gets caught it will be you two."

"But he can't run away, he's like a cripple," Davette said.

Dave looked at her. "What?"

"Yeah, remember he told us he had only one liver?"

Nicola stared at her. She could hear a foghorn somewhere over the water. Her hands were even colder now and she wanted to get out of the wind. But she stayed where she was.

"Only one liver? He told you that?"

"He's on dialysis, he said."

"Are you sure he didn't say kidney?"

"He said liver; he said it was from drinking grain alcohol when he was in grade school."

"I don't think we should be saying all this," Dave said.

"It's okay," Nicola said. "But you know, Dave, everyone has only one liver."

She waited two beats. The Daves looked at her, not understanding.

"Everyone is born with just one liver."

They stopped looking at her and looked at each other. The wind whipped their hair in unison and Nicola watched them get it. Suddenly she felt this was easy; she could play it by ear.

"Is that true?" Davette asked. Her nose was running a little from the cold.

"Let's just go," Nicola told her.

She started walking back and in a moment the Daves followed her. The sidewalk was sandy and ripped up and the fog had thickened into something like suspended rain.

"If he lied about the liver, he could have lied about the other thing, too," Davette muttered to Dave. She sniffed, and her hands were crossed over her chest as she walked. Dave said nothing but his face was pale.

At the door to the van Nicola stood still while Davette wrapped the scarf around her eyes again. Then she said, "It's better to take Evans to Third. If you listen to me I'll get us back quicker."

The Daves said nothing but they took her advice. They were in something like shock.

"Get into the right-hand lane," Nicola told Davette, who was driving. "At the first major light make a right."

"On Third?" Davette asked.

"That's it."

She waited for the boy to speak. At last he said, "You know where we're taking you."

"Not really," Nicola lied.

"That complicates things," he said.

"Not really."

They skimmed along making green lights. Nicola could feel when they were on wide streets or narrow. Traffic was light since the muni trains had stopped and the buses were on their night schedules.

"If you know where we're taking you things will have to be different," Dave said.

"Tell the guy to come," Nicola said.

"Huh?"

"The liver guy. Tell him to come to the warehouse."

"What for?" Dave asked.

"So we can talk."

Davette sniffed again and wiped her nose on her sleeve. "We might as well, Dave. What if it's true, what if he lied? And now she knows where she's been."

Dave thought for a minute. "You really fucked up," he told Davette.

"Fuck you," she said calmly. "I did not."

"I knew we should have never untaped her mouth."

"We had to sometime. For water and stuff."

"He never said."

"He said it to me."

"*When* did he say?" Dave asked. His voice was like a cat's, small and sleek. "Listen, I want to know this: when did he say so much to you when he didn't to me?"

"He called me last night. He told me I was the lead role."

"The lead role? *I'm* the lead role."

"No, you're supporting."

"No way do I support!"

"Take a left at Mariposa," Nicola told Davette.

Davette pulled at the blinker. "Do you want the blindfold off?" she asked.

"Dave!" Dave said.

"Well, what's the point?"

"Actually I'm enjoying the challenge," Nicola told her.

The girl was dead.

He stood over the body, looking at it. The camisole was in pieces. A bad taste filled his mouth. It had all worked out.

The video camera was still running.

"Shambhala," he told her, "is a way of life."

He took a step back, thinking maybe his arm or hand had strayed into camera range. It was late, very late. Downstairs, Marlina at last was quiet. Asleep, probably. He himself was tired, but he had much more to do.

"Shambhala is about waking up and bringing buddhism into your life. It's a warrior's buddhism, inspired by the ancient kingdom of Shambhala, an enlightened society based on wisdom and fearless action. Fearless action. It has a tradition of meditation and bravery combined. I myself went to a meditation center for eleven months and completed five levels of Shambhala training, beginning with the 'Birth of the Warrior.' "

Chorizo paused, and looked at the girl.

"But you don't care about any of this," he said.

Later Nicola would realize that the smell on the street that was almost like urine was really yeast from the brewing factory across the street. She would realize how close they were to Potrero Hill—only a block away, with projects and a schoolyard in between. There were plants in plant boxes and small stunted trees lining the sidewalk and a few blocks up antique dealers showed their merchandise upon appointment.

After Dave made the phone call they sat like before in the cold upstairs room, not so tired now although it was almost two in the morning. When at last they heard the garage door open, the boy got up and started downstairs. Nicola heard his footsteps going down and another pair coming up, then a pause as they met in the middle of the staircase. They spoke for a minute. The man with one liver said, "I'm not going in, then."

"She's still got the blindfold."

"Is she taped up?"

"Her hands are . . . are tied."

"Not her mouth? Why not her mouth?"

Nicola held her breath to hear better.

"Why did you call me?" the man asked. "Christ, you scared me. I thought she was dead or something."

"She wants to talk to you."

There was a pause.

"Do you know how stupid you are?" the man asked.

Nicola exhaled and waited. It would feel so good to get out of this chair.

As they walked into the room a bird from next door screeched loudly, and for a second Nicola wasn't sure who was where; it sounded like maybe the girl got up as the men came in and the different noises competed with each other. She thought she heard heavy footsteps cross the room.

No one spoke for a moment. Nicola tried to guess where they were all standing so she could turn her face toward them.

She said, "Scooter. I thought that was you."

The bird shrieked again. Nicola almost laughed—she could feel his surprise fill the room. Scooter, her ex-husband.

"Come here," she said. "Come on, Scooter; undo my hands now."

She could imagine him standing there weighing his choices. After a moment he came toward her. Even under Dave's soft cotton shirt her skin was burning, the effect of so much tape coming on and off, and when Scooter untied her hands she reached up to her face and pulled hard at the blindfold. Jesus, thank God, Nicola thought. She was finished with all this. She was finished.

"Nicola," Scooter began weakly. "But how did you . . . ?"

"The liver story," she said. "You've used that one before."

"You told her that?" Scooter asked the Daves.

"Plus I know about the grain alcohol in kindergarten."

"That was first grade. My dad's still telling the story."

"Your dad's a sick man," Nicola said. She looked around her. The room was larger than she had imagined. She glanced at the Daves, who were crouching by the dry wall staring at her. Dave looked a little surly. And there was Scooter, wearing the same brown overcoat she'd seen that morning—or was it yesterday by now?

"I saw you this morning, you know," Nicola told him, "at the muni station. What is that coat you're wearing?"

"I'm sort of in disguise."

"Well, like everything else that almost worked."

She felt sorry for him, a feeling she remembered better than anything else but not the feeling that ultimately made her leave him. Scooter felt for his wallet; the gesture was like a surrender. He was a small man, physically jumpy in a way that had been attractive in college.

Dave and Davette were staring at them. Davette stood with her hands dangling at her sides, her spiky hair in a mass over one shoulder, while Dave little by little pasted himself to the one wall: first his heels, then his back, his elbows, his head. Each of his motions seemed designed to look casual.

"Are we still gonna get paid?" he asked.

Nicola felt a spurt of anger. "I don't think so, Dave."

"Well, you can't blame us for trying."

"I can blame you for failing," Nicola answered. She didn't know what annoyed her more: the fact that they kidnapped her or that they were so bad at it. Scooter was watching her with the expression of a man used to conceding the point. He looked even smaller in his large overcoat, and when he sat down his eyes narrowed as if he were ordering the events in his head, still trying to work out how it all had come to this.

"So what's the story this time?" she asked him.

"It's more or less more of the same," Scooter said.

"Money?"

"Pretty much."

"Well you could have just asked."

Scooter shrugged. "I thought you'd say no."

"That you were right about. But hold on—" Nicola turned to Davette. "Are you both really called Dave?"

"Yeah," Davette said.

"That's just much too confusing. From here on you're Davette. Okay? Okay, good. Now listen, Davette, this is the most important thing you'll do tonight. Get my black bag and take out the address book, which is in the inside pocket—I believe you found it before. Go to 'P' and look under 'pizza' and call the number I have there, then order the largest pizza you can with tomatoes and anchovies.

Got that? Tomatoes and anchovies. And I want one of their cornmeal crusts."

Davette went off for the purse, her big black jacket making its usual puffy noises as she went, while Dave picked at his nails with his minitool. Meanwhile Nicola could feel Scooter watching her. Waiting for instructions.

So now things were different. Scooter, in fact, was a game she knew how to play. Nicola felt as though sometime in the night she had finally figured out how to get what she wanted. Now she knew. It was not about the situation, any situation, it was who you were— and trusting that. It was *knowing* you could get what you want. And what she wanted was to be the one in charge.

She pulled off her shoes and stretched, making Scooter wait. Here she was, the one in charge. She was in charge now and it felt great. Tonight she'll sleep in her own bed on the white silk sheets she bought the day the divorce became final. She will wash her face, she will put on her silk jammies, and she will sleep in her own bed. And tomorrow, Nicola thought, I'll get on with everything else. Davette came back into the room and Nicola checked the purse over quickly but everything was still there: her money, her credit cards, her keys, her picture of Lester.

"Okay," Nicola said, and she turned back to Scooter. "Now tell me the whole story," she said.

Eight

The story began in the usual way: Scooter got tired of what he was doing and wanted to make money faster. He'd been working as a partner in a door-to-door seafood-and-steak operation in L.A. when he met a guy who knew a guy with a dog kennel in Apache Junction, and when the guy he knew headed out that way (actually he was on his way to Tempe to buy or sell or do something with a car), Scooter decided to hitch a lift and check out some races he'd heard about.

"Greyhounds pay better than horses," Scooter told them. He was sitting in the desk chair, swiveling it slightly with his foot. "The trick is to stay out of the dog cage."

The Daves were sitting near him on the floor while Nicola stood against the doorframe, drinking a bottle of water she'd found in the half-finished kitchenette. She watched Scooter swivel his chair again, then use one of the levers to adjust the backrest back and forth, back and forth—probably, she thought, without even noticing. Scooter was small but his body was lit with a constant nervous energy that made him seem larger. He had thick, rough hair in a light shade that was not quite blond, and his nose was noticeably long. Still, there was something attractive about him: the way he held his body, his excited interest in each project du jour.

She took a long sip of water. How long had it been, three years, since she'd seen him? Not counting this morning. As he spoke Nicola found herself thinking with no nostalgia about their old apartment above the bicycle shop (now an Asian fusion restaurant) near Golden Gate Park, which they decorated from catalogs—the Danish floor lamp, the futon couch, the mounted posters, a rough jute rug—when the only difference between them and their other coupley friends was that they were actually married. Married! Because that was another one of Scooter's hot ideas: let's get married!

Well, at the time it had seemed like it might be fun. At first Nicola imagined life with a visionary, someone surprising and entertaining, but as it turned out all his ideas were about the same thing: money. Once he got someone to pay him in cash, five hundred dollars in tens and fives, and he threw all the bills into their empty bathtub and brought her in: look at that! This was motivation.

"What's the dog's cage?" she asked.

"The Saturday night crowd, the house number crowd," Scooter explained. "It's hard at first for rookies because there are no pool totals posted on the tote board. You have to choose your race and wait."

He adjusted the angle of the chair back then swiveled back and forth and back and forth.

"So one night I was talking to one of the announcers just to, you know, sound him out a little because in something like this you want to find an insider. And this announcer let me in on a secret: the dogs run faster when they're in their favorite box."

"How do you know which is their favorite?" Nicola asked.

"That's where the skill lies."

He smiled and swiveled. Nicola looked at the Daves, who were sitting on the floor like kindergartners looking up at him. Rapt.

She put down her water bottle. "What's the bottom line here," she said. "How much did you lose."

"Wait, let me just finish, it's pretty exciting. In fact, I would definitely advise you to try this sometime. I found this one dog that was really fast and I watched him for a couple of races. Primogeniture. The races where Primo did well he was in an inside box. So in his last race I went with him in four to seven all and keyed him in with five other dogs for sixty bucks and then I did seven six-dollar keys with Primo on top plus one hundred bucks to show plus the quinella."

Nicola had never been to a racetrack. "I have no idea what that means."

"What it means is, when Primo won I got fifteen hundred dollars. Fifteen hundred dollars in thirty point oh two seconds!"

"NFW," Dave said.

"FW," Scooter told him.

Nicola looked over at Dave, annoyed. Had he already forgotten that Scooter had tricked him into perpetrating a felony? Her wrists were still burning and she thought there might be something in the corner of her eye, a piece of silk or something from the blindfold, which she couldn't blink out. Dave was sitting on a strip of carpet looking very rugged with his army haircut and his untied boots and his legs stretched out before him. Part of her wanted to humiliate him, which surprised her—she had no idea she was so retaliatory. On the other hand, she was also willing for him to wait around until it was time to do her tedious chores.

She looked at her watch. "You should pick up that pizza now," she told Dave.

"But I want to hear the end!"

"The end is, he lost it."

"Not lost, not lost, because what I'm doing here is developing a system," Scooter said. "I just need to plug up a couple of holes."

He hadn't changed, she could see that. She asked him how much he lost. The whole fifteen hundred?

"Actually," Scooter said, "and this I admit was another mistake, I borrowed some money too because that's how sure I was about Primo, I was thinking this could be it for the year, no more door-to-door lobsters."

"How much?" Nicola asked again.

"You know, not much, I don't know, about twice that again, or what's that come to, maybe four times. But the people I borrowed from, they're pretty cool. It's a small business, family-owned. Right now they just need the interest, you know how that works," Scooter told her. "I have to show my good faith. So I thought, cool, I'll get like six hundred dollars and that will tide them over a while. I thought of you right away. Only I knew that with you the bank was closed. I knew that. So I thought I'd just . . ."

" 'Borrow' a little something?"

Scooter stopped swiveling and smiled at her. "Exactly! But I couldn't actually, you know, do the kidnapping myself. For one, you'd know my voice. Plus I'm too nice."

"Hey, we're nice," Dave protested.

"Technically," said Nicola, "I don't think that's true."

"I thought we did a pretty good job."

Nicola stared at him. "Dave, you failed."

"We learned something, though," he said.

Scooter caught Nicola's eye and smiled, and Nicola smiled back, thinking one of the things she always liked about him was how he had absolutely no sense of irony. He was misguided but upfront. He was not cynical, not usually. Once just before she left him Nicola found one of his lists:

New house with new appliances (alarm systems etc.)
Flat-screen TV
More olives, mangoes, avocados, organic fruit (organic OJ)
Exercise room (hardwood floor)
Pool? Outdoor/indoor?
Child's name: Griffin

It was a list of things he wanted. Why did she think he was idealistic? He was practical and literal, and in many ways she was the same, although it was his perceived difference that had originally attracted her.

Nicola sent the Daves out for the pizza, then she went around the room opening the heating vents. The room grew noticeably warmer. Meanwhile Scooter swiveled around in the desk chair and played the backrest back and forth. No doubt cooking up some new plan, Nicola thought.

Already, it seemed, he was over not getting her money. Well, he had always been good at bouncing past a setback. He was the idea man, the man with a plan. A fast talker, her mother had told her. She was right. The whole time they were married Scooter talked and talked, first about this and then about that, always changing the subject after a few days. He talked and talked and talked and talked. Once when Nicola was in her car stopped at a light she watched Scooter cross the street muttering to himself in the crosswalk and she thought, *Look* at him, he's *still talking.*

Nicola went to the window. If she stood in the right spot she could see the orange lights from downtown. All she wanted was to eat and then go home and sleep for three days.

She said, "So how did you find those two anyway?"

"Who, the Daves? I put a sign up at their school."

"Jesus, Scooter! You put up a sign in a *high* school?"

"They were really looking for computer work," he said. "Davette's pretty good—she got behind Bank of America's main firewall twice. I'm still trying to work that angle somewhere."

Nicola looked outside again. The minivan was just pulling up. "You are headed for serious trouble," she told him.

But he had given her an idea.

Later, while they were eating the pizza, she asked him about his loan shark. Was he in Los Angeles?

"Yeah," Scooter said, looping a piece of cheese over his slice. "But I'm meeting his son or his nephew or someone here tomorrow. After that I'm going to check out a race at Golden Gate Fields. Did you know that genetically wolves and dogs are the same species? Every dog is a wolf."

"I had a dog once who was an epileptic," Dave told him. He picked off an anchovy and ate it. "Turns out it was the plastic bowl. Plastic really absorbs the chlorine in water, which is highly toxic to dogs."

"I thought it was chocolate that was so bad for dogs," Davette said.

"We got a metal bowl and his fits just stopped."

Dave pulled up his legs to his chest and Davette stretched, then took off her tundra boots. Nicola took another bite of pizza. She watched them for a moment. Davette had a sharp look to her; she was someone who paid attention but not always to the right things. Dave's strengths were less apparent. He knew how to start a job then keep it moving, you could say that for him.

"Listen, I might have some work for you two," Nicola told them. "If you're interested."

"I'm not doing the kidnapping thing again," Davette said.

"No, this should be legal."

"Should be," Dave repeated. "What's it pay?"

"Same as he paid."

"Don't you think we should get a raise?"

This she could not believe.

"You're lucky I'm not going to the police," she said.

"But you wouldn't," Dave said, "because of *him*." A gesture toward Scooter.

"As if I haven't set the police on him before," Nicola lied. She turned back to Scooter. "Tell me more about the guy you're meeting tomorrow."

"His name is Lou," Scooter said. "I'm meeting him for breakfast downtown."

"You're having breakfast with your loan shark?"

"Like I said, he's the nephew or something, I don't know. He's from New Jersey. He told me he'll be carrying around a big notebook, like a sketch pad, or I can't remember exactly what he said. Maybe he's a painter or something."

"Christ, a loan shark with a hobby," said Nicola.

"Or he sketches, I don't know. Does something with charcoal. He said I would know him," Scooter said.

"How would you know him?"

"Maybe he'll look very New Jersey."

"Lou from New Jersey," Nicola said. She stretched and rolled her neck. It was time to go home.

"Listen, where are your car keys?" she asked Scooter.

"Why?"

"You're driving me home. I'm going to sleep for, let's see," she looked at her watch, "about three hours. Then I'm taking your meeting with Lou."

Scooter stared at her, his mouth slightly open. A thin cheese strand was dangling from his chin, and his eyes were wild from sleeplessness. "You're taking my meeting?"

Nicola almost smiled—he looked like a five-year-old who'd been playing outside too long. "Alone," she told him.

The meeting with New Jersey Lou was way across town near the bay. After she slept Nicola showered, then put on a dark red chemise and a short black skirt and black pumps and a half-buttoned black blouse, the chemise clearly visible underneath. She wanted to look good. Serious, but good. Traffic was light at this hour and it was only when she turned up Jones Street and began to look for parking that she realized where the meeting was: the San Francisco School of Art. Was Scooter's loan shark or bookie or whoever he was—Lou—was he a student, someone who considered himself knowledgeable in art? She could already imagine the lectures about chiaroscuro or whatnot. How many times had she listened to a man explain away his opinion as fact with the air of bestowing a gift? It was best to be defended beforehand, and she tried out various distracting remarks:

"Excuse me but do you think there are tampons in the bathroom?"

"I'm using this very drying lice medication."

"That always makes me think about sex."

Nicola parked, then walked through a large arch leading into a courtyard. In the middle of the courtyard stood a round tiled fish pool with a rim wide enough to be used as a bench.

She walked toward the pool, where a man was sitting with a notebook open in front of him. He wore a white and blue sticky label on his shirt that said HI! MY NAME IS: LOU.

Was this a joke? He was much younger than she had imagined.

"Are you waiting for Scott Whitmore?"

The man looked up from his notebook. He was about her age and had dark hair and dark eyes. He wore a white button-down shirt and his face had been recently shaved.

"I'm taking Scott's meeting for him," Nicola told him.

Lou looked her over.

"You're not a lawyer," he said.

"No," she agreed.

"Is Scott all right?"

"He's either asleep on a floor or asleep on a bus."

At that Lou smiled. He was not what she had expected. His skin was very clear and this combined with his white shirt and clean shave made him look like a boy in a Catholic high school. His face was serious but not threatening, the face of a student. He didn't look like the kind of guy someone owed money to, but except for bad skin she didn't really know what that kind of guy would look like.

Nicola watched him flip close his notebook. She hoped he wasn't going to show her his sketches now or any time in the future, and she practiced the line about tampons in her head.

"Are you hungry?" he asked. "Have you had breakfast? There's a café right here."

Nicola knew it—a divey student-run kind of place with great food and a fantastic view of the bay. A bank of windows took up one wall and Alcatraz lay directly outside, for once displayed in its natural context: a tiny rock dwarfed by the huge green state park, Angel Island, which lay behind it.

"Let me suggest one of their muffins," said Lou as they went into the building. "This place specializes in homey baked goods, still warm from the oven."

Homey baked goods? Nicola glanced at him, but he had an absolutely deadpan expression. Who was this guy? He was still wearing his nametag. The café was self-serve with a counter facing the short-order cook, and since it was early they were the only ones there. A chalkboard on the counter claimed there were banana muffins and cranberry-orange; Lou asked for banana but when Nicola wanted that too he changed to the cranberry.

"These are the best lattes in town," he said. "Whole milk, organic, no hormones, no milk machines." Lou turned back to the cook. "Are the coffee beans from shade plants or sun?" he asked.

Clearly this was a man who breakfasted seriously. Nicola, who had planned to ask for a latte, ordered a large coffee instead.

"Guatemalan or Aged Sumatra?" the clerk asked.

"Whatever's closest."

Lou seemed not to have heard but she thought he was listening. He can't help himself, Nicola thought, he's going to tell me which is better. But he just settled his latte on his tray and looked at the fry range. He was moderately built and handled objects attentively, not like Scooter, who moved fast and was always on the verge of spilling something or dropping something else. Lou, on the other hand, seemed—Nicola searched for the word—comfortable. He seemed comfortable.

"That bacon smells excellent," Lou said to the cook, a young man wearing a tie-dyed scarf around his head.

"Smoked and peppered," the cook said, and handed him a piece. "Taste."

As they walked to a table Lou said, "Extremely friendly student staff."

Nicola glanced at him. "You sound like a restaurant critic," she said.

He looked at her sharply. "Really? In what way?"

"The baked goods comment, the comment about the staff."

They put their trays down on a long trestle table overlooking the bay. Below them, ferries carried people to Oakland or Sausalito, while huge dirty sailboats tacked up and down the bay for pleasure. Lou was watching Nicola with his serious dark eyes.

"I've gone out to eat with a lot of clients," he said. "No one has ever said that before."

"Oh, well." Nicola was dismissive. She began pouring some half-and-half into her coffee.

"I mean," Lou continued. "I'm just very surprised you picked up on that. Because you're right."

"You're a restaurant critic?"

"Or more generally food."

"Really? A food critic?" She couldn't tell if she was being put on or not. "I thought you loaned money, then charged exorbitant rates of interest."

"Not exorbitant, never exorbitant," Lou protested. "And, anyway, that's just my profession; food is my hobby."

"How many reviews have you done?" Nicola asked.

"This would be my first," Lou said. He smelled the muffin. "But I've been practicing for years."

Nicola laughed. This is one weird guy, she thought. She liked him and supposed this was part of his game. A few students came into the café and looked at the food display as if they were waiting at a bus stop and had just spotted a bus.

"So what's wrong with the loan business?" Nicola asked.

"It's my uncle's business. It's a fine business; it's just not mine."

She watched him get ready to taste the muffin. He broke it open and looked inside at the yellow marbly texture, then touched it with his fingertip.

"A strong orange flavor," he pronounced after he bit into it. "But not too strong. Actually, the degree of tartness is perfect. How's yours?"

"I don't know. It's good."

"Can you say anything more?"

"I like its crunchy top," Nicola said.

"Let me taste."

She gave him her muffin and he broke a piece off.

"Mmm. This is very good. A strong taste of banana, but it does not overwhelm." He took another bite. "Neither does the sweetness. I think this one is better. You know, banana muffins are among the more difficult ones to bake. Bake well, that is."

"So you cook, too?" Nicola asked.

"Only dishes someone has taught me. My mom and my uncle are both great cooks. I like to know what I'm doing."

"But you know, they have these things now called recipes," Nicola told him. "They're like directions."

Lou smiled. "Well, yeah, recipes. I'm waiting for the recipe that says, Skin the meat from the bone and dice into small pieces; this could take upwards of five hours."

The café's cement walls and ceiling made Nicola feel as if she was in a soundproof box. They sat at the long table, too big for two people, and while Nicola finished her muffin Lou explained how it was important, when reviewing food, to go with other people so you could sample as many dishes as possible. At the same time discretion is necessary—you want the typical fare, not something prepared especially well this one time to please a reviewer.

Lou opened his notebook and wrote something down.

"This sort of place," he said, "is perfect for a beginner like me. An undiscovered studenty place with some unknown cook."

"Actually, the man who runs this is a well-known chef."

"Really?" Lou looked disappointed. "How do you know?"

"I've eaten here a lot."

"Were you a student?"

"I took some classes years ago," Nicola said. He nodded, sipping his latte, and waited for her to say more. Obviously he was in no rush. As far as he knew she was someone—who?—there to agree to his terms.

Nicola blew on her coffee. Well, he could bring up the topic whenever he liked, he could talk about food forever, that was fine with her. She knew she looked good and she felt great, her adrenaline was up, and although she was tired she hardly felt it. Also her skirt was the exact right amount of tightness, just enough so she felt it without being binding.

"It's pretty, isn't it?" Lou said. He was looking at the inside of the muffin. Around them students began talking about art supply places, and although they were loud there was a friendly, uplifting tone to their talk. Their artwork hung everywhere—in the courtyard, in the hallways, in the bathrooms (the toilet seats featured colorful embalmed fish)—and the café tables were stained with smears of paint. It was beginning to get crowded; soon someone would sit with them.

"Maybe we should talk about Scott," Nicola said.

"I can't do business while I'm eating," Lou said. "Let's walk down to the wharf after this."

Nicola got a refill of coffee and took it with her when they were ready to go. Outside the sky was white with fog and they crossed Columbus Avenue then walked down the hill toward the bay, following the cable car tracks. They passed the soft-shell crab restaurants and the souvenir hat and T-shirt shops and the racks of postcards and dangling cable car key chains and then they walked out onto the wooden pier.

Lou was not much taller than she was—a couple of inches maybe. Nicola liked that; it made them seem more equal somehow. They stopped halfway down the pier and Nicola sat down on a bench overlooking the water. In the distance she could hear seals barking for popcorn or whatever it was tourists were feeding them.

She wrapped her hands around her cardboard cup. It was windy and cold and she couldn't see much past the few ships that were permanently docked—a submarine and an old navy clipper. Lou wore a comfortable-looking suede jacket.

"Would you like to wear my coat?" he asked.

"I have on silk underwear," she said, and looked at him. She wanted to see him look surprised; she wanted to throw him off a little bit before they began. But Lou's expression didn't change. He watched her steadily, waiting for more.

"Which is very warm," she finished.

He smiled then, and looked out at the water. She wasn't sure if he was disconcerted or not. She took a sip of her coffee but it was still too hot.

"You really should have tried their lattes," he said. "They were excellent."

"In what way?"

"A good combination of hot liquid with full flavor. Some places think a high degree of heat is enough."

"That last needs some rewording," Nicola said.

Lou got out his notebook and wrote something down. The seagulls called to each other without stopping and there was a heavy clang of boat equipment—an anchor chain hitting the side of the dock. Soon the tourists would arrive wearing thick sweatshirts and baseball caps. Nicola looked at the band of restaurants along the south shore.

"So can we talk about Scott now?" she asked.

"Is he prepared to agree to whatever terms you and I come to?"

"He agrees."

"Then let's get started," Lou said. He opened his briefcase. "Here's his bill."

Nicola looked at it, then frowned. "It's a little higher than he led me to believe."

"It always is."

She read it over carefully. One loan was incurred three years before.

"We offer an initial two-month grace period and you'll notice our terms of interest are *not* exorbitant; they're very competitive," Lou was saying. "And here's a form you can fill out if for any reason you need to miss a payment—if you submit this within two weeks you are eligible for another two-month grace period, pending review. Just check the applicable category: death, illness, emotional turmoil. We're usually good for one per year. Oh, and here, I guess I can give you this." Lou shuffled through his briefcase and took something out.

"A complimentary key ring. We also have movie coupons but I seem to be out."

Nicola said nothing. Lou must have thought she was stalling because he said, "Should I show you where to sign?"

"No I don't think so." She handed him back the bill. "I have a proposition for you, Lou."

Lou raised his eyebrows.

"I can pay off Scott's loan today, right now if you want," she said. "In return for a favor."

"What's that?"

"I have a problem. My landlord wants to evict me. He served me a notice that stated that one of his family members wants to move into my house, but I don't believe him. I don't think he has any family members, in which case this is an unlawful eviction. I've lived in the house for four years, and the first two years I lived with a friend who had lived there alone for three years before that. In all that time— seven years—rent prices on the open market have gone up over eighty percent."

"How much do you pay now?"

"Let me just say that I think my landlord could get eight hundred dollars more a month for the house. And I would pay eight hundred dollars or more a month for a comparable situation. There have been cases where landlords in the Mission District have paid their tenants thousands of dollars to move out so they could raise the prices to market levels. In some places they were able to triple the rent. *Triple* it."

"Why don't you just buy a house?"

"With twelve thousand dollars?" Nicola asked. "Maybe if I were married and my husband and I both had high salaries and we were willing to take on a three-hundred-thousand-dollar mortgage, maybe then I could."

Lou watched a seagull pick at some gum on the ground a few feet away. "So what's the favor," he asked.

"I would like you to help me prove my landlord has no family members, or at least none in the area, and none that want to move in."

"What makes you think I can do that?"

"Your profession. You follow people, right? You dig up a little dirt, you scare them."

"All I do is keep track of people and every once in a while remind them what they owe," he said mildly. "They bring their own fear."

She watched him watching the seagull. "I think you can help me," she said. "I imagine you find people who don't want to be found, and that must take some skill."

The seagull stopped picking at the gum and flew off. Lou turned back to Nicola.

"And in return you'll give me twelve thousand dollars," he said.

"Which I'll save up again in just over a year if my rent doesn't increase. After that I can start saving again. But if I have to start paying eight hundred dollars more every month in rent I might as well leave the city; I'll never be able to save a dime."

"But the twelve thousand dollars, the money you'll give me, that's mine anyway," Lou said. "It's money Scott owes me. Why should I do anything more to get it?"

"Have you ever gotten money from Scott?"

"I've gotten a lot of money from a lot of people."

"Yes, but it takes time, and from Scott it will take a lot of time. Believe me, I know this. And your time is valuable," Nicola said.

"It's really not that valuable."

"Maybe to your uncle it is."

Lou looked at the pier again and again Nicola waited out the silence. She liked his deliberate motions; she felt he was competent, he could be counted on. At the same time there was something casual about him; she could almost see him on a surf board. Someone she might have gone to school with. He was not a loan shark by nature, or if he was then the whole business seemed tame and orderly, men who sold a product—money—then delivered the bill.

"How long have you been in this business anyway?" she asked.

"Only a couple of years." Lou smiled. "I needed a job after I was kicked out of law school."

"You've got to be kidding."

"Well, actually I just left, but being kicked out sounds better."

He got up to walk her back to her car. As they left the pier he said, "We usually count on a few months of interest. If you could kick that in, then I'll do it."

"A few or a couple?"

"Three."

"I can do that," Nicola said. She had been prepared to go as high as five.

"But what if your landlord is telling the truth?" Lou asked.

"If he is, then I've lost my investment. But my belief in humanity will have risen."

She smiled at him. The wind had died down and the sun was coming out and she was feeling better and better. In fact she was almost cheerful in spite of a damp spongy sensation near her eyes and temple—fatigue probably—and the sore edges around her mouth where duct tape had been ripped off again and again.

But she had won the first round. She had been kidnapped and she had gotten away. Her six hundred dollars was back in her purse and her purse was safely back over her own shoulder. And her mysterious persecutor was Scooter! Scooter, whose own mother once told him he was born to be an ex-husband.

Now it looked like she might solve her eviction problem too. At least she was on her way. Nicola offered to write Lou a check for half the amount now and the other half in a week, and Lou agreed. Then, as they waited to cross Beach Street, Nicola wrote down her landlord's name and address and gave it to him.

Lou looked at the paper. "Twelve Bliss Street," he read. "Where's that?"

"I have no idea. Knowing Robert, it's probably some seedy little alley near the highway."

The light changed and they stepped out into the street where a few tourists were parking their cars or reading posted menus. Nicola looked at her watch.

"Why do you meet for breakfast if you can't do business while you're eating?" she asked Lou.

"Actually," he said, "I usually *do* do business while I'm eating. I just, I didn't want to this time."

"Why not?"

"Well," Lou hesitated. "For one thing I wanted to see the wharf," he said.

She took a chance. "You were impressed when I guessed you were a restaurant critic," she said.

"Food critic," he corrected.

"A food critic. You were impressed. You wanted to see more of me."

Lou smiled an easy kind of grin. "Who wouldn't," he said.

They walked by the restaurants, then turned down a smaller street with a line of motel signs: Wharf Motel, Piedmont Motel, Daily and Weekly Rates. As she passed one open doorway, a man standing in the vestibule wearing a silver bracelet reached out to close the door—Nicola's attention was caught by the bracelet and she looked up in time to see the man's face. It was Chorizo.

"That's strange," she said.

"What?" Lou asked.

"The man in there—we eat lunch sometimes at the same time in a café near my office. He told me he lived in Noe Valley."

Lou stopped for a moment and looked back at the motel.

"Golden Gate Rooms," he said. "Maybe he works there."

"And eats lunch in West Portal? It's way across town."

"Did he see you, too?"

"I'm not sure," Nicola said, looking at the closed door.

Nine

Chorizo locked the motel door after he closed it, yawned, then set the Vacancy sign to NO. He was tired from last night—he didn't get done until almost four in the morning, and he still had some, what should he call it, some tidying up to do.

When he walked back to the small room he used as an office the accountant was still sitting in front of the computer, an accounting log on her lap and two more open on the desk. She played with a strand of her hair as she examined one of the books, turned a page, then positioned the book better under the desk lamp.

The room was dark. Although there were two square windows looking out into the yard—a small patch of sandy dirt with a few abandoned paint buckets and irregular fencing—the room was always dark. It was also crowded. Junk mail and phone books and accounting records were stacked on every conceivable surface, and a large ancient copier took up one corner. A fat gray and black cat lay on top of the copier and a litter box was positioned on the floor beside it. The room smelled of paper and pine-scented kitty litter. Chorizo picked up a small manicure case that was on his desk, the desk with the phone, and looked at the tiny steel instruments inside.

"Is your brother coming?" he asked.

"He said he would."

He moved a log book and sat down on the only other chair in the office. Then he selected an emery board and began filing his thumbnail carefully, leveling the nail in one direction. The woman's fingernails were terrible, bitten and split. She chewed on her thumbnail as she sat there.

"You're very restless," Chorizo said.

"I've been here all night," she reminded him.

"You have until Friday," Chorizo said. "I'm sure you can make everything clean and pretty by then."

"They should have audited you years ago."

She was young and pretty and wore small oval eyeglasses and had long dark hair and dark eyes. As she studied the book on her lap she crossed one leg over the other, then began jiggling her foot.

"Restlessness is a form of fear, you know," Chorizo told her. He looked at his thumbnail, then began filing the nail of his index finger. "A fear of death. We play with our hair, we jiggle our knees, all in the vain attempt to prove we are still alive. We think that if we just keep moving we won't die on the spot."

The woman did not appear to be listening. "I'm putting all the receipts with no dates in this envelope," she told him.

Chorizo selected a small rosewood stick from his manicure set and began to push back his cuticles.

"And yet fear is good," he went on. "It's the primary attribute of a warrior. Without fear, we cannot experience fearlessness. One feels afraid, one moves beyond it. I'm speaking of the spiritual warrior."

He paused again, then took out a small blue bottle of cuticle complex and squeezed some onto his fingers. The woman looked from book to computer to book again, and in the silence noises from the outside could be heard—a shout, the screech of bus brakes. Chorizo rubbed lotion into his skin, then stopped as if to listen.

"I'm looking for nineteen ninety-eight," the woman said.

Chorizo looked at his hands again. "The spiritual warrior is an optimist. He does not give up on anyone or anything."

The woman swiveled in her chair and began looking through another pile.

"Even lost records," he said.

His silver bracelet clinked on the desktop and he turned it around, pulling a few dark hairs away from the chain links, then looked at his cuticles again.

"Did you know men's nails grow faster than women's? But the increased surface area makes them more vulnerable to bumps and bangs, which can cause splitting. Some say you should never cut your nails on a boat; this brings bad luck. But if you cut your nails on a Sunday, you will bring someone else bad luck. I like that one. My mother told me that one."

There was a knock on the door and Chorizo swung back in his desk chair and rolled over to the door to open it. A tall, heavyset man with dark hair and dark eyes walked in and went immediately over to the woman at the desk, who glanced up at him.

"What do you think?" Chorizo said.

The man looked at Chorizo's outstretched hands. "About what?"

"My nails! I'm thinking of buffing, though the effect of that has not been proven. The trouble is there, do you see the bulges in the middle of my thumbnails? It's a certain sign of an early death. However, on the other hand, you see these white spots? They bring good luck. Never go to a palm reader; hand reading is so uncertain."

"Are you all right?" the man asked his sister. "Have you eaten anything?"

"Never mind her," Chorizo said. "Let her work. Listen, I want you to do something for me."

The man looked at Chorizo. "What?"

"I want you to find someone for me, a woman named Nicola something. I don't know her last name, but she works somewhere on West Portal. She's a dental hygienist," he said.

Ten

It **was hard** to believe that after that whole weekend, after the kidnapping and the night tied to a chair and the breakfast meeting with a bookie, for Christ's sake, which she never dreamed would be a scheduled item in her day, after all that today was still just a Monday—*Monday*—and the feeling of Monday doesn't change no matter what comes before it. Nicola mentally divided the morning into its major segments: power walk, muni, coffee. The minor segments, like work, fit in without much thought and it was better that way.

On Mondays, Nicola found, it's best not to think too much. It's best to just get on with the schedule, just start it all up again. This she did well.

At the office she hung up her jacket and turned on work mode. The meeting with Fred was scheduled for eleven. At ten-thirty Nicola could hear Guy sneezing down the hall and she knew that any minute he would pop his head in and complain about dust, which was usually his prelude before unleashing his anxiety du jour and asking Nicola to step into his office.

The fact was this: she was second in command here and she hated it. Alia, the nominal boss, was too busy looking after her spiritual condition to do much, so Guy made the decisions and had Nicola carry them out. In Nicola's favorite fantasy, Guy was forced to move to New York City and find work as a house cleaner. She liked to picture him wearing a mesh hairnet.

"Nicola, could I see you a minute?" Guy asked from the doorway. "Jesus, the air in this room could kill you."

As Nicola left, Audrey gave her a thumb's-up and Carlos said, "Be brave, young soldier." Nicola followed Guy to his office. She felt her short suede skirt rub against her legs as she walked. That morning she had looked through her closet feeling strong and smart and wanting to look fantastic. She chose the skirt and a tight brown top and a black silk camisole, which was only just visible. She knew she looked great, but all of it was wasted on Guy. He sat down at his desk and barely even glanced at her.

"About Fred," he said, looking at his computer screen.

"Yes," Nicola began. She had given this a lot of thought on the muni this morning. "You know, I was thinking about what you said last Friday, and I agree, you should definitely sit in on the meeting."

"Oh, I should?" Guy was surprised. "Why is that?"

"We could do a little good cop bad cop. I tell him the bad news, you tell him the good."

"There's good news?"

"I outlined it in that memo, the goNetURI solution."

Guy was dismissive. "Oh right. Like I said on Friday, I don't think that will work. Don't waste your time."

Nicola pulled her chair closer to Guy's desk, then swiveled his computer so she could work on it. "I put up the test site this morning," she said. "Watch."

Images fell from the screen. Nicola clicked on one at random, and a new window opened.

"Huh," Guy said.

"Just what Fred wanted. He'll want to know how it worked, and as the good cop you can explain it. I put it all in my memo. Just spell it out in layman's terms."

"I didn't get a memo," Guy said.

"Here's a copy."

Guy looked it over. "Huh. Huh. Huh," he said, frowning. "Okay. Well, since you got it working, okay, but it seems overly complicated."

Nicola looked at him steadily. She was not afraid of him, not anymore. Had she really been *afraid* of him?

"Oh Fred loves that," she said. "He likes to think he's hiring rocket scientists to work exclusively on his site. Just explain it in detail."

"Is that right," Guy said. He was still looking at the memo. Then he looked at his computer screen. Awkwardly, he moved the mouse over and clicked one of the images.

"It seems to work," he said.

"It's beautiful," Nicola told him. She shifted a little in her seat and pulled at her skirt. Guy looked down at her leg.

"But I have an idea," he said. "Why don't I be the bad cop? That way you could explain all this in detail and as you do it you could flirt, smile with him a little. Remember how you were going to smile? Butter him up. Make him feel, you know, wanted."

"Wanted?"

"Well just a little." Guy smirked.

Nicola pretended to consider it. "We could do it that way," she said.

"Good. Okay, then."

"We could do it that way except for the obvious problem."

"What's that?"

"Fred's gay."

"He's gay?"

Nicola smiled. "So really it should be you smiling and flirting."

"Me?" Guy laughed. "Oh I couldn't do that."

"Why not?"

"Well why do you think?"

"I have no idea."

"Because I'm not gay!"

"Does that matter?"

"Of course it does! He won't believe me. You should do it," Guy said.

Nicola raised her eyebrows; this should be interesting, she thought.

"You're the *woman*," Guy explained, "so you should flirt. It'll be more effective."

"A woman flirting with a gay man is effective?"

"More believable, then."

Nicola swung a little in her chair and looked pointedly at Guy. "So you're saying it will be more believable if I flirt with someone whom I know does not desire me or anyone like me? Is that what you're saying? It will work better if the one flirting is the one not desired? Is that what you're saying?"

Guy looked down, then looked around the room. "Hunh," he mumbled.

"Okay, then."

"Well," he said.

Nicola smiled. "So, okay."

She took the meeting alone.

Fred walked in late, wearing the sour expression of a man who might bag groceries for a living; in fact, come to think of it, he did look a lot like the man who bagged Nicola's groceries for her and who had once told her he was fertile every fourteen years. A come-on? Fred had a full red face and wore crumpled trousers and a shirt that always seemed to hang on him crookedly, like a flag at half mast. Probably, Nicola thought, he had never flirted with a woman in his life. He had one outstanding skill: he could slow a meeting down to a standstill.

But Nicola brought chocolate cookies to the table and every time there was a pause she fed another one to Fred. Meanwhile she talked and talked, and she said she understood his problems, and said she thought she could solve them, and she said here take another cookie while I explain something we've done that might help with that, and in the end Fred was on a vast happy sugar high and all the features Nicola particularly wanted stayed in. In fact, Fred even went so far as to promise the next check on time—a first, if he could be trusted.

"Thank you, Nicola," Fred said at the elevator, and he held out his hand.

Had Fred ever thanked her before? As she walked down the hall to the bathroom she was smiling to herself. Unbelievable—a Monday that is better than a Friday. She's got it, she sang to herself in the bathroom mirror. Yeah, baby, she's got it. Nicola touched her face, trying to see herself in profile. Her hair looked great.

"Admit it, you get off on the pressure," Audrey said to her later, when they went to pick up sandwiches for the team. It was cloudy out and cold and Nicola buttoned her leather jacket as they walked down the street.

"I'm not saying I don't like a little adrenaline flow," she admitted.

"Fred is your favorite customer because he puts up a good fight."

"And today," Nicola said, "I won. What could be better?"

They crossed the street quickly, their heads bent against the sudden gusts of wind. The rain started in a meagerly way, then stopped again, and a few homeless men sat on tarps on the sidewalk.

"I could never do what you do; it would make me too nervous," Audrey said. "When things get tense I have to go outside so I can relax for a minute. And these days even that doesn't help. I mean, look at it." Audrey gestured around. The street did seem very bleak. It was gray and cold and the palm trees looked like great sad, hairy Dr. Seuss beasts bending in the wind. But Nicola herself felt great. How long had it been, three days since the kidnapping? Still, she felt completely different. Either it was real change or it wasn't. Either she would go back to the way she had been, or she wouldn't.

She stepped around a flower cart, thinking about Friday night. She had been tied up, she had been kidnapped, her purse had been taken from her and rifled through, and they had laughed at her hair. But through it all, strangely, she did not feel like a victim. She was a victim, but she didn't feel like a victim. She knew one thing—now she was going to fight for what she wanted. She was going to fight, and she was going to fight hard. This wasn't bravery; it was sanity.

"I have a fantasy that Declan and I quit all this and move in with my brother," Audrey went on. "We could help him make his bamboo flutes."

"Your brother makes a living making bamboo flutes?"

"And bamboo headjoints. He also tutors people on breaking them in; they have to be played in gradually and protected against sudden temperature changes. He advises rubbing the finger holes with edible oil."

"Is this the brother who went to Princeton?" Nicola asked.

"Brian. But he's trying to get his name changed legally to Yevgeny."

Nicola laughed.

"I know, I know," Audrey said. "But it *would* be nice to live right on the ocean."

Nicola glanced at her. Her face looked suddenly wistful. They walked past the record store and the place with incredible fudge. A giant chocolate Santa stood in the store window.

Nicola said, "I wish I had just one friend who didn't talk about leaving."

Audrey looked away. "Oh, San Francisco is so overrated—the fog, the palm trees, the paint jobs. But go to McDonald's and it looks just like anywhere else."

"In Hawaii McDonald's serves mahi mahi," Nicola told her.

"Really?"

"Mahi mahi on a stick."

They stepped into the café and out of habit Nicola looked around the room, but Chorizo wasn't there. Well, she didn't really expect to see him. She was sure he had been the man at that hotel, and, hey, you know what, she thought, he was probably there with some other woman. Actually, it surprised her that she hadn't considered that before.

She thought about his birthmark, his smooth conversation. I must have been a disappointment, she thought. Not that she wanted Chorizo to ask her out again. Or maybe she did. Maybe she would like to play one man against the other—she was thinking of Lou. Nicola hoped she was not turning into someone like that, although she could see the attraction. No, she wanted something else with Chorizo: a chance to redeem herself. She didn't know what exactly. Some kind of makeup test. Because she knew she would do it better this time around. She wouldn't back down at the last minute out of fear or insecurity or whatever it was.

Their sandwiches came and Nicola handed the bags over to Audrey, then turned back to pay for them. It was then that she noticed the missing-girl sign taped to the counter.

"This is new," she said.

"Just happened," the owner told her. He was a dark, unfriendly man from some former Soviet State or another. He never showed any signs of recognizing her, although she had been coming here almost every day for two years. Nicola read the Xeroxed flyer. Missing: Melissa Snider, twenty-six years old, brown hair, brown eyes. Last seen at her place of work two blocks away. Nicola's mouth puckered. Missing since Friday.

"Recognize her?" the owner asked, taking Nicola's money.

Nicola looked at the picture again. "No."

"She came in here a lot. Sweet girl."

She glanced at him, but his sour expression remained. I could be the one on this sign, Nicola thought.

"Pretty," Audrey commented.

"Always gives me correct change. None of this twenty-dollar bill for a cup of coffee business." He looked at the bills Nicola gave him.

"Hey, it's what the bank machine spits out," she protested.

His expression didn't change. "Yes, yes, yes," he said wearily.

Out on the street Audrey shifted the bag of food to her other hand and said, "Creepy."

"I agree," Nicola said. She felt oddly shaken. The flyer seemed to represent something—a lesson or a warning or at least something too coincidental to ignore. The girl, Melissa Snider, had disappeared at about the same time the Daves were tying her up in the van. It could have been her face on the flyer if the Daves had been more competent. Or less.

"There's something so sad about those missing-person flyers," Audrey was saying. "Or those flyers you see about lost pets. You know they'll never come back, although you can't say they're gone for sure."

"Maybe they'll come back," Nicola said.

"Face it; it's terrible here. I mean, look what happened to you!"

"But that was just Scooter."

"The crime's getting worse. I really want to get out of here and go someplace warm. Get out of the city."

"That's the difference between you and me," Nicola said. "I like where I am. I like my job, I like my home, I like my friends. And if anybody tries to take them away, any of them, I'll fight them. Hard."

"Really," Audrey said. "And when did you get so testy?"

"Around midnight on Friday," Nicola told her.

From across the street Chorizo watched Nicola and the other woman, thinking how awful they looked in the wind, their terrible postures, like weakened animals heading for shelter. Their jaws moved, but of course he could hear nothing. Not that he needed to, he knew it all— work complaints, last night's sitcom, the price of lunch. Husbands or boyfriends. Landlords.

A muni rang its bell as it moved up the street toward the tunnel, cutting off his view. He walked in their direction anyway; he could tell they were in no hurry to get back to the office with their lunches in bags. Eating at their desks—another mistake. Bent over a keyboard. It's bad enough, but when you're digesting? Walking or sitting, how you carry yourself is important. He himself meditated every day in the standard lotus position. "Leave your body and dissolve. Now come back to your posture." This had carried him through some rough times. The muni passed on, and there they were again with their buckling torsos. He recognized Nicola, of course, but not the young woman with her. He was sad for them, almost. It is so very important to synchronize body and mind.

At the corner the women stopped for a moment, still talking, then entered a building. He took out a pencil and wrote down the address and at that moment the cellular telephone in his pocket began to ring.

"Yes," Chorizo said.

It was Robert.

"I'm in West Portal," Robert told him.

Chorizo looked up the street. Robert was nowhere in sight. "Are you," he said ironically.

"I'm checking up on that woman, Nicola."

"All right."

"The woman you wanted me to check up on."

"All right."

"And I checked every doctor's office on the street, but I couldn't find an employee named Nicola anywhere."

"Excuse me?"

"What?"

"You went to *doctors'* offices?" Chorizo asked.

"Yeah and there weren't any Nicolas, but there was one Nicole. Could that have been her? At a podiatrist's. Was it Nicole, do you think? Anyway I have the address."

"I told you dentist, not doctor," Chorizo said.

"What's that?"

"She works at a *dentist's* office, she works for a *dentist*. Oh, never mind. Just meet me back at the office."

Chorizo turned off the phone and looked at his watch. Robert was such an idiot—really, he'd been hoping for more. Maybe he should spend more time with him, teach him not to be such a fool. Was Robert teachable? Chorizo crossed the street and looked in through the glass door of Nicola's building. A shaft of sunlight cut through some tempered glass creating a momentary prism, and he was reminded of the second principle of Shambhala—Discover goodness by finding beauty in the everyday world. Chorizo took a moment to watch the prism as it floated lightly against the painted stucco wall.

Beauty in the everyday world.

Then he looked around the foyer. The women weren't there. He entered the building and studied the office listings pinned by the elevator. A café on the ground floor. A design firm on the top floor. Two dentists in between. Chorizo smiled. She must work for one or the other. The spiritual warrior prevails, he thought, as he copied down the dentists' names.

Eleven

Go on, say it: You're in my way!"

Nicola shifted her weight and kicked. Her foot reached sternum level. "You're in my way!"

"Fighting stance!" shouted Alicia. "Left side forward, now bounce! Switch to the other foot! Bounce! Exercise your legs and heart, come on! Five more! Now switch! Two more! Now switch!"

The music turned into heavy bass beats and Nicola turned and began her cross punches. She was standing on the red wrinkled karate mats with twelve other women facing a wall of mirrors. The room was brightly lit and smelled slightly of foot fungus.

"Guard up!" shouted Alicia. "Get a rhythm, come on! Tina, where's your elbow? Nicola, very good!"

They finished their cross punches, practiced their obliques, then started the whole sequence over in double time. By the time they got to the snap kicks, Nicola felt sweat running down her temple and she could hear someone behind her start to groan.

"All set for handrail drills! Four count front, round, side kick!"

Nicola let her mind go blank as she copied Alicia's movements. It was important to forget how tired you were. The karate mats felt thin beneath her feet and for a while she tried to imagine an opponent—her landlord? Guy?—but when she let go of specifics, her movements felt cleaner. Clear your mind, Alicia liked to say. Anyone could be an opponent. Nicola kicked the air, then jabbed with a closed fist. Her heart felt like a revved motor.

"Sideways, kick! You're in my way!"

Nicola turned and kicked. She was mean and serious. During her match she practiced lateral movements, hitting, then stepping aside. Speed was the important factor. Alicia demonstrated a spinning back kick and Nicola thought, I want to do that.

After class she noticed Lou sitting on one of the spectator benches. She smiled at him as she walked over, surprised and glad to see him. He was wearing another white button-down shirt and his face looked recently shaved.

"I thought we were going to meet at the restaurant?" she asked.

He said, "I wanted to see how tough you California women really are."

Nicola pulled her hair out of its ponytail. She was dripping with sweat.

"And what did you decide?"

"You have a vicious hook," he told her.

He smiled at her. He had a great, slow smile. The surfer grin, Nicola thought. But his eyes were sharp, like a cat's.

"Nicola," Alicia said, coming up to her. Her forehead was clear and dry and her blonde ponytail was still perfectly in place. "Good work tonight. Very good. Have you been practicing?"

"You might say I've had a shift in attitude."

"Well, your focus has really improved. You're letting yourself empty out, which is great. Soon you can fill up the cup." She touched

Nicola's shoulder, then moved on to another student.

"Fill up the cup?" Lou asked.

Nicola shrugged. "It's a zen thing," she explained.

She showered and changed, then walked with Lou to his car, a dark blue rental with a spoiler over the trunk. Lou unlocked her door before unlocking his own. Well, well, Nicola thought. Inside it smelled like damp newspapers and Lou fastened his seat belt, then sat for a moment with his hands on the steering wheel.

The night was dry and windy, the kind of wind that seemed to swoop up from underneath you. Drivers were just beginning to turn on their headlights. Nicola glanced at Lou's hands, which were thick, kind of muscular. Can fingers be muscular?

"What's up?" she asked after a few moments.

"I'm doing my traffic prayer," Lou said, looking out the windshield.

"Your traffic prayer?" Nicola almost laughed. "You have a traffic prayer?"

"It's very effective."

"Can I hear it?"

"Really?"

"Definitely."

Lou cleared his throat. His two top buttons were unbuttoned and beneath the V-shaped opening she could see the small rise of his collarbone. Lou from New Jersey. He had the dark good looks of an Italian—or was he Irish, dark Irish? He had dark eyes, straight dark hair, a small nose. Irish, she thought. She could see him growing up in the suburbs: going to mass on Good Friday, then playing pool at a bar with a bunch of his buddies.

"Let my car pass undamaged through the streets," he began. "And let the vehicles part before me. Let the red lights turn green and let the green lights linger. Let my tires remain unpunctured. And let me

neither be stopped nor cited now until I reach my destination, amen."
He looked over at Nicola and started the engine. "Sometimes I add
a few lines about animals, too."

Nicola laughed.

"Or storms, if the weather looks bad."

"You're an odd one, aren't you?" Nicola asked.

"I don't know what I am," Lou said.

She wasn't sure if that was all just for her amusement or what,
but she liked it. Lou reached over to adjust the rearview mirror and
as his hand came near her Nicola remembered the sudden strange
intimacy of sitting in a car with a stranger. Was this a date, she wondered? The phrase "business associate" conjured up something disreputable, possibly unlawful, but probably that was closer to the
truth.

"I think you could use something more at the end," she said.

Lou flicked on his blinker. "At the end of the prayer?"

"Something about a place to park."

"Curbside parking," Lou said. "That's good."

The restaurant was in the financial district with long windows facing the
cable car tracks. The hostess seated them in the back. Sea nets hung
on the walls and there were rows of sconces shaped like clamshells.
A good restaurant: expensive, well-lit, comfortable. As they sat down
Nicola found herself checking her fingernails.

"Last night I went to an Italian restaurant," Lou was saying. He
fluffed out the thick white napkin and spread it on his lap, then he
opened a small notepad. "Dinner took almost four hours."

"What did you have?"

"Panzerotti salsi di noci." He was reading from his notes. "That's
white sauce with walnuts. Now a few days ago I went to a vegan
restaurant. Ever try that? I had a drink called Doctor Telma's Chinese

Potion. Actually I liked the food, but as soon as I was outside I started to crave pastrami. Like when you leave an aquarium and head for the sushi bar."

"Are you going to write any of this up anywhere?" Nicola asked him.

"That's the plan."

He had been in San Francisco for only a week but already had checked off Russian, Mediterranean, and Vietnamese food from his list. Tomorrow he was planning to go to a Turkish restaurant and try something called kota voskou.

They opened their menus. The restaurant was full but not noisy, and Nicola felt easy with herself. Comfortable. They faced each other across the table, which was much less intimate than sitting side by side in a dark car. In his neat white shirt Lou looked young and polite. But anyone can be an opponent, as Alicia would say. Nicola looked at his hand for a wedding ring.

"I was engaged once," Lou said.

"What?"

"I see you're looking at my left hand."

"I wasn't," Nicola began. Then she shrugged. "All right," she said.

"Do you want to hear about it?"

"Oh, that's a story I've heard many times. Second date stuff. How the woman you never understood broke your heart."

"Actually I broke hers."

"Well, that I might listen to," she said.

The waiter came to tell them the specials. Lou listened carefully, then ordered appetizers for both of them to share: black mussel soufflé (the restaurant's specialty), salad, and a consommé of wild mushrooms and sweet bay scallops. Nicola noticed his dark eyes again, the careful way he spoke, his casual confidence. He watched the busboy fill their water glasses, then he took up his notebook again.

"So this is a second date," he said. It was a question.

Nicola sipped her water. "That depends on the food."

She found herself comparing him to Chorizo. They were both attractive in the style she liked: dark, not too thin, not too hairy. Chorizo was the fatherly version. Lou was polite in a way that Nicola had learned to distrust; it sometimes masked chauvinism. Still, there was something about a man in a white button-down shirt, Nicola thought, his pale skin underneath like something protected by Brooks Brothers.

Their appetizers came and Lou divided them neatly in half. He gave Nicola a plate. "She wanted to have puzzle rings as wedding bands," he told her.

"Your fiancée?"

"And there were other differences. The wedding meal was supposed to be color coordinated with the bridesmaids' dresses. What food can you serve that's blue?"

"Delicious," Nicola said. She was eating a Greek salad with red wine vinaigrette and smelt fries.

"Really?" Lou picked up his pencil. "Tell me more."

"I could just eat and eat," she said.

She concentrated on the arrangement of flavors: sweet, salty, smoky. As they ate Lou wrote down each dish and timed the servings and asked Nicola for her opinion. She liked that. The restaurant was a real restaurant with white tablecloths and white candles and a branch of unusual flower buds in every vase. She liked that too. They were sitting in a row of two-person tables and the large room spread out before Nicola in soft gold and orange. Her hunger seemed to increase as she ate and she leaned the tines of her fork inward to retrieve every last small leafy tidbit.

"Now tell me something about Scott," Lou said.

Nicola took a small sip of wine. "When I was married to him everyone still called him Scooter."

"Well that tells me something," he said. "What else?"

She thought for a moment. "Once he bought a used cocktail piano even though neither one of us could play. We were supposed to make money on it. But although we listed it in the classifieds week after week, no one ever came by to see it. For years it just sat in a corner and once in a while Scooter would pay someone to come in and tune it." She took another sip of wine. "I wonder whatever happened to that," she said.

It had been a relief, when she left him, to also leave all their possessions—the piano, the leaky water bed, the Star Trek commemorative plates, the boxes of carefully preserved third-rate comics. Nicola pictured Scooter in a room that grew increasingly crowded and narrow. He was always coming home with surprises.

"How long were you married?" Lou asked.

"Four years. He always had a new idea about how to make money. Once he invested an entire paycheck in an animal rest home," she said.

"What, for senile retrievers?"

"Actually, that one didn't do too badly."

Two waiters served their entrees on small gold-rimmed plates. Behind them the curved restaurant bar with its shiny top and silver mirror and well-dressed drinkers seemed like a scene on an ocean liner.

"What is a cocktail piano anyway?" Nicola asked.

She had ordered caramelized Chilean sea bass in sweetened onion sauce with fried okra, and Lou chose the medallions of rare ahi tuna. Midway through the meal they switched plates.

"Excellent," said Lou about the sea bass. "This has really brought me into the zone."

"The zone?"

Lou looked at his watch. "So far I've been in for just under ten minutes."

"What's the record?"

"Oh, the record is a long story."

Nicola put down her fork. "Okay," she said.

"Really?"

"I'd like to know."

"Really? All right," he said. "Well, one day I was walking in the park. This was in New York. Although it was only about five o'clock, I was hungry because I'd just played racquetball with this woman who turned out to be not so interesting, and when she went home I decided to go to this restaurant she had told me about, but I wasn't optimistic because, you know, she wasn't interesting."

"Okay," Nicola said.

"So I get there and even though it was early there were only about three free tables, but still they could seat me right away."

"Because there were three free tables."

"Right." Lou smiled. "Okay, anyway. It starts out they have this huge cavernous dining room, like some medieval cave with a fire going in a huge fireplace that was really like a hole in the wall with sticks on the bottom—it was so big the logs looked like sticks—and almost everything is cooked right there on that big open fire. I started out with mussels in the shell, which tasted like they had been caught about ten minutes before, and then I had smoke-licked pork loin. If the mussels hadn't kick-started me into the zone, then the pork definitely did. Then there was grilled asparagus with parmesan cheese, and roasted yukon potatoes with arugula, and Italian wine, and, oh yeah, a basket of tiny fresh-baked rolls, like minimuffins, that a waiter kept replenishing. That was his whole job, replenishing minimuffins."

"I want that job," Nicola said.

Lou took another bite of fish. "Then there was warm caramelized tart with house-made vanilla ice cream, and coffee. I was worried I might overdo it, but that night I could do no wrong. I had been planning to go see a movie but I didn't want to get out of myself; I didn't want to break the spell."

"So what did you do?"

"I walked around the city. I went into a bookshop. I felt I could do anything as long as I didn't engage in someone else's life. I know it sounds hokey."

"It doesn't sound hokey."

"It sounds completely hokey but I think that was the best night I ever spent in my life. I walked along Columbus Avenue and looked at all the stores, which of course were all closed and gated. But, see, that was the best part. I wanted nothing. For the first time I wanted nothing. I was content just to look."

He stopped and kind of smiled a little. The surfer grin.

Nicola couldn't help smiling back. "That's the story?" she asked.

"That's the story. That's the record for the zone. And that's when I decided I wanted to do this for a living, to get out of my uncle's business and go after the zone in a legitimate way."

"And you're in the zone now?"

Lou smiled again. "Here I am," he said.

It wasn't until they were at the coffee and dessert phase that Nicola brought up the topic of Robert.

Lou told her what he had found. Apparently Robert was from Vacaville, California, a place that literally meant cow town. Fifteen years ago Robert started buying real estate in Berkeley, then eventually moved to San Francisco and bought a few lots near the ocean. He lived alone and although he owned a lot of property he was seriously in debt.

"But that's not unusual," Lou told her.

"I'm sure you see it a lot."

"It's pretty much all I see," he said.

There was no sign of a sister so far, but Lou had put in a few calls about that. Still, it was a lot of work for, what was it, one day?

Two days if you count Sunday. Nicola was impressed.

"How did you do this so fast?"

Lou handed her a folder. "I have excellent phone skills," he said. "And here's something else you might find interesting."

It was a Xerox of some legal document—a title deed. In capital letters was the name GOLDEN GATE ROOMS.

"Golden Gate Rooms?" Nicola looked at Lou. "That motel?"

"I took a look around his place the other night. How much do you know about him? Like for instance, is he a geek?"

Nicola laughed. "Robert?"

"I found lots of computer equipment in his garage."

"You broke into his house?"

"I looked in the window. Do you want to taste this?"

He sliced off a bite of his dessert—Meyer lemon tart with sherbet—and placed it on her saucer.

"Mmm," Nicola said. It was delicious. She took another bite. "I thought it would be cold and flaky."

He grinned, agreeing. "No, it's warm and melty."

"But not at all mushy." Nicola took another bite, then leaned back in her seat with her coffee. And looked at Lou.

She was enjoying herself. She was liking him more and more.

"I wouldn't guess that Robert had anything to do with comput-ers," she said. "He's kind of an idiot."

"This is good for us."

"But in truth nothing would surprise me. He's shifty and greedy. You won't believe the rent he charges the poor Russians who live in the main house. I'm always surprised that in all these years he's never raised my rent. It makes me more suspicious, in fact. Like he's lying in wait for something. He has his little plans."

"Has he spoken to you about any of them?"

"Robert would never talk to me about anything. But there's a way he looks at everything—you can see the little wheels turning. It's easy to see them since they turn so slowly."

The waiter came over with the bill.

"One computer was left on," Lou told her, "though I didn't see any applications running. It could be he just forgot to turn it off."

"Or it could be an open connection," Nicola said.

"An open connection?"

"To the Internet. Maybe he's hosting a Web site or something. Though I can't believe that's true. I know a couple of kids who could find out."

"College students?"

"High-school kids. Last weekend they kidnapped me and tied me up. Turns out they worked for Scooter."

Lou laughed.

"You think I'm kidding," Nicola said. She put on her coat. Outside the wind had died down but it was still chilly. A street light flickered as they passed underneath it.

"I gave them my landlord's name and address. They're going to search the Internet, see if they can find anything there. They work for me now."

She felt for the top button of her coat. They walked side by side on the sidewalk, almost touching, and Nicola felt full and warm, satisfied, a little spacy. When they got to the street Lou unlocked her car door for her.

"So how did you like the meal?" he asked.

Nicola smiled. "I enjoyed it."

"Enjoyed it as in, for instance, a second date?"

He stood with his hand on the door handle, watching her. They were on a busy downtown street, noisy but dark, and although Nicola couldn't see Lou's face very well still she could feel something happening, she could feel how he looked at her and she knew that all it would take from her was one step forward. Her heart seemed to squeeze in on itself. I like him, she thought. His shirt collar was bent under his coat and she felt a strong desire to put her arm up to his neck and straighten out his collar, but at the same time she knew she should wait, go slowly, figure him out, find out his secrets, assess, direct, plan this thing, whatever it is, or is it just part of the loan sharking business, the part where they kiss you then pat you and say now now now little missy? One step forward, that's all it would take. A car slowed, then stopped, just behind them and its right blinker lit up. They had been discovered. Their parking spot had been claimed. Just a step, Nicola was thinking, one step. But instead she held her ground.

"I'll tell you tomorrow," she said.

Twelve

After Lou dropped her off, Nicola walked down the path next to the main house toward her cottage, a small one-bedroom hidden from the street.

The path was short, constructed of crumbling octagonal stones, and unlit. Lights were on in the main house where the Russians lived, and the white December roses that grew in their yard seemed tinged with blue in the moonlight. As she passed, someone in the house drew back a curtain. A woman with a baby. Nicola held up her hand. The curtain fell back.

Inside her own house she locked the door and put on the tea kettle. It was easier not to think of Lou as a bookie, or whatever he was. She saw him as an easygoing type, a surfer, a gourmand, though he also mentioned law school. Nothing quite fit together. Her camisole strap had gotten tangled with her bra, and she was looking forward to her terrycloth robe, a silk nightshirt, or maybe nothing underneath. But first she would have tea the way she liked it, steeped for three and a half minutes, then sugared. Nicola watched the clock on the microwave, then turned back for the sugar bowl. And gasped.

There was a face at the window.

"Christ," she said, stepping back.

His eyes were dark holes and his face seemed outlined in silver, and when he saw that she saw him, he knocked sharply on the glass. Nicola took another step away, thinking about phone cords and other household weapons, then she realized it was her landlord, Robert.

Her hand was on her throat. She went to the door but didn't open it. Instead she opened the small brass peep window next to the chain and spoke through that. "What," she said.

"Nicola, can I come in?"

"What are you doing here?"

"I want to talk to you. Can I come in for a minute?"

"I don't think so."

"Did you get my notice?" Robert asked.

"You know I did. I was served."

"There's someone I want you to meet. Can I come in? Just for a second? My sister is with me."

Nicola stepped to the side and looked through the peep window at an angle. It was true; a small woman with long dark hair stood beside him.

"She doesn't look anything like you," she said.

"Just for a second," Robert said.

Nicola closed the peep window. She felt her collarbone absently, considering options.

"It's beginning to rain," he complained.

She slid back the chain and opened the door. Robert stepped inside. He was wearing a baseball cap and an extra-large white T-shirt. His eyes were small and red and tired.

"See, I told you this was nice," he said to the woman.

"What is it you want?" Nicola asked.

"Just a quick look around. This is my sister, Carmen. Carmen wants to measure the oven space. She's thinking of getting a Viking."

Nicola stared at him.

"I don't believe this. You came here at ten o'clock at night to measure my oven space?" She didn't know if she was angry or just completely astonished.

"Look at that tile. And over here, see? Leaded glass."

"Listen, Robert, you're going to have to wait until you get me out for this," Nicola said.

"Let me just take two steps around," Robert said.

She shook her head. "Oh, so I should do you a favor? First you kick out my dog, and then me."

"When you weren't home I waited for you, even though I have a key."

"Because that's the law."

"And I'm doing everything legal," Robert said. He opened the pantry door. "Lots of shelf space," he pointed out.

Nicola's face felt suddenly hot. "That's enough," she said.

Why had she let them in? For a moment at the door she had thought Robert was going to tell her he'd changed his mind; she could stay in her house. Or that maybe she and the sister could be roommates or something. Why didn't she know better?

Anyway she didn't buy the sister deal. The woman was pretty and spoke English with a faint accent. In her hand was a tape measure and Nicola noticed that her fingernails were bitten into odd, angular shapes.

Robert took off his baseball cap and pulled his fingers through his hair. His eyes looked very tired. "She has a right to know what she's getting," he said.

"Does she know about the ants she's getting?"

"Well, but every house around here . . ." Robert began.

"And you can't poison them because they lead the poison back to their nests and then it gets into the ground water. I never drink out of taps anymore." She turned to Carmen and put her hand out sharply, gesturing to the wall. "Also, the whole property is built on a pond. That means landfill. If there's an earthquake, this sinks."

"How do you know this?" Robert asked. He rested his hand on the chipped tile countertop, claiming ownership.

"Survey maps. But before the house sinks, the walls will collapse. That's the real worry, getting out in time."

"You mean you could be buried alive?" Carmen asked.

"Carmen," Robert warned.

"But you know all this, Robert," Nicola continued. She turned away from him, hiding her face. And started to fish. "You own a lot of property around here. You own the house in front."

"Yes I do," Robert said.

"And other places over the years. A few buildings along the beach. A duplex in Parkside. Oh, and something by the wharf, what was it, the Golden Gate Rooms?"

Robert looked at her quickly. "How do you know all this?" he asked.

"Well it's a matter of public record. You have to know where to look, sure, but anyone can find it."

"Public record?" Robert repeated. He fidgeted with his watch strap, then dropped it on the floor. Carmen picked it up for him.

"We've got to go," Robert said suddenly. "Come on, Carmen. I need to . . . you should get back to that place." They left abruptly without saying good-bye. Robert seemed shaken.

Nicola closed the door behind them. Her tea was now cold and she tipped it out over the sink as she listened for the sound of footsteps on the stone path. After a moment a single foghorn sounded distantly, to the north.

Now what was that about, she wondered?

Thirteen

The next morning the phone began ringing when the light was still unevenly gray. Nicola had been dreaming—something about handcuffs. But was she in the handcuffs, or was somebody else? She had to clear her throat twice. "Hello," she said finally.

"Guess who's here."

"Audrey?"

"Guess who's here at my house."

"Oh God, Audrey," Nicola said. She tried to focus on the clock. "By tradition, shouldn't I tell you what time it is?"

"One guess."

"Someone I used to be married to?"

"I came downstairs and there he was on my couch. When I went through his pockets, there wasn't even a pause in his snoring."

"You looked through his pockets?"

"For my key."

"I didn't know he had your key."

"It was news to me, too," Audrey told her. Nicola laughed. "So, can you come over? Because Lester's kind of under the couch."

An hour later Nicola was standing at Audrey's door carrying cardboard cups of coffee and a bag of croissants. The morning was still dark. Audrey and Declan lived across the street from the ocean, near a block of project housing. Someone had hung kites, five or six of them, from the drainpipes of the house next door. The wind looped them sideways. Soon it would probably rain.

"Hey," someone said behind her.

Nicola turned. It was Dave, walking up the driveway wearing an army cap and an oversized sheepskin-like coat. But what was he doing here? And at only—Nicola looked at her watch—seven in the morning?

"What's up?" she asked.

Dave looked around kind of awkwardly. "Scooter told me to come. I called him this morning. I found something," he said.

That was fast, Nicola thought. "That's great," she said, trying not to sound surprised. She rang the doorbell again.

"Well, he's up," Audrey announced when she answered.

"Is it noon already?" Nicola asked.

"I heard that," Scooter said from the living room.

He looked terrible, tired and rumpled, and his face had a dirty, waxy cast to it. Her ex-husband: what didn't she know, or could guess, about him? Nicola gave him a coffee and the pastry bag.

"What's this?" he asked.

"I'm trying to be nice."

She took in the state of his hair—dirty and flat on one side—and wondered where he'd been sleeping before this. But instead of asking she looked around the living room. "So where's my baby?" she asked. "Where's my sweetpea?"

From under the couch came a couple of thumps. Dave, who was still standing, looked around in confusion.

"Lesty," Nicola called, "come here. Lesty. Come on over here and give me some sugar."

Lester eased herself out from under the couch on her belly and then walked stiffly toward Nicola. She was old, small, fat, and shaped like a bullhorn. Nicola picked her up and sat down on an overstuffed ottoman.

"Lester Pearl," she said, scratching between her eyes. "What do you think? Do you like that?"

Scooter yawned. "I really thought that dog would be dead by now."

"She just keeps eating," Audrey said. She was wearing a black T-shirt and men's pajama bottoms and she was sitting with her feet pulled up on the couch. Outside, small birds no bigger than Ping-Pong balls hopped up and down the tree branches. A second later it began to rain.

Nicola turned to Dave. "So, what have you got?" she asked.

Dave pulled out his laptop and set it up on the coffee table, then looked around for a phone line. "You're gonna love this," he said.

Audrey finished up her coffee, then stood. "I've got to get going. But listen, Nicola, will you tell Scooter he can't stay here? He won't listen to me."

"You can't stay here, Scooter," Nicola said.

Scooter was watching Dave. "I'm thinking of going back to Scott," he said.

"What?"

"My name. I'm thinking of going back to my given name, Scott."

Audrey said, "You see what I'm up against."

"Because I just don't see a man over thirty in the name Scooter."

Nicola said, "That's funny, I don't either."

Scooter frowned. "Ha ha."

"Do you remember that video you made for him?" Audrey asked Nicola. "Step-by-step instructions on how to change a toilet paper roll?"

"That was a joke," Scooter said.

"I mean he's just barely domesticated," Audrey said.

Nicola finished her coffee and threw the cup into the wastepaper basket in the fireplace.

"Well, he can't stay with me," she told Audrey.

"Here it is. Watch. You're gonna love this," Dave said. He shifted the monitor slightly toward Scooter. "I found a couple of good sites, but this is the best; you can actually follow the races in real time with a live feed. Here it comes. Look. Well, it's empty now because the next race isn't until eight."

Nicola stopped scratching Lester's head and looked at the screen. "What is this?" she asked.

"You can follow any dog race in the country. You can even search for a specific dog," Dave went on. He typed a name into the search engine window.

"And there's Primogeniture!" he said.

Scooter bent over to see. "Cool!" he said.

Nicola was momentarily confused. Robert owns a racetrack, too? Then she realized this had nothing to do with Robert. "You're researching dog races?" she asked.

"Yeah, well, I thought about your problem and I decided what you really need is more money," Dave said. "And I think we could make lots of money with this."

Scooter took the mouse. "It looks like you can place your bets online," he said.

"Dude," Dave said. "No need to travel the country."

Reason number eighty-nine to be glad you're a woman, Nicola thought. No one will address you as "Dude."

"And here, look at this," Dave went on. "A Web site all about dog care. Here's a cool recipe for killing parasites; it's like ground-up grapefruit seeds and something."

"Okay, but Dave, this isn't what I wanted," Nicola said.

"You can use it for acne, too. I was thinking we could e-mail

Primo's owner. You know, help him keep up with the latest."

"What I asked you," Nicola tried again, "was to dig up some dirt on my landlord."

Scooter was scrolling down the page. "Did you find Primo's owner?" he asked.

"I'm still looking for the e-mail address," Dave told him.

"*Listen*," Nicola said. Lester jumped off her lap. Dave and Scooter were looking at the computer together and she noticed they were both jiggling something—a thumb, a foot. Also, Scooter was nodding a little as he scrolled. Their heads were almost touching. Nicola thought, what's the use.

Still watching the screen, Dave pulled a piece of paper from his pocket. "Here's my bill for my time so far," he said without looking at her, and he stretched out his hand more or less in her direction. "I also added lunch."

Nicola didn't take it. "I don't think so," she told him. She looked at her watch. It was time to get to work.

Dave turned. "What do you mean, 'I don't think so?' "

"I mean, Dave, that in business you pay for something you've agreed upon in advance. We did not agree you would research citrus cures for racing dogs. We agreed you would look for my landlord. So I don't think I'll be paying you."

"But I told you, on that thing you're screwed."

"How do you know?"

Dave said, "Because he's a landlord."

Nicola shook her head. "I've really got to go."

"Wait," Dave said fiercely. "I need the money."

Nicola said nothing.

"But I *really* need the money," he said. His neck was turning blotchy and red.

The doorbell rang and Lester went back under the couch.

"Lesty," Nicola called.

"And that will be Davette," Scooter said, going for the door. A moment later he came back with Davette, who was carrying a plastic white airlines bag. Her hair was dyed a bright magenta.

Dave watched her walk in. "She won't pay up," he announced in a loud sulky voice.

Davette took off her coat. "What?"

"She won't pay up for the work we've done."

"Did you check the IP address?" Davette asked. She sat down on the rug cross-legged and took a new colorful laptop out of the airlines bag and put it on the coffee table.

"Not exactly. But it's the principle."

"What did you show her?"

"It's also the needing the cash."

"Just show me what you found," Davette said patiently.

"Okay," Dave said sulkily. "Here. Look." He turned his computer slightly toward her.

Davette turned it more. "What's this? I told you to check the IP address."

"I like the dog racing angle."

"Oh, my God, Dave, YSL."

Nicola looked at her. "What?"

"You're so lame," Scooter explained.

"I asked him to check the IP address," Davette told Nicola.

"What IP address?"

"Here. It's easier just to show you."

Davette booted up her laptop and connected it to the phone line. Nicola sat down on the rug beside her and stared at the monitor. After a moment Davette said, "We're in. Okay, here. Wait a sec. Okay, look."

As Nicola watched a wide, black-and-white photograph was forming itself on the screen. It was fuzzy at first, drawing itself in as they watched, but there were definitely naked breasts there and long stockinged legs and no clothes in between.

"I found this in the library yesterday," Davette said. "During lunch."

"You can get this on a school's computer?" Nicola asked her.

"Oh, those Puritan blocking programs do nothing."

One naked woman, then two, appeared on the screen. Below them were a couple of female head shots and a form to fill out credit card information.

Scooter stood behind Nicola. "If you are looking for the girl who can satisfy all your senses . . . ," he read aloud.

"This is his site," Davette said. She was sitting cross-legged on the floor with her legs bent in some intricate yoga position. "Your landlord's, I mean. I found the IP address and the site is running off of his computer."

"Are you sure?"

"That's what Dave was supposed to double-check. But I'm pretty sure I got it right."

Audrey's husband, Declan, walked in wearing a dark wetsuit and a towel around his neck. "Hey," he said to Nicola. "What's up?"

"Porn site," she told him, gesturing to the computer.

"Cool," he said, looking at the takeout coffee. "Can I have one?"

"Be my guest."

He took a coffee and went down to the garage, probably, Nicola thought, to wax his surf board or do whatever you did to them when it was too rainy to surf. Meanwhile Scooter edged in next to Davette and began scrolling down the screen. "Pretty standard stuff," he said.

"You familiar with porn sites?" Nicola asked.

"Familiar," Scooter repeated. "Familiar. I don't know about familiar. But I've done some research."

Dave crossed his arms. He was still wearing his coat. "This is useless," he said. "There's nothing illegal here. So he makes a little money showing dirty pictures around, so what. There's nothing about him moving in somewhere or whatever, or his sister or whatever. I'm telling you, go with the dogs."

Nicola turned to Davette. "I'll write you a check."

"Cash only," Dave said.

"I think this payment is for Davette," Nicola told him.

"Hey, we're partners, remember?"

His voice had turned snotty, but it wasn't worth struggling over. Dave didn't like her, that was clear. And she wasn't too sure how she felt about him either. Nicola turned away. She could hear Audrey's shower going, and she remembered that at first she wasn't too fond of Audrey either, but look at them now. Still, bonding with Dave seemed pretty unlikely.

Scooter squatted in front of the coffee table to get a better view. He turned the computer more toward him and scrolled up and down, looking at images.

"So what do you think; you think maybe *you're* up here somewhere?" he asked Nicola.

She was caught off guard. "What?"

Dave snorted a laugh.

"Could this be you?" Scooter asked, pointing to a woman wearing a strawberry-colored bustier.

"Of course not!" Nicola said.

Scooter scrolled further down the screen.

"Well. Not to your knowledge," he said.

Nicola looked at him. "What are you saying?"

"I'm saying that not to your *knowledge* are you on this site."

She thought about that.

"That is a very creepy thought," she told him.

"Do your bedroom windows have shades?"

"Shades and, thank God, good strong locks."

"Any hidden cameras?" Scooter asked. He looked like he was

enjoying this. "Like in the closet or something? Above the bed? Or I know, on the showerhead. A landlord could do that."

"Oh, for God's sake," Nicola said.

"A little tiny camera on the showerhead. Away from the spray. Or maybe disguised as a little spray hole, a little black spray hole. I can just picture it."

"I bet you can," Nicola said.

But the idea disturbed her. When was the last time Robert was in her house? Discounting the visit last night with his so-called sister. Nicola was sure, relatively sure, that there could be no obscurely placed cameras in any of her rooms. On-the-spot surveillance; good God. She had once seen a Web site that monitored patients in a periodontist's office as they were being worked on. She couldn't understand it. Who wanted to watch that stuff? Nicola liked sitcoms because the actresses dressed so much better than anyone she knew and the kitchens were all very attractive.

After the Daves left she let Scooter walk her to her muni stop, and as they climbed up to the paved jogging path above the beach Nicola remembered there was that one day when Robert came in to do some work on the kitchen sink. A Saturday. Had she stayed in the house the whole time? Beside her feet the ice plants were turning from red to brown and the sand dunes were a slightly lighter shade of brown leading down to the foamy water. It was cold out, and although it had stopped raining it seemed ready to start up again at any time. Nicola looked out to the ocean. Low, nickel-colored waves reared up one by one, then collapsed. The thought of going home was beginning to feel creepy.

"Three nights," she said. "That is absolutely the limit."

Scooter said, "You won't be sorry."

"That means by Saturday you have to be gone."

"I can look around the place for you. Maybe take down a few things, check for cameras. You don't want to be alone right now."

"Do you even know how a screwdriver works?"

"I know what one looks like." Scooter smiled.

They were walking north, toward Marin, and the hills were covered with a layer of low dense fog moving inland. Nicola loved these hills; they seemed so soft and brown, and although they were fairly far away you could see every bend leading up to the top. Or were those shadows from clouds? In any case, there was nothing like them back in Cleveland. She thought about the trees there, and the wide suburban streets and the green front lawns and the spaces between houses. Her mother expected her to marry a Cleveland boy who was well-spoken and involved in local politics, who went to Amherst or Princeton, then came back home to settle. But instead Nicola moved to San Franciso and married a man who had dreams but no money or skills. At first Nicola was pleased with the strangeness of California, but later, after leaving Scooter, she was frustrated by her own inability to make happen whatever it was she came out here for. Because she did want something. She was definite about that.

She stepped over a stray rope of kelp on the path. "Have you kept in touch with Bill Lopez?" she asked Scooter. "Is he still working at Mission Legal Aid?"

"I think so. Why?"

"I have a bunch of questions I want you to ask him. There was some recent legislation in the rent control laws; he should know what's going on."

"What questions?"

"I'll give you a printout." She looked at him pointedly. "As well as the itemized bill from Lou."

"Lou?"

"The shark's nephew, remember?"

"You call him Lou?"

"Well, what do you think I'd call him?"

"But the way you say it."

"Scooter, I say it in the way of the guy I paid a lot of money to so you could postpone your life of crime."

"I know, I know, I know," Scooter said. "Really, thank you for doing that. I mean it. Once again you've bailed me out."

"Well, remember you're going to be helping me now," she said.

"Whatever I can do," he said, gesturing with one hand. This was something he said when he meant to do nothing.

"Call Bill for a start."

"I mean it, how many ex-wives would do this?"

Nicola looked over at him. He had fixed his face into an earnest expression. The sand beside the bicycle path had become black with dirt and foam, and she thought she could smell an oily scent drifting inland.

"It all makes me think maybe we're not what you call 'over,'" Scooter said.

"We're divorced," she said. "Legally that means what you call over."

"My cousin Mark married the same woman three times."

"He and Bonnie are back together?"

"They're kind of trying out an open-marriage-type thing."

"Scooter," Nicola said. "We haven't seen each other in almost three years. I cannot believe you've thought much about us in all that time."

"No," he admitted.

They had stopped beside the path leading down to the muni stop. Nicola looked at Scooter. She could tell an idea was beginning to form in his mind.

"But you know," he was saying, "things have not been so great with me right now. I mean that's obvious. That whole kidnapping thing, that whole stupid scheme. Well, you can kind of get an idea of where I was at to do something like that. I was definitely at the bottom there. But let me tell you, seeing you, when I walked into that room and I saw you tied up there, blindfolded and everything, a little saliva on your chin—did you know you had that?"

"No," Nicola said.

"Yeah, there was a little strand of saliva there but it wasn't gross at all; it was like, here was this woman I know so well, a woman I once thought I would have kids with, a woman I loved . . ." He hesitated.

"Scooter, what?" Nicola said impatiently. "I'm already late."

"Well I'm fumbling around because I don't know how to put it exactly, but something changed in me when I saw you."

"And my strand of saliva," Nicola said.

"You laugh, but I say this because it was the *humanity* of your appearance that did something to me. Your saliva, yes, which showed me your *humanity*. A woman tied up, blindfolded—this was no longer some abstract way of getting money, but it was you, a real person in discomfort and possibly pain, all because I made a bad bet or two and my credit went to pieces."

"Okay, well, you're welcome." She turned to go.

"No, no; I mean yes, thank you, but what I'm also trying to say is that I've thought a lot about it and I want you to know I'm through with all that. That kind of living. Waiting for the monster deal, the monster payoff, whatever. I can see getting a real job and buying a house somewhere, like maybe Vallejo, where it's much cheaper and you can get a yard."

"Scooter—"

"That was definitely the bottom for me. The turning point. People evolve, Nicola."

"It's called mutation."

"No, I mean it."

"So do I. Nature evolves in an effort to keep the status quo."

"That's just what I'm saying," Scooter said.

She looked at him. His hair was being blown forward by the wind and he had a plaintive puppy look about him. She couldn't believe he really wanted to get back together; it was only the idea of it he liked.

"Plus I don't want to live in Vallejo," she said.

"Or here's an idea, we could move to Cleveland and I could work for your father. He always liked me."

"It was my mother who liked you."

"Well it only takes one," Scooter said.

He took her hand. Nicola looked up at him, surprised, and he bent forward, then kissed her on her mouth. His lips were very soft and warm and Nicola remembered the spot on the back of his neck she liked to touch when they embraced. It was unexpected and comfortable and for a moment she had the feeling she could fall right back into it again. It would be so easy; it would take no effort at all. The wind pulled at her jacket and blew foam along the beach and she could hear a not-so-distant muni train ringing its bell. A warning, or a sign of arrival? She pulled away.

"We've already done this," she said.

"They say experience is everything."

"Scooter, I'm not kidding."

"Neither am I. Nicola, we could have fun together. Didn't we have fun together? At least part of the time?"

He was using that voice again, that let's-have-an-adventure-together voice. For years it had worked so well on her. Nicola looked at his pale green eyes, which turned up at the corners, giving him the appearance that he always was smiling, always having a good time. Well, he was still a charmer; she would give him that much.

"I can't do all that again," she told him.

Scooter smiled. "You might surprise yourself," he said.

Fourteen

Chorizo drove down Geary Boulevard listening to the radio, Mama Cass singing "Dream a Little Dream of Me." A woman with a large soul, a heart like a beating drum. He liked large women. His wife was a large woman. These women here, these women in California, they were small women, and he didn't just mean their skinny shoulders and legs and their tiny little breasts. Their, what should he call it, their compassion? Their compassion was small. Their understanding. And it was sad, really, the way they starved their bodies.

He parked on the street and began walking down the sidewalk thinking that his own body felt heavy and out of synch. It had been like this since Friday—a sense that the fluids inside him were moving in the wrong direction, the blood coursing rapidly out of his heart and away. A slight edge of sadness. His wife used to tell him he was too tender-hearted. Would she still think so?

He came to a glass door with a simple gold and red sign: KABUKI BATHS. Come back to your body, said the voice on his yoga tape. He pushed open the door. Well, that was why he was here.

Inside he showed the receptionist identification and paid with cash. "No massage today?" she asked. She had a small wire heart on the end of her nose ring. As he put his ID back in his wallet he saw the list he'd made of dentists and thought about that woman, Nicola, the dental hygienist.

He thought, Everything follows a course.

The lobby was warm and dark with a deep-red rug runner and wood-paneled walls. Chorizo looked at his watch. Robert was late. He began to examine the various articles for sale—chakra oils, straw bath slippers, a palmistry chart, a chart about dreams. He picked up the chart about dreams. What had he dreamed last night? He could never remember his dreams.

The bell on the front door tinkled and Robert stepped inside, looking lost and uncomfortable.

"This is . . . ?" he began. Then he saw Chorizo.

"I've paid for you already," Chorizo said. "But she needs to see your ID."

"Why is that?" Robert asked, feeling for his wallet.

"Too many whackos, I guess."

"What?"

Chorizo smiled. "That is a joke."

Another man entered and two more left. Robert's face took in everything. He was jittery; he was always jittery. He should really stop with the coffee, Chorizo thought.

"Did you know that if you dream of cake that means you will get a pleasant surprise?" Chorizo asked him. He was still holding the laminated dream chart. Four dollars, it sold for. But Robert was look-ing at the shrine at the end of the hallway—a somber, cross-legged Buddha with items arranged in a semicircle around it: a candle, worn glass shards, two shells, a dime. Robert's face was tight, defended. A Catholic, Chorizo remembered.

"And if you dream about handcuffs you will find satisfaction," he said.

"Oh, ha," Robert said.

"That is not a joke." Chorizo replaced the chart. "This way."

They went into the locker room where men were changing into loose white terry-cloth robes. Robert fidgeted with his watch while Chorizo found his locker and began to unbutton his shirt.

"Maybe I'll just meet you after," Robert said.

"Nonsense. This will be good for you," Chorizo told him. "Water calms, it relaxes. Some say just washing your hands can help."

Chorizo took off his shirt but Robert didn't move. "I don't get this," he said.

"Get what?"

"Why we're doing this."

Chorizo hung his shirt in the locker. "The plan is you and I spend time together."

"Why would you want to spend time together?"

"Spend time together, get to know each other better," Chorizo continued. He stopped and looked at Robert. "What is it, don't you trust me?"

"Trust you, right," Robert said.

"I want to see you more involved in the business. But first I want to . . . to teach you a few things. No, teach is not the word. Introduce you to a few things."

"What? Why?"

"I want us to be partners."

Robert snorted. "Partners, right." But he seemed pleased. After a moment he looked around, then he turned slightly and began to unbutton his shirt. When they were both in their white robes, Robert followed Chorizo down the small hallway to the baths.

Chorizo opened the door and allowed Robert to go first. Inside it was clean and bright with piped-in music—harp and flute. To the right were seven small foot baths, each with its own bar of soap and wooden stool and white enamel basin. To the left, at the end of the room, there were two doors: one to the dry sauna and one to the wet.

The baths themselves were in the center of the room: a warm bath, a hot bath, and a cold plunge.

"I don't know," Robert said.

"I'll take your robe."

"Maybe I'll keep it on for a while."

"It will get very wet," Chorizo said. He smiled. There were maybe twenty, twenty-five naked men in the room. He could tell Robert was trying not to look at anyone below the neck.

"Right now the feet," he said.

He went to a stool and motioned for Robert. Then he tested the warm water, adjusted the temperature, and filled the basin.

"First soak, then spray," Chorizo said. "The spray feels wonderful."

"Just my feet?"

"It opens the pores."

Afterwards they moved to the warm bath, which was circular and covered in small blue tiles. Chorizo sat on the built-in bench. He was aware of every part of himself, the wetness on his skin, the small strands of black hair. Hips, thighs, calves, feet. Beside him, Robert, also naked, sat down more cautiously. He was more square shaped, Chorizo noticed, like a child's wooden block. Robert moved his hands under the water, but his jerky, jittery motions were beginning to subside. Water calms, water relaxes. After a few minutes Robert allowed himself to look up, to look around the room. Chorizo sank his hands in the water. A feeling of power washed over him.

"Is it me, or is this not that hot?" someone asked—a young man, maybe twenty, who was just stepping into the tub. His head was shaved and he had a tattoo on his scalp.

"It's preparation," Chorizo explained. "The large tub there is hotter."

White towels hung neatly on hooks around the room. In the center stood a wide wooden table with a stack of waxed paper cups and two pitchers of water. There was also a basin filled with ice cubes and another one with coarse white salt.

"This isn't bad," Robert said. Near them a Filipino man was brushing his stomach with a hard plastic brush.

Chorizo smiled. "Let's do the next level."

He was beginning to feel himself again, his body, his mind, though the feeling of sadness persisted. It was always this way after one of those nights: first his body returned, then his heart. Sometimes it took as long as a week. He walked across the room to the hotter tub, which was large and square with multiple levels of benches. Yes, this was good. His pores were pinpoints of heat. His arms and legs no longer felt like part of a costume.

"Whew," Robert said, stepping in. He paused midway. "I'm just getting used to it," he said.

A few men on the other end of the tub talked quietly, but other than this the room was quiet. Peaceful. Some sat in tubs, some relaxed on chairs which were arranged in small clusters around the room. A large, red-headed man sat in an Adirondack chair, naked, reading the newspaper. Next to him was a small fountain, the water trickling over shiny black rocks.

"You were right about this," Robert said. He frowned. "I'm thinking I maybe misjudged you a little."

"That's easy to do."

"Maybe you're not so bad."

Chorizo smiled. "Maybe not."

Robert swirled at the water with his hand.

"So you're thinking along the line of partners, you and me?"

"I'd like to move in that direction," Chorizo said. "If you can see yourself that way."

"I can see it." Robert hesitated. "But I'm wondering," he said, "what this means for my sister."

Chorizo smiled. "Yes, we can talk about that."

The floor and walls were white. Robert sank into the tub until the water reached his chest. He was beginning to go gray there, Chorizo noticed.

"So. Is it always just men here?" Robert asked.

"Men on Tuesdays and Thursdays, women on Wednesdays and Fridays. On Mondays it's coed."

"There's a coed day?"

"You have to wear a bathing suit."

"You ever come on a coed day?"

"On occasion," Chorizo said. "But I prefer to be naked."

"You meet any women here?"

"A few."

"I'd like to come on a coed day."

"I did meet a woman here recently."

"The one from Friday night?"

Chorizo shifted in the tub. "What was that?"

"The woman you were with last Friday night. Did you meet her here?"

Chorizo paused and looked at his hands. Then he stood and waded over to Robert's bench and sat down next to him. Here the water came only to Chorizo's hips. He settled himself and looked at his hands and pulled a few hairs away from the links on his bracelet. He did not look at Robert.

"Did I see you on Friday night?" he asked casually.

"I don't know," Robert said. "I don't think so. I was in the office, I forgot my wallet and I had to go back. You were just going upstairs with a woman."

Chorizo lowered his hands in the water. How much had Robert seen?

"You mean the blonde," Chorizo said.

"Huh," Robert said. "She looked darker than that. Anyway, I thought about calling out, hey, but then I thought, I don't know, don't break the moment. You two seemed pretty intense."

"Mmm."

"So was she from here?"

"Oh. No. No, she wasn't from here."

He began thinking fast. Robert clearly hadn't seen the posters yet, but he might. He hadn't put two and two together, but he might. He might not. But he might. Chorizo was silent for a moment. Then he said, "It's time for the sauna."

The heat hit their faces as they opened the door and all the steam made it difficult to see. They made their way to the long wooden benches and arranged their towels to sit on them.

"Here," Chorizo said. He had filled two paper Dixie cups halfway with salt and he gave one to Robert.

"What's this for?"

"Watch."

He took a pinch of salt and began rubbing his feet and legs. Now he could feel his warm skin in a way that he didn't usually. The salt was a tactile reminder, small rough grains on his skin saying pay attention to this.

"Polishing the body," he said.

Robert said, "What?"

White steam floated like fog curling out from the center of the room and they sat back letting the soft wet heat enter their bodies. Robert held the paper cup of salt in his hand and closed his eyes. They were the only ones there.

"Would you like some ice water?" Chorizo asked.

"Thank you," Robert said.

Chorizo used the standing shower in the corner to rinse the salt off his legs. Then he went to the counter and poured water into two cups and added a lemon slice for each.

"I've been thinking about sadness," Chorizo said as he sat down. He took a sip of cold water. "I recently read that scientists believe this feeling may have Darwinian roots."

"Hunh," Robert said with his eyes closed.

"Imagine our ancestor is lost in the wood and needs to get back before nightfall. He is a hunter-gatherer with only simple weapons; it is dangerous to be out after night. He takes the wrong turn and a feeling comes over him—a sense that something is wrong. Sadness. Depression. This is a signal from the body."

"He should turn around," Robert said.

"Bravery is a kind of sadness," Chorizo continued. "The ideal warrior should be sad and tender. He doesn't act out of anger, out of fear. He acts out of necessity. But that doesn't mean he is cold, that he is a stone."

"What warrior?"

"Each of us is a warrior. We do battle every day."

"In traffic, yeah." Robert laughed.

"Warriors assess what *is*. We act according to what *is*. That's why we need to let the world in. But to let the world in is to be sad. To act on that is to be brave."

"You have completely lost me," Robert said.

Chorizo sipped his water. Sadness, duty, bravery, he thought. These were important concepts. Lost concepts. Here they were in a Japanese sauna, participating in the great tradition of the Japanese public bath. The Japanese with their honor, their sense of duty. A great warrior race.

"I've grown fond of you, Robert, you know that?" Chorizo said.

They were sweating. The towels they were sitting on were wet.

Robert smiled, pleased. "Oh, right," he said.

Afterwards, in the locker room, Chorizo watched Robert examine his face in the mirror.

"Look at me, I look so relaxed. I can't believe it."

"I told you, this is very good for you."

"I feel so great," Robert said. "I might even sleep tonight."

Chorizo bent to tie his shoe.

"I didn't know you had trouble sleeping," he lied. He straightened up. Robert was still looking at his own face, which looked pink and healthy in the mirror. Pink and healthy and alive.

"I can fall asleep but then I'm up an hour later. It's like that all night: asleep, awake, asleep, awake."

"Do you take anything for it?"

"Brandy," Robert said.

"Just one?"

"Or two or three."

Chorizo thought: I could make it look like a suicide.

"I have something that might help with that," he told him.

"What's that?"

"It's a natural cure for sleeplessness. Like homeopathy. A pill. Two actually. You should take them with brandy." He thought: a suicide or an overdose, either way. "I have some on me; you can try two tonight. If you try them tonight and they work, I can get more tomorrow."

"Homeopathy?"

"But you have to take two," Chorizo said.

Fifteen

Wednesday evening Lou knocked on Nicola's door with a large Tupperware container under his arm.

"I've brought some beans," he said when she answered.

"What's this?"

"I'm making you dinner."

"I thought you didn't cook."

"Barlotti beans," Lou said. "Soaked overnight."

"They let you soak beans overnight in your hotel?"

"I'm not staying at a hotel," he said. "Do you have an eight-quart soup pot?"

He carried in a shopping bag and took out square plastic cartons with fresh rosemary and fresh sage leaves, bags of carrots and celery, a small onion, and about twelve red potatoes the size of crab apples.

Nicola watched him line ingredients along the counter. "Are you wooing me?" she asked.

Lou smiled and two patches of red appeared under his cheekbones. Unreal, a loan shark who blushes.

"You're wooing me with soup," she said.

"Not just soup. These are Lamon Barlotti beans, from Australia. They say Italian migrants brought them over. They're best if they're grown on a wire fence."

"You grew these, too?"

"I did not grow them," Lou said. He rolled up his white shirt-sleeves and began washing his hands at her sink. "I very carefully bought them," he said.

Who was this guy? Four days ago she had paid him six thousand dollars of her own money, she had written him a personal check for six thousand dollars, and in return he was making her soup. She wanted just to stand and look at him. Nice hands, nice arms, a good face. Makes money in the time-honored tradition of helping others when no legitimate institution will touch them.

"Beans are one of the richest sources of vegetable protein," he was saying. "Did you know that bean soup is on the menu of the United States Senate Restaurant every day?"

"Is that so?"

"Every single day," he said.

He held a stalk of rosemary under the faucet then began cutting it into tiny herbal points.

"It's like a law," he said.

He had everything: peppercorns, garlic, extra virgin olive oil, chicken stock, salt. He crushed a sage leaf between his fingers then held out his hand. "Smell," he said.

He was wearing black jeans and the inevitable white shirt, and although the hair on his head was dark, the hair on his arms looked like fine strands of deep gold.

"So where are you staying?" Nicola asked.

"What?"

"If you're not in a hotel?"

Lou began washing potatoes with a scrub brush.

"My uncle."

"Your uncle the loan shark?"

"My uncle the doctor."

"I thought you came from a crime family?"

"That's my mother's side," he told her. A warm smell of garlic frying in olive oil wafted over from the range. Lou added the diced herbs and vegetables, then covered the sauté pan.

Nicola said, "So Uncle Doctor lives in San Francisco?"

"He's trying to get me to move here, too."

"I didn't know you were thinking of moving."

"Of course it depends."

"On what?"

Lou looked at her steadily. "On the food," he said.

Nicola smiled and looked at her reflection in the window and realized she was still wearing her work clothes. She told Lou she'd just be a minute. In her bedroom she pulled on jeans and a black China silk camisole and a small pink T-shirt. Her lipstick was the creasy kind and she rubbed it all off, then applied another color that wasn't as good but stayed on longer. Pressed her lips together. Blotted. Is this really necessary, Nicola wondered? She applied more lipstick and blotted. I look okay, she thought. She smiled. I look great. For the first time in she didn't know how many months her eyes looked alive. She held out her palm and looked in the mirror and thought: I can feel him right here.

But before she went back to the kitchen she turned away from the door and dialed Scooter's cell phone number. When he answered she asked him not to come back to her house before ten. She said, "I'm kind of, I need to do some work."

"What's going on?" Scooter asked. She could hear bar noises in the background.

"I'm working on something," she explained, and she thought well that's pretty much the truth.

When she came out Lou was in the living room looking through her compact disks. A woman's voice filled the room. Mama Cass.

"Is the soup done?"

"The first stage," he said, and sat down on the couch. "You look nice."

"Thank you."

"Though I liked the suit, too."

She sat down on the couch halfway facing him. Again she noticed how dark his eyes were. Their legs were almost touching.

"So do you do this at everyone's home?" she asked.

"What, make them dinner?"

"I meant take charge."

Lou looked her over.

"I can't imagine anyone taking charge of you," he said.

She thought of Guy. "Really?"

"You're so I'm-in-control."

She laughed. "You think so, huh?"

"It's kind of a turn-on," Lou said.

He took her hand. Her heart gave a sudden hard beat. She tried to think of what to say. "You smell nice," she told him.

Lou smiled. "I always smell nice."

Again her heart seemed to tighten. What is this, she asked herself? She was excited and nervous and she didn't want to be, she wanted to be in control, comfortable, setting the pace. Lou's legs were stretched out in front of the couch and he looked up at her with a serious expression. His sleeves were still rolled up from cooking. Nicola tried to picture him in an apron. He had fine dark eyebrows and a perfect complexion. Again she noticed his arms, how strong they were. She thought of her father, who when he first met Scooter said you can do better. But a bookie?

"So who was that on the phone?" Lou asked.

"You heard that? It was nothing, just a . . . a thing I had to check."

"Is someone staying here?"

"Why do you ask?"

He motioned to the duffel bag underneath the window.

"Oh yeah. Yeah," Nicola said slowly. "Well, actually, Scooter."

"And you called him," Lou said.

"Well. Yes."

"You told him not to come by."

"Yes."

"Until a certain time."

"Yes."

"And what time was that?"

"Ten."

"Ten tomorrow morning?"

Nicola smiled. "Ten o'clock," she said. "Tonight."

Lou said, "Then I have to move fast."

But instead of moving fast he leaned his head back on the couch cushion and closed his eyes. A shark, a law-school dropout, a man who makes soup. Who was he really? For a while they sat there saying nothing, holding hands, listening to the music.

It was nice, actually. The warm room, the smell of garlic, a woman's voice on the stereo. Nicola began to feel more comfortable, more like this wasn't so strange to be sitting here on her couch with a slightly disreputable man, and anyway it's not like the last man wasn't slightly disreputable, and the one before that. She moved her foot toward his and when her shoe made contact he turned and looked at her, he looked at her face and at her T-shirt and her jeans, and Nicola wondered if the camisole she was wearing was visible and she hoped that it was. Lou smiled and she smiled and she felt kind of dopey smiling together like that but she liked it too.

After a moment he touched her cheekbone with his thumb. "You know what I really like?" he asked.

"What," she said.

"Your arms."

She laughed.

"I really like your arms," he said.

She said, "I like yours, too. I was noticing them while you chopped."

"Really?"

"I like a man who can chop with inferior cutlery."

At that he grinned and moved closer and took her other hand and what else could she do? She closed her eyes and kissed him. His lips were very warm. She was thinking, It's always such a surprise, the first time you kiss someone. It feels so oh, so this is who you are. All these people I don't know, I will never know, because I will never kiss them. Mama Cass sang, "Every time I see that girl you know I want to lay down and die." Nicola opened her eyes and saw that Lou had his eyes open too. He was watching her. "But you know I'm living a lie," sang Mama Cass.

"All right?" Lou asked.

She felt extraordinary. She didn't know what to say.

Lou pulled back a little. "Is this good?"

"It's good," she finally said.

"Good. Listen. Tell me when thirty minutes are up."

"Thirty minutes?"

"I have to add the herbs to the soup."

She laughed. She felt that something large and wonderful was happening, a feeling that pressed upwards on her heart. Lou took her face in his hands. They moved backwards on the couch and the couch cushion bent under their weight and Nicola heard the CD click into the next song. They began to kiss in earnest. She didn't open her eyes. All she wanted was to lie there in the warm room kissing him and smelling the aroma of soup cooking on the other side of the wall and feeling his hands on her face and feeling the corduroy couch fabric against her neck when suddenly there was a terrific banging on the front door, a banging and banging, like two fists going at it at once.

"Quick, quick," someone, a woman, was shouting. She banged again. "Open the door!"

"Jesus," Nicola said sitting up quickly.

"Is anyone in there? I can see lights," the woman shouted.

Lou and Nicola jumped up at the same time and Nicola ran to the door and didn't even think but opened it without looking to see who it was—a woman in trouble, that's all she knew. As the door opened the woman seemed to fall inside.

It was Robert's sister. She was holding a suitcase and a laptop computer and her face was swollen from crying.

"Oh my God, he's dead," Carmen said. She was sobbing. "He's dead, Robert's dead."

Sixteen

She had lovely wide hips and small breasts and a small waist and she told him that she tried and tried to take some inches off her thighs but her body didn't work that way—"it all goes from my breasts," she told him at dinner, "that's the first place that shrinks."

Three hours later he was watching her through the viewfinder. It was true about her breasts. Her face now was calm and trancelike, in the stage he liked best. Her fingernails were blue.

She lay on her back on the bed, barely conscious, and Chorizo moved the camera in for a close-up of her face, her brown eyes hidden under half-closed lids, her lips pale, her face pale, her naked shoulders pale, pale. Panning in and out: the close-up, the long body shot, the longer shot of two bodies, a man and a woman's, on the bed.

They were not naked. They were not even touching. Chorizo pulled back for another shot of the two of them. He could see how filmmakers got off on this: making other people see things the way they were seeing them; the way they experimented with seeing them.

Moving his fingers over the camera buttons, opening and shutting the audience's eyes, moving them into position: you're looking in from the doorway, now you're on the ceiling peering down.

It's a physical thing, Chorizo was thinking, what you do to the ones who watch what you do.

He pulled the small slick gray knob forward and back with his thumb and said to the boy, "Now touch the fabric."

The boy moved toward the girl but it was clear he was not very interested. Later he would shoot up next to his girlfriend Marlina on her Navajo bedspread, and much later they would fall asleep chastely, side by side. These days what they had was more intimate than sex, based as it was on mutually assured survival. The boy was wearing a white T-shirt and briefs and he lazily pulled on the spaghetti strap of the girl's embroidered silk top. Chorizo could see old needle marks that peppered the backs of his thighs. He kept the camera off that. The bedspread was deep blue and red, the pillowcases yellow. Chorizo liked lots of colors for these shots. The room was well-lit but with thick black curtains; still, he could hear noises from the outside, a steady stream of talking and laughing and shouting and sometimes the breaking of bottles. There was a popular club across the street and an all-night diner on the corner. It was just about eight o'clock.

"Ricky," Chorizo ordered.

The boy was lazy, and the girl was already asleep. Technically, comatose. He wished he could remember her name. Lake, was that it? River? Rive? When he had told her the story of the crocodile and the monkey she had fixed her brown eyes on his mouth as if watching the words themselves, living creatures that sprang from his lips. He had said, "The story is a wonderful example of what you need to succeed: courage and faith and luck.

"What you are missing," he said to the girl, "is luck."

She had smiled then, a crooked kind of acceptance. Did she actually understand him? Most of them didn't understand by then. But he would swear there was something in—Rive, was it?—there was something in her that grasped his meaning. Grasped it, accepted it, let it go.

"Ricky," he said again.

The boy stirred, then pulled on the straps of her chemise again. The girl showed no response. There would be a moment when the body stiffened; it actually seemed to grow hard in an instant. The death instant. Maybe it wasn't so much hard as still; very very still. Riva? Was her name Riva?

Chorizo panned back for another shot of the two of them. The moment was coming. He had given her two pills but they were working fast. He was a little afraid the moment would get here too soon.

Carmen was sitting on Nicola's couch sobbing in gulps while Nicola watched her, trying to think of what she could possibly say. Only a few minutes before she had been sitting in the same spot with her legs entwined in Lou's. Now here was Carmen with her head down, her hair over her face. Lou had turned off the music. Right now he was half-sitting on the couch arm with a glass of water in one hand and his other hand on his knee. After a minute, when she seemed to have quieted down a little, he touched Carmen's shoulder and she looked up and took the glass then she gave it back without drinking. She gulped some air and put her head down and everything started all over again.

"Oh dear," Lou said.

Nicola gently pulled Carmen's hair back behind her shoulders. She almost said, It's all right, but she stopped herself because of course it wasn't.

The sister, she was thinking. She must really be the sister.

What could she say to her? After a while Carmen's breath came back and her sobs began to slow down. Nicola stroked her hair and

Carmen said, hiccuping, "You must really be wondering." She took the water Lou gave her and wiped her eyes with her fingers and Nicola went into the bathroom for a wet washcloth wondering, Should I offer her something stronger to drink? She put her fingers beneath the tap waiting for the spray to get colder. She had a few bottles of beer, but that didn't seem right.

When she walked back to the room she tried to think what she would want to hear if their positions were reversed. The clock ticked loudly over the mantelpiece and Carmen took the washcloth without looking at Nicola and held it over her eyes. What would I want someone to say, Nicola wondered?

She said, "Carmen, we're going to help you."

At that Lou looked over at her.

"What," she said, meeting his stare.

"We should find out what's going on first," he told her.

"Of course. We find out what happened. Then we fix it," Nicola said.

"I agree we need to help, but . . ."

"But?"

"We really need to find out what's going on."

"Look at this woman," she said.

Carmen was still holding the washcloth over her eyes. She took it off and dried her face on her sleeve.

"I'll get you a towel," Lou said.

"No, wait." Carmen took a breath and drank some water. "I know you're wondering and I want to explain," she began. "Robert always said . . ." She hiccuped and started to cry again then tried to stop herself.

"It's all right," Lou said. "You don't need to talk."

"No," Carmen said. "I want . . . you must really be wondering. I want to tell you."

"Well, take your time," Lou told her.

Carmen took a breath and almost smiled. "What a nice guy. He's a nice guy," she said to Nicola. "Is he your boyfriend?"

"We were just sort of getting to that," Nicola said.

"Oh, Christ. Did I . . . ? I mean here you were having a nice evening, a date—was it a date?"

"Yes," Lou said.

"And I show up," Carmen said.

"Stop apologizing," Nicola said. "We can pick all that up again whenever."

"And I barge in, a total stranger."

"Stop," Nicola said again. "Look, I'm going to take the washcloth away if you don't stop."

"Because Robert always told me if anything happened, if anything strange or frightening or just anything, I don't know, anything happened I should come to this house. This cottage. I'd be safe here, he said."

"Safe here?" Nicola asked.

"So I barge right in because I didn't know what else to do after I found . . . I found him . . . he was sitting in his TV chair with his eyes open . . ." Carmen began losing her voice. "But I don't believe he killed himself," she said, losing control.

Lou and Nicola looked at each other. Killed himself?

"I don't . . . I don't want to cry," Carmen said.

"But you should be crying," Nicola said. "Robert is your brother. You should be crying." She took Carmen's hand. The clock ticked loudly; it was just after eight.

"Listen, why don't you lie down," she said. "Whenever you want, you talk to us, you tell us what happened. But first I'm going to make you some tea. And then after that we're going to feed you. And after that we're going to help you." She looked at Lou. "Aren't we?" she said.

"Oh my God," Lou said, getting up suddenly.

"What?"

"The soup," he said.

But Chorizo needn't have worried; as it turned out the timing was perfect. It was dark now and slowly the sounds from the street increased as more and more people left restaurants and headed for the clubs. Chorizo looked through the camera lens.

"Awakening is to know what reality is not," he said aloud. That was good; he liked that. A pity he would have to delete the soundtrack. Later he would add music, then convert it all to quicktime. Last time he did Brian Eno. This time, who knows, some retro seventies band? A big-hair band? She had a seventies look with her puffy hair, her wide-cut blue jeans. Not that she was wearing blue jeans now.

He could definitely picture a seventies soundtrack. Something light and frivolous. A good juxtaposition, he was thinking, as she died. Not that he thought of himself as an artist. He thought of himself as a businessman.

A businessman with a wife in trouble.

"It's time," he told Ricky.

He looked at the girl. Beneath the overhead light a thin stream of dust moved down from the ceiling and he focused the camera for a moment on the girl's pale face, what he could see of it. They had eaten garlicky Chinese food for dinner and afterwards they stopped for a mojito—rum mixed with mint and lime juice. His mouth felt slightly sour and he ran his tongue over his bottom teeth. "Awakening is to know," he said again. But what did that mean exactly? She will not awaken, he thought. She will not know.

Ricky moved over and, without disengaging himself from her, picked up the scissors from the metal bedside table.

———

A half an hour later Carmen combed her hair, then sat down with a cup of chamomile tea at Nicola's small kitchen table, a forties-style metal table wedged into the corner of the room. The soup smelled delicious. Lou was cutting potato rosemary bread with a long serrated knife.

"I don't know what to do," Carmen said. She was still wearing her coat.

Nicola pulled out bowls from a cupboard. All her dishes suddenly seemed too bright and festive. What was this, dinner in Disneyland? She poured bubbly mineral water into tall Mexican glasses with stems.

"Drink this," she said.

"Do you have anything stronger?" Carmen asked. So Nicola brought her a bottle of beer. Her mind kept circling around two things: curiosity about Robert, and trying to comfort Carmen. About Robert she wanted to know the particulars, but, about Carmen, she felt she could not ask.

Carmen said she wasn't hungry, but Lou put soup and bread in front of her anyway and soon she was eating in small, rushed bites. Lou washed his hands and grated parmesan cheese over her soup, then took out a bottle of wine.

Nicola found three glasses; one she had to wash first. She thought of a story she had read in the news that day about how women don't have the same fight or flight tendencies that men have; instead, this particular report claimed, they tend and befriend. Tend and befriend. Nicola hated that phrase the minute she read it and she hated it now, remembering.

Because she *would* fight. Even for Carmen, and who was Carmen? Pretty much a stranger, someone who might take my home away, okay, but also someone in trouble. It wasn't Carmen's fault that her brother tried to screw her, Nicola, over, and then went and killed himself or whatever it was that happened—in any case something that Carmen will now have to deal with for the rest of her life.

Nicola sat down beside her. Lou ladled out more soup from the pot and like a mother kept getting up from the table to fetch something else—the parmesan cheese, napkins, a pepper grinder.

After her second bowl Carmen slowed down and began talking.

She told them that her brother worked for a man he didn't trust, someone she worked for too, and that last week Robert told her about this cottage and said that if anything ever happened she should come here. She would be safe here.

To be honest, Carmen said, she never trusted the man. Adam Lightwell was his name—but she didn't think that was his real name.

"He looks like a sausage," she said.

"What did you do for this man?" Lou asked.

Carmen tore the crust from her bread and added it to the pile on her plate. "Originally accounting. That's what my degree is in."

She said Lightwell and Robert had done a few deals together, some real estate stuff, but something strange happened over the last one—Carmen thought maybe Robert somehow lost his portion and became indebted to Lightwell as well. But Lightwell wasn't only involved in real estate. He had ideas about making money on the Internet. Carmen found herself helping him set up a Web site, nothing very interesting except that he had her upload files through an anonymous remailer that went through Finland. That was when she realized he didn't want to be traced.

Lou was standing at the table, stacking the empty soup bowls. "What's a remailer?" he asked.

"A remailer," Nicola explained, "is kind of like an e-mail go-between. You send your files, or your e-mail, to a server in a protected country—in this case Finland. The server in Finland consults its secret database and forwards your files to another server, one which you've set up beforehand, say one in California. Your Web site is on the server in California, and the files are published there. But if someone wants to know who uploaded the files onto the California Web site, all they get is the address of the anonymous server in Finland."

"You leave no trail," Lou said.

"You leave no trail," Nicola agreed.

"It sounds fishy." He turned to Carmen. "Weren't you suspicious?"

"Well, but this is the Internet; so many people are a little crazy," Carmen said. "You know—paranoid about privacy. That's all I thought it was at first."

"And then?" Lou asked. "After a while you changed your mind?"

"And then—oh, I don't know. I began to wonder, I guess. That soup was delicious."

Lou took the stack of bowls to the sink and closed the kitchen blinds, then set the skillet to soak. The night had lost all of its original romance. A woman sitting at the kitchen table, crying over her brother who was—murdered? As she listened to Carmen, Nicola could feel her heart start to race. She didn't know if she was being very, very stupid or not.

"At a certain point we should consider the police," she said.

Carmen tore more crust. "What can they do? They'll say it was suicide."

"You said that before. Why do you think that?" Lou asked.

"There was a note in the printer tray. Not even signed. Also, I found an empty bottle of pills—methadone. But when does Robert take methadone? He's not a junkie; maybe he drinks a little too much, but that's it. I just don't buy it."

Nicola tried to be gentle. "You say he was seriously in debt to this man? This Lightwell?"

"He owed him a lot of money."

Nicola took a breath, then paused. She and Lou looked across the room at each other. But Carmen caught their look.

"It was *not* suicide," she said again fiercely. She pulled out her laptop and put it on the kitchen chair beside her and turned it on. "Look at this," she said.

The scissors caught the light from the bare bulb and he was glad he just had them sharpened. He threw away the bedspread each time and he bought new pillowcases and new posters for the wall but the scissors were always the same—German hairstyling scissors with long blades and small finger holes. The boy had thin fingers, which is why Chorizo hired him. Not that there was much competition.

The boy put his fingers in the finger holes, then, blades closed, he lay the metal over the girl's throat. No movement. Her chest went up and down only slightly as she breathed and the end of the scissors pointed straight out at the camera. Chorizo stepped quickly to the other side of the bed for a better angle and the boy opened the scissors and cut once into the air.

"This is what he does," Carmen said.

She opened an image file on her computer.

"I'm not sure," she said, "but I think the girl is dead."

Nicola and Lou stared at the image.

"Now," Chorizo said.

The boy moved down over the girl's body—thank God she was still hanging on—and began cutting. First the white straps, exposing her shoulders. Then the bodice. He made a long incision lengthwise, smoothly rending the white silk into two pieces. Her chemise opened, became a vest, but the boy did not pull it aside; instead he cut a strip of material out and then another. He was cutting her clothes off. She was absolutely still.

"Good, good," Chorizo said. "Be careful of her skin."

Ricky cut some more, making smaller and smaller cuts, drawing the process out. Sometimes he made shapes: long flat ovals, trapezoids. A not-very-good squiggle of lightning. Flaps of white material fell away from her or hung like feathers near her skin.

Chorizo watched through the viewfinder. "I want only the suggestion of blood."

The idea was a kind of transference—you didn't see the skin cut but you felt the skin was cut. In a few minutes the chemise lay in pieces. When there was no more to slice, the boy looked down for a moment then moved to her panties.

"Careful, careful," Chorizo told him.

The panties were white silk too. Ricky started at one leg hole then cut a line to the opposite one.

"Careful."

The material fell away. It took only a few seconds. The boy was visible from behind. The girl's arms were at her sides, limp, palms up. Her head was turned and her eyes were not fully closed. Her lips had turned a deeper blue.

"That's it," Chorizo said.

The boy fell forward for a moment, losing his balance, and nicked her with the scissors. "Ooh," said the boy.

"Christ," Chorizo said. He stopped filming. A small dot of blood appeared on her thigh.

"Christ," Chorizo said again. The inside of his mouth felt slick, as if lined with sesame oil from that night's Kung Pao chicken. He wanted to take the audience to the edge, make them see the blood without seeing it. Feel the death without doing it. The spiritual warrior is at one with the physical plane, but in a sense he moves beyond it. He finds the spirit within the object. There would be no blood and yet the audience would swear there was blood, because the sense—the *spirit*—of blood is there.

Chorizo felt the back of his hair with his fingers while Ricky looked up at him, waiting to hear what to do. He thought about the audience, middle-aged men with credit cards sitting at a desk chair holding the crotch of their blue jeans or chinos or suit pants, what have you, watching the scissors snip snip at what might have been her throat, watching the clothes fall away, both their hands moving together, sitting in the den or in the family room with the television off, late at night, the family in bed, or maybe they lived alone, maybe they lived with their mother, maybe they were getting a business degree at night or they were in some frat house in a college on the eastern seaboard and they were saying to a frat brother man you gotta see this. Look at this, man, come here a minute, oh shit, oh my God! Their voices getting higher. He thought about all the men with their credit cards and their secret desire to duck under society, to get out of its tedious grip, and why shouldn't he give them that pleasure for a fee? He would give them that pleasure and he would see his wife out of jail with their money, why not? Because they were not warriors. They were not priests. They were not shamans. They were not healers. They ate, they watched, they took anything offered without thought. The underlying meaning would be lost to them, absolutely—this he always knew. Still, one wants to do one's best.

Chorizo adjusted the chain of his bracelet and felt his hair with his hand again then looked back through the lens. Ricky was still waiting.

"Oh well, fuck it," he said to Ricky, "go ahead."

It was difficult to tell if the girl in the image was alive or not. Nicola moved the laptop from the chair to the table.

"When did you find the picture?" she asked.

"I didn't find it, I copied it. I took it home. Now I realize how incredibly stupid that was. I never looked at any of the files before."

"Were they all images?"

"What if Robert was killed because I . . ."

"Wait," Nicola said. "First I want to know, were all the files images like this one?"

"I don't really know," Carmen said. "They were compressed in various ways."

"How did you decide to take this one?"

"It was one of the ones he threw away, that's all. I found it in the computer's trash can."

There was a knock on the door and Carmen gasped. "Do you know who it is? Don't open it!" she said quickly. As she took hold of the kitchen table, Nicola noticed she wore a small silver ring on her thumb in the shape of a snake.

"It's all right," Nicola said. "I know who it is. I made a phone call a few minutes ago. Don't worry."

She came back with Davette.

"See," Lou said. "It's all right."

"This is Davette," Nicola said. "She's our resident hacker."

Davette looked around the kitchen. She had dyed her hair an orangy-yellow color and was wearing a short black skirt underneath her puffy coat.

"Where's Dave?" she asked.

"I didn't call Dave," Nicola told her.

Carmen was still clutching the edge of the table. Davette took off her coat and set her airline laptop case down on the floor. After Nicola offered her food and gave her a glass of mineral water, she told her what had happened to Robert. She watched Davette's face closely. Her expression didn't change although her color deepened.

"This is the landlord?" she asked.

"And we think there's more going on," Nicola said. She pulled Carmen's computer onto the table and showed Davette the image of the girl on a bed. "Carmen feels that . . . well maybe you should say what you think, Carmen."

"The man who did that is going to kill me," she said.

Davette glanced at Nicola. Nicola suddenly remembered she was only sixteen or seventeen, a girl. But Davette only said, "Well, we won't let him."

Lou said, "Do you think you can find out more about Robert's Web site? There might be a connection between that and this . . . this girl here."

"I think so," Davette said. "But first." She reached inside her airline bag and searched around until she finally found something. It looked like a matchbox.

"Pocket spell for luck," Lou read aloud, looking over Davette's shoulder. "What's that?"

"A pocket spell," Davette explained. "For luck."

She did the spell with tiny white candles on a white saucer and a small gray pebble glued to a leaf. "Lucky rock," Davette chanted, "lucky circle, lucky day, lucky hour, lucky me."

Afterwards she looked up at Nicola, who was still standing next to her. Nicola blew out the candles.

"There," Davette said. She gave the plate with the spell circle to Lou, then looked at Carmen.

"You'll be all right," she told her, and pulled the laptop closer.

The girl's silk camisole lay—if not in threads, then in long white strips that led away from her body like snakes leaving a log. But she was not dead. Not yet. Ricky sat next to her and began making himself hard. He had to get himself ready on his own because nothing worked too well in that area these days. Chorizo, bored, watched him do it.

Meanwhile the girl breathed slowly and unevenly. Her skin was that extraordinary color. He wished he could pick it up better on video.

"All right, then," he said.

Ricky climbed on top of her and began to move. The girl groaned; she was still hanging on. She didn't know what was happening, it was probably like a wonderfully vague dream. Or so Chorizo hoped. For her sake, he hoped so.

His wife accused him of being tender-hearted, but surely she couldn't accuse him of that now. She was the one who wrote letters and sabotaged—or tried to—various Turkish or Greek offices of government. She, with her Turkish father and her Greek mother, hated both sides. What did she want? Anarchy, she would say. The end of nationalism. But she didn't really know what she wanted. She was angry; she was well read. At various times she said various things. For the press she had all sorts of ridiculous statements.

And the most ridiculous thing of all was the way she'd been caught—a prematurely exploding bomb. Her own bomb. She was lucky she wasn't dead herself. But her hands . . . her hands! thought Chorizo. At the trial she had hoped she could make some statements, but they wouldn't admit political discourse. So it was all for nothing! Chorizo's face contorted. Her beautiful hands.

He made himself focus on the bed. Ricky was right there, moving on top of the girl, her filmy skin, a coldness that seemed to start from her heart. These Americans, Chorizo thought. For a moment he felt the bitterness his wife felt—although in her case it was all about who governed Cyprus—the sense of being with the wrong people and hating the people for being wrong. Americans. Everything on the surface, everything easy, everything in control. A narrowness of mind that was almost staggering.

And the remarkable thing was that they *liked* this, this what Ricky was doing. The Americans *liked* this. It was for them a turn-on. A man on top of a comatose women, naked, her clothes cut away. Fucking her to her death.

He had to sit a minute. Take a breath, center himself. It was his fault for letting thoughts of his wife creep in.

The spiritual warrior is at one with the world.

When he looked back up the scene seemed different. Was the girl still breathing? He listened for the death rattle—each time it sounded slightly different. The first time he thought it was a cough, a cough without movement, a cough without opening her mouth. Then he realized. Now he watched closely as the girl's eyes opened slightly, two slits looking at something halfway across the room. Her skin, he knew, was growing colder. The sound was forming in her throat.

"What the fuck," Ricky said suddenly. He started to get off of the girl.

"Don't stop!" Chorizo ordered. But he was surprised, too.

It was remarkable. Her eyes had opened fully, looking Ricky right in the face. Like she knew exactly what they were doing.

"She's freakin me out. Man, stop it."

He started to cover the girl's face with his hand.

"No, don't do that."

Then all at once she relaxed and closed her eyes again.

"Man," Ricky said. And settled back down.

Chorizo panned back. River? Was that the girl's name?

Davette found the Web site they had gotten to before and began running a program in the background to get more information about it.

"It has a different IP address than Robert's," she said. "I'm going to hack into the server. Find out when it was last updated."

A line of files and dates appeared in a separate window.

"Any of these names look familiar?" she asked Carmen.

"Those are the files I copied for him. Look, there's one that's still compressed."

"Hmm," Davette said, frowning.

"What?" asked Nicola.

"Not all of these filenames match what's on the site. It could just be that he didn't end up using all the files. Let's just see. Let's just look around a little."

Davette launched several programs at once and after the third one got going Nicola watched the screen, amazed. Davette was really a pro for someone so young. Nicola found herself thinking about her own days in high school. She was such a good student, so active, so competent, and yet always the vice president—the one who ran around organizing what everyone else wanted. Now she was the one making decisions while someone else did the work.

Carmen washed her face at the kitchen sink, then went into the living room to lie down, and Nicola brought her a Mexican blanket. After that she had nothing to do.

"Do you mind if I load your dishwasher?" Lou asked her. He was standing at the sink.

"What?"

"Some people are particular."

He had wet hands and Nicola pictured him wearing rubber gloves as he sprayed the bottom of the skillet. Why did this turn her on?

"Do you want some help?" she asked.

"Under control," he told her.

"What's this?" Davette said suddenly from the table.

She was looking at another Web site on screen.

"A semi-invisible link," she said.

"Semi-invisible?"

"From your landlord's site. The porn site. There's a semi-invisible link. Which means you have to know where it is. Let's see where it goes."

She pressed the link. Nicola moved closer. A new screen appeared: the face of a rubber doll looking up. It was heavily made-up and dressed like a cabaret dancer in, say, Berlin around 1930.

Lou came over to see. "Dolls for sale," he read.

"A site selling rubber dolls," Nicola said.

"A site behind a site."

"Strange."

"But still nothing illegal."

"I bet there's more," Davette told them.

Nicola stared at another doll, which was dressed in a turquoise negligee that looked familiar. "More?" she asked.

"Just a sec," Davette said.

Lou pulled a chair up behind Davette and after a few minutes Davette found what she was looking for: another transparent link on the rubber doll site. There was only the slightest change in the cursor arrow as Davette passed over it, like a faint ripple on the surface of the moon.

"Here we go," she said.

"Should I wake up Carmen?" Lou asked.

"Let's just take a peek," Davette told them, and clicked on the link.

Nicola was watching over Davette's shoulder as a window popped up on the screen.

"It's asking for a credit card number," Nicola said. Lou reached for his wallet. "No, wait," she said. She went into the living room past the sleeping Carmen and knelt beside Scooter's duffel. Carmen was breathing lightly. Inside the duffel, at the toe of one of the shoes, was a credit card.

"Okay, here," she said coming back into the kitchen.

Davette typed in the number and confirmed.

"How much does this cost?" Lou asked.

"I didn't look."

The screen had faded and was now a flat dull uniform gray. Then a small window popped up indicating that a video file was loading. After a moment music began.

"Hawaiian," Lou said. "The Guy Pardos band. I think I have this album."

"You have Hawaiian music?"

But the video was starting—hula dancers on a stage, filmed from the waist up, their dark hair held back by large pink flowers. It was some sort of old documentary clip. When the drums began, they started to dance.

"Weird," Lou said.

Nicola looked over at him. "Do you think this is it?"

The drums got louder and louder and the women shook their hips though you couldn't see their hips, you could only see their naked navels and their tanned stomachs and their shoulders and their shiny black hair with the flowers. They moved faster and faster with concentration and precision but with smiles on their faces. The drums beat harder. The women moved their hands. Mahalo, they mouthed. Their palms were up, giving. Mahalo.

"WTF," Davette said.

"Here comes the finale," Lou said.

But just as the drums got very loud and the camera began to pull back to show the whole shot—tanned women with grass skirts and bare feet on a wooden stage—the video sort of just crinkled—crinkle was the only word Nicola could think of to describe it—crinkled into a new video, though still accompanied by Hawaiian music. She stared as the image of the dancing women faded and the new image crinkled in.

It was a woman lying on a bed.

Next to her, a man. He had scissors in his left hand and he snipped at the air above her throat. As he snipped, new music began—Brian Eno.

"What's he doing to her?" Davette asked.

Her clothes were in shreds and the boy was raping her and she was going to die right there on camera.

Call a spade a spade.

Her eyes didn't open again. Chorizo listened to the rattle in her throat as her breaths unevenly came and went. Was that her last breath? He waited, listening hard. No, there was another. That one, then? He waited again. Ricky moved up and down, up and down, but the girl was absolutely still. Nothing. No more breath. That was it, then, there would be nothing more. The body was so still, so still, as though something had evaporated and moved away, just moved away. So that was the end. A spirit dispersing. Chorizo kept the videotape rolling.

He thought about how in the final version the music would build to a climax, and just as the viewers adjusted to the snipped clothes the camera would cut suddenly to Ricky climbing on top of her and then they would get to see a long shot of the girl dying while Ricky worked himself over her, raping her, killing her, and then if they were lucky a long last take of her strangely still and strangely colored body. If they were very lucky there would be a little blood, just a trickle, slithering down from her nose. Her clothes cut away from her. Her clothes in shreds. He always appreciated that added effect. A woman whose most intimate clothing, a symbol of her deeper side, her sensuality—her secret thoughts of sex—all of this stripped away, destroyed.

God is in the details, his wife used to say as she made her inferior bombs.

Ricky rolled off the girl and rubbed his eyes with his thumbs. For a moment the noise outside abated and Chorizo could hear Ricky breathe heavily, then cough once into his hands. No doubt about it then, the girl was dead. She'd passed over. Or, as Chorizo considered it, she'd passed through. Ricky moved his legs over the edge of the bed and began to pull on his pants. Dead bodies—it seemed they meant nothing to him. He would get paid and he would get the junk that Chorizo had purchased that morning and he would eat something and find a hotel room and shoot up in peace while Marlina finished with her john in the room just below them. He would save some food for her.

And meanwhile Chorizo would do all the rest—get rid of the bedspread, the posters, the girl. Anything that appeared on the video. The main thing was not to allow himself caught on camera, and how could he be, if he were the cameraman? There would be no trace of him on the Internet. There would only be poor Ricky: one indistinguishable junkie in a country of a thousand indistinguishable junkies.

Chorizo stopped the video and examined the lens of the camera. Everything appeared normal. He was always very careful with the disk files even though technically he was not very proficient; but he was learning, he was watching Carmen and asking her questions and soon he would be able to handle the nuts and bolts of the Web site himself. Carmen knew so little of what really went on. Still, she would have to die.

She was so pretty; almost certainly she would be photogenic. He wished he could do it on video. But there must be no links back to himself; that was important.

Chorizo covered the girl's body with the bedsheet, tucking the edges in around her shoulders and head. Be true to yourself: this is the first rule of Shambhala. No backward links: this is the first rule of crime.

Seventeen

Nicola woke early the next morning, scared out of sleep by a dream—what was it? But no, it wasn't a dream, it was a video. It was that video. Jesus, that girl, she thought. Her bare bluish shoulders and feet. The strange color of her lips. Nicola turned and looked at the clock. What had she gotten herself into? Fear: this is what it felt like. She wanted to stay in bed.

But the screech of a garbage truck coming down the street got her up—as usual she had forgotten to put out the cans. "Oh shit," Nicola said and she threw herself out of bed and onto Carmen, who was sleeping on a foam pad on the floor. "What?" said Carmen, still mostly asleep.

"Oh shit, oh shit," Nicola said, pulling a sweatshirt over her nightgown.

In the kitchen, a faint pearl-gray light was filtering through the blinds. She opened a paper grocery bag and began throwing cans and bottles inside. The recycling truck always came first. From the street she could hear it start up, then brake again, and also the sound of a

second truck starting and braking not far behind. Nicola quickly began throwing old newspapers and junk mail into another empty paper
bag, then she picked up all the bags and ran.

The recycling guy—Ulyssey—was grinning at her as she opened
the front gate.

"I'm waiting for you," he called.

"One of these days I'm going to surprise you," she told him.

He swung the bags up into the truck and jumped into the cab,
driving with one foot and one hand. Nicola looked up. It was cold
out, but surprisingly clear. The sky was a soft baby blue. She shivered.
She would never get back to sleep.

When Lou called later Nicola was on her computer looking again
at the snuff video, which she had illegally copied onto her computer
using software she got off a hacker who occasionally freelanced for
her. She was running the video over and over, pausing to look at
something more closely, then running it and pausing it and running
it and pausing it, trying to find something . . . she didn't know what.
She was thinking about Carmen, who was still asleep on her bedroom
floor. Was this what was in store for her? The video scared her every
time.

"I wasn't sure if I would wake you," Lou said.

"I was just about to do my power-walk. This girl is a size eight,
like me."

"The girl?"

"The dead video girl. There's something about her that seems
familiar."

"Can you see her face?"

"Not clearly, no. I've tried to zoom in, but then everything gets
so blurry." She pointed her mouse to a frame in the video then
stopped and picked up her coffee instead. It was ice cold. She was
sitting at her kitchen table, her back to the door.

"Scooter never came back last night," she told Lou.

"Does this worry you?"

"Not really. Not normally. But right now I guess everything worries me. I've decided to call in sick for work."

"I'm with you on that," Lou said.

"You call in?"

"From time to time."

Nicola stood up and went to the sink to pour out her coffee. She cradled the phone against her shoulder and told Lou she wanted to ask him a favor. Had he by any chance cashed her check yet?

"Oh that's long gone," he said.

"Because I was thinking I might need money . . . I'm not sure now what might come up."

"I'm sorry, princess," Lou said.

Nicola looked out her kitchen window. The fog was beginning to come in. Long stalks of grass swayed in the wind like a row of musicians. She closed the blind. It was a good day to stay inside and hide. But was she thinking about Carmen or herself?

She asked Lou if he wanted to come over.

"I mean as long as you're sick," she said.

Nicola and Lou watched the video maybe fifteen times together, taking time off to ask Carmen, when she emerged, if she wanted breakfast. Lou poured her a cup of strong black coffee and Nicola started the video, explaining what had happened last night after Carmen fell asleep.

"Oh my God, oh my God," Carmen kept saying as she watched. "This is what I did for him?"

"You did not kill this girl," Nicola said.

"Oh my God in heaven," said Carmen.

She drank her coffee and watched it for a second time. They looked at every sequence. It was Carmen who noticed a small item by the foot of the bed, seen only once, very briefly. A jar? A wine glass? A glass, they decided. Lou said the woman was definitely drugged; she had probably died from an overdose.

"I mean you can see she's dying the whole time," he said. "Maybe he slipped something into a drink. Or maybe he gave her pills, and she used a glass of water to wash them down."

It was hard to tell the exact moment of death. But clearly the girl was gone by the end.

"I can't look at this anymore," Carmen said after the fourth round.

But Nicola felt both scared and hardened—she was determined to watch the video until she figured things out. The wineglass was important. Was it important? If it wasn't important, then she had nothing.

She handed Carmen a pad of paper and a pen.

"Okay. Then write down everything about this man," she told her. "His name, anything he owns, what kind of car he drives—anything you can think of."

Carmen took the pen. Adam Lightwell. Age—mid fifties? Dark hair, dark eyes, drives a Toyota station wagon. Nicola went to the cupboard and opened a box of pretzels. The kitchen brightened as sunlight pushed through the fog. Already it was past noon. Carmen had pulled her hair into a ponytail and was wearing a T-shirt and a pair of Nicola's sweat pants. Nicola realized she had never gone for her walk.

"We should break for lunch," she said, eating a pretzel. "I mean go out somewhere."

"I don't want to go out," Carmen said. She handed Nicola the list.

"This is it?"

"This is all I can think of."

Nicola read through it. All of a sudden her left hand dropped to her side. "Wait a minute," she said. "He owns the Golden Gate Arms?"

"With my brother."

"He's maybe five, five eleven, with dark hair? He wears a silver chainlink bracelet and has a birthmark on his neck?"

"You know him?"

Nicola turned to Lou, who was sitting on the counter. "He's the one at the motel. Remember? The one we saw by the wharf."

It was Chorizo. Why hadn't she made the connection before? He was the motel owner, or at least a partial owner, but at any rate not a guest like she had assumed or whatever it is you call people who go to places like that. Johns? Or in his case. . . . And, Jesus, he had asked her out. He had asked her to go out with him, alone; he wanted her to take off work and go off with him that day. That Friday. The day that . . . Nicola's eyes lost focus and she looked down at the list until it became just a sheet with lined patterns. Carmen and Lou were quiet, watching her. A car honked outside, and the door to the Russian's house slammed shut, but Nicola didn't hear it; she didn't hear anything. She was thinking hard—something was coming together.

"Oh my God," she said suddenly. "I know who the video girl is."

The phone rang and someone knocked at the door at almost the exact same time. Carmen jumped. "Who's that?"

"Carmen," Nicola said, "if you're going to jump every time the door bell rings. . . ."

"I don't want to see anybody," Carmen said, looking at the door behind them. The window blind was still drawn; they could see nothing. "Please, send them away. Please."

"Carmen," Nicola said.

"My brother is dead," Carmen said.

Nicola looked at her. The phone stopped ringing. "Let me just look through the peephole," Nicola said. A moment later she turned back.

"Who is it?"

"It's my ex-husband," Nicola said. "And his new buddy. Believe me, no one to worry about."

"Don't let them in! Please."

"Carmen," Nicola started, but Lou interrupted. "It's all right, Nicola. Carmen, listen to me. Don't take this the wrong way, but why don't you take a shower. Take a long, long, long shower. Or take a bath. Bring a book in with you. Stay there a while."

"That's a good idea," Nicola said.

"Run a bath, lock the door, stay in the bathroom. If you want we won't tell anyone you're here. We'll say we're letting the water get hot or something if they notice."

"Which they won't," Nicola said.

"My brother is dead," Carmen said again, twisting the ring on her thumb.

"I know, sweetheart," Lou said. "But Nicola has to act normal too. She can't hide out with you."

The doorbell rang again.

Nicola put a hand on her arm. "We won't tell anyone you're here unless you say it's okay."

"Well," Carmen said. She touched her forehead. "Okay. Wait, I didn't mean okay, I meant okay."

"I know."

"I just meant okay."

"I know."

Nicola got a clean towel and gave Carmen her new robe from Victoria's Secret, and when she heard the bathroom door lock she turned back to the door.

"Well, well," she said as she opened it.

"What the hell took you so long?"

Scooter walked in, followed by Dave. They both looked like they hadn't slept all night—Scooter was wearing the same clothes he had on yesterday. With Dave it was hard to tell.

"Hey, boys," Nicola said.

Scooter stopped, seeing Lou. "And who's this?"

But Lou was still watching Nicola.

"Listen, don't keep me in suspense any longer," he said. "Who is the girl in the video?"

"It's the girl from the flyer," she told him.

"What flyer?" Lou asked.

"What girl?" Scooter said. "What flyer?" He looked at Lou. "And who are you? Wait, you must be the loan, uh, guy."

"I'm Lou," Lou said, jumping down from the counter. He held out his hand.

Nicola introduced them quickly. "The video girl is the girl on the flyer," she explained, "the missing girl flyer from the café where I first met Chorizo."

"Who's Chorizo? Why the hell would someone be named after a sausage?" Dave asked.

"Show them the video," Lou suggested.

"Shouldn't you be in school?" she asked Dave.

"I called in sick," he said.

"Today's the day," Lou commented.

Nicola set up the video again. "Christ, I'm hungry," she said. "I'll show this once and then I really have to eat."

But as the video loaded yet again there was another knock at the door; it was Davette, carrying a bag of deli sandwiches.

"You are an angel," Nicola told her, opening the door.

"I tried to call from the road," Davette said. "I decided to just skip fifth period."

They turned off the kitchen lights. The colors on the computer seemed overly bright, commanding attention. Still, Scooter seemed to be watching Lou more than the video.

"She must have been faking," Dave said at the end. But his voice sounded uncertain. He looked at Davette. "She's not really dead, right?"

"She wasn't faking," said Lou.

"That's right, you're the loan shark, you must see dead bodies all the time," Scooter said. "That's like your business."

Nicola shot Lou a look. "Really?"

"Really, no," he said. "We're small time. On the verge of unsuccessful, actually. Dead bodies—well, that's way beyond our league."

Scooter scoffed. "Right."

"And I'm basically the errand boy anyway. I do some research, I tell my uncle what I find. Sometimes he sends me out if there's a problem, but only the relatively tame ones."

"He sent you to deal with me," Scooter pointed out.

"Exactly," Lou said.

They were all standing around the table except for Davette, who was sitting. Lou turned to get more coffee. There were small lines of wrinkles along the back of his shirt.

Nicola pulled out a chair but didn't sit down. "Anyway, you can see now how important this is," she said. "That video was made by a man named Mehmet Pamuk—at least, that's the name he gave me. He also goes by Adam Lightwell, and I myself call him Chorizo for reasons too uninteresting to explain. Anyway, he tried to pick me up in a café last Friday afternoon but instead he picked up this poor girl, the one you just watched die on the video. I recognized her from the missing-girl poster that the owner of the café put up. I'm going to go to the police, but also we should make some plans."

"Are you taking your computer with you?" Scooter asked.

"Why?"

Scooter looked at Dave. "We've come up with our own plan," he said. "I didn't know about this . . . about all this you were doing, but I think I can see a way to dovetail our two projects."

"Our *two* projects?" Nicola asked.

Scooter and Dave sat down at the table and Scooter took out a ragged piece of paper from his pocket and smoothed it.

"I didn't know there were *two* projects," Nicola said.

"The dog racing, remember?" Dave told her.

"I thought we shelved the dog racing."

Dave took the paper from Scooter. He had a sulky expression on his face and his upper lip needed a shave.

"Scooter and I have been hunting around on the Internet. We found those racing sites, remember? Well, we definitely found a way to make some money, enough money so that you can find a new apartment, Davette can take her class this summer, and I can get the hell out of San Francisco. We have a new theory."

Nicola looked at him. "A new dog racing theory."

Davette shook her head and said, "Dave."

"Wait, hear me out. It's based on a tip we found on the Internet— a chart you can use to beat the odds, which basically looks at weight, averages, percentages—I forget what all. We have it loaded into my computer but Scooter was thinking we could run it on yours, too. I'm gonna design a program that automatically downloads racing stats every day to feed to the chart. Do you want to see how much we made last night?"

Scooter grinned.

"Almost four thousand dollars," he said, and showed Nicola the paper. It had some figures written down, nothing very legible. "I was hoping we could borrow your computer and do twice as well."

"We hit ten out of the last thirteen trifectas that we played," Dave said. "And that was only in, what, six hours?"

"I think five," Scooter said.

"Five hours. That's like a thousand dollars an hour."

"Eight hundred dollars an hour," Nicola corrected.

"Oh, yeah? And how much do *you* make an hour?" Dave sneered.

"Okay, okay," Nicola said. She looked at Lou—he was standing by the refrigerator now, drinking coffee, saying nothing. Probably wisely. "It's great that you, uh, made some money last night, but I don't want to go any farther with this. I'm not interested in betting."

Dave tugged impatiently on his T-shirt. "Listen, you're not listening," he said petulantly. "We can solve all your problems!"

"I don't think you can, Dave," Nicola said. "Not by just getting some money, you can't."

"You are so naive," Dave said.

"Maybe."

"Dave," Lou said. "If you want to help, maybe you could go with Nicola to the police. Bring the computer for her."

"I'm not her lackey!" Dave told him. "I'm not computer-bearer boy! Scooter and I come up with this great angle and you guys are too . . . too weak to use it! You gotta have some guts! You gotta have balls! Jesus."

"You're right, Dave," Nicola said. "I don't have balls."

"Jesus."

"Also, I'm cheap. I hate losing money."

"But this is what we're trying to tell you! You can't go wrong!"

"Maybe afterward, when this is over. But right now I need you and Davette to find some more information on Chorizo."

"Hold on," Dave said. "I'm not going to put off the dog chart. I need the money to get to Nevada. Maybe afterward," he sneered, imitating her.

Nicola looked at him for a long moment, trying to decide what to do. His face looked young and soft, and his hardened, angry expression seemed like a very thin mask. "Okay," she finally said. "I get it. Well, I guess . . . I'm sorry but, look, I can't pay you to keep doing that."

"What are you saying?"

"You're fired," she told him.

"I'm not fired, you never hired me! Well maybe you did hire me but you can't fire me."

"A parting of ways, then," Nicola said gently.

"I do not believe this. You know what? I'm gone. I'm out of this party. But not because you so-called said you're fired. Because I need to do my thing. *My* thing. Come on, Dave, let's get the hell out of here," he said, glancing over at Davette.

"Davette," Davette corrected. She was sitting very still.

"Dave, Davette, whatever," Dave said. "Let's go."

She didn't look at him. "I'm not going," she said. "I'm staying."

"What?"

"Yeah, I'm kinda with Nicola on this. I just don't think betting on a couple of dogs is going to help that girl on the video there."

"Don't you get it? *Nothing* is going to help that girl there. That girl is dead. We are the ones who need help, and money is the way help is given. Jersey boy over there can testify to that, right J.B.?"

Lou said, "Sometimes. But I don't think entering information about certain races with certain dogs is going to help you make money on the next race with different dogs."

"You're fucked, you're all fucked," Dave said. "You *know* I'm right about the money. You of all people. Money talks."

"It does," Lou agreed. He put his coffee cup in the sink. "When it's actually in your hand, it does talk. Or at least it makes an impression," he said.

"I'm going to make a bundle," Dave said. He was still standing by the table, pulling on his T-shirt.

"All right," Nicola said.

"You're going to be sorry," he said.

"All right."

He turned to go. "Scooter?"

Scooter grinned embarrassingly at Nicola and pressed his lips together, then moved up and down on the balls of his feet. Nicola said, "That's okay, Scooter."

He said, "But I am going to help you; it's just that right now I have to, I just have to get myself together a little bit first and so on and so forth."

"It's okay," Nicola said again, and she watched him get his duffel bag from the living room. His hair was sticking up in the back and his eyes were lit with the excited expression she knew so well, the expression that comes with the roller coaster ride down. Well, she was no longer interested in the thrill of decline. Wait, was that true? Nicola paid attention to herself for a moment. It was true, she realized. It was absolutely true. Was she finally over Scooter? She didn't want to be a scared passenger anymore, no matter how much fun the ride.

"Sayonara," Dave said, slamming the door behind them.

Afterwards, Nicola and Davette and Lou looked at each other in the kitchen. Davette gave out a little humorless laugh and Lou opened his hands as if to say what can you do? It was warm in the room and Nicola could hear faint noises coming from the bathroom. She had almost forgotten about Carmen. Nicola looked at her watch. The deli bag was still on the table and she took out a wrapped sandwich and a pickle and a can of Sprite and she set a place for herself at the table. Then she opened the can.

"Just a little downsizing," she said calmly, taking a sip.

Eighteen

outh San Francisco, The Industrial City. These words, spelled out in flat block letters, lay on the low hills just outside of the city, surrounded by transformers and a few six-story cranes in use at the airport.

As she passed by them on the highway Nicola checked the rearview mirror to see if her hair was rebelling. Her computer was on the car seat beside her. Although she said she was going to the police station, she wanted to make a personal stop first.

Carmen and Lou were at the Golden Gate Arms looking for more data files—Carmen finally had agreed to leave Nicola's house, but only if Lou went with her. He was taking her to the office. He would not let her out of his sight.

Carmen had never seen Chorizo in the office on a weekday. Still, it was risky.

"In cases like this," Carmen had said, "the unexpected always happens."

"Cases like what?" Nicola asked.

"Murder."

Nicola looked in the side mirror and changed lanes. It was really windy out. Fog swirled like chalk dust over the hood of her car. Murder—that's what Carmen said. Nicola thought that Chorizo probably gave Robert the pills and told him they were something else. Afterward, he brought the empty pill bottle over then typed up a suicide note and left it on the printer tray.

Was he really after Carmen? Carmen seemed to think so. Nicola tried to remember everything she could about Chorizo—his good manners, his hands, his awful shoes. He said he worked with computers. Well that at least was true.

But why had he killed Robert? His business partner. Carmen claimed Robert didn't know anything about the girls in the video. Well, maybe he found out.

And so did I, Nicola thought. She looked in the rearview mirror again, this time more nervously.

Ten minutes later she parked in front of a short strip mall, then sat for a minute looking around. There wasn't much to see. Some construction guys were walking around talking into cell phones, a couple of teenagers were sitting on the curb, and a woman wearing a button-down shirt and a tie walked out of the gun shop carrying a plastic handle bag.

Nicola had never been to a gun shop before. In fact, she didn't even *know* anyone who had been to a gun shop before. She pictured the customers: badly dressed teenagers carrying rolled-up *American Survivor* magazines and comparing—what, the size of their Remingtons?

She had to admit she was curious.

But inside, the shop was a little disappointing—she expected something grittier, something more American West. The place had a polished floor and fluorescent lights and impulse-buy items clipped to the counter. To be honest it looked like a 7-Eleven.

Nicola chose a random aisle and wandered along looking at displays of cleaning devices, gun handles, and holsters. She picked up a three-tine frog spear that was for what, fishing? Defense? I guess this could poke out someone's tiny tiny eyes, she thought. Near the rifle counter two Asian men were having a heated conversation in Mandarin—she guessed Mandarin—and she noticed that the clerks behind the counter were two mod San Francisco hipsters wearing unusual T-shirts.

"It's called tuna quiche," said the one with square glasses.

The second clerk was shorter and his head was shaved bald. Above them hung a sign with small white letters, "AMMUNITION IN STOCK," and next to that a stocky no-nonsense girl was talking into a wall phone: "We have the merchandise but his papers haven't come through."

"Tuna quiche? Tuna *quiche*?" said the bald one.

"Just listen, Jer."

"I've never heard of tuna in quiche."

"Just listen. My mom made it."

"Your mom's a good cook," Jer said, bouncing on his toes a little. "But I don't know about tuna in quiche."

"You get a package of pie crust mix," explained the one with the glasses.

They were young, in their early twenties, and could have been transported with no change of clothing to a comic book store. Where were their camouflage pants? Where were their T-shirts imprinted with American flags? Nicola noticed that Jer had a dark blue tattoo on his scalp and that reassured her a little. She had imagined gun shops to be full of Republicans or registered Democrats who voted Libertarian.

She looked at her watch. "Excuse me," she said.

The one with the glasses turned slightly and Nicola read his name tag: Morgan. "Oh I'm sorry," he said politely. "Do you need some help?"

"I'm looking for your self-defense items."

"Self-defense, self-defense," Morgan said. His eyes looked over the store. "Self-defense."

Was he confused?

"Like if you're attacked," she explained.

"Right. Self-defense in case you're attacked." He kept looking around the room.

"Which is what self-defense usually means," she said.

"You're right, you're right."

"They're over here," Jer told her.

"You're absolutely right," Morgan said.

Jer was gesturing to the wall shelves behind him which, as Nicola looked more closely, were filled with pepper spray guns, stun guns, mini stun guns, and various other minor assault devices camouflaged as ordinary objects. Some were shaped like flashlights or pens. Others were canisters of noxious fumes which could be concealed in hand weights. There were bear deterrent sprays and strobe lights and sonic alarms and some of them came with naugahyde hip holsters in black or maroon.

"Let me take this," Jer said to Morgan, and Morgan swept his hand toward Nicola, offering her up.

"We have many levels of self-defense," Jer told her. He pointed to a lower shelf. "First off we have our pepper spray collection. That's a level one. Then you go up a level to alarms and lights. This one's called The Screecher and comes with a handy push-top activator. And over here, what's this called, oh yeah, The Cry for Help. That one's programmable in five different languages. Also you can change it to say FIRE instead of HELP. Some people think you're more likely to get help if you say fire, it's less threatening somehow, or I don't know, maybe they're less likely to scamper off in fear. Like they won't get hurt if it's a fire? Hah hah."

Nicola looked Jer over again—he was clearly enjoying this. Did everyone think people were so dangerous? She tried to imagine him twenty years from now, living off of roasted insects and roots in the wilderness.

"And then over there," Jer continued, "no over there, yeah, those are the stun guns and the very latest in stun gun pens. Now those are great; you can carry them anywhere. You can fit one in your hip pocket if you don't want to carry a purse. I recommend them for guys actually. They're small but highly effective. Up here is our cross-bow collection. That's the top level."

"Crossbows?" Nicola asked. "It's legal to carry a crossbow?"

"It's the highest level of personal protection without the hassle of paperwork—felon checks and so forth. I could sell you one right now with nothing more needed. You can't do that with guns."

"So if I'm a felon I go for the crossbow?"

"Are you a felon?" Morgan asked.

"Not yet," Nicola said.

"Of course they're harder to conceal," Jer said. "Some women I know carry them around in a shopping bag. But that means you have to carry them around in a shopping bag."

"I was thinking more of pepper spray, a stun gun—something small like that."

"Of the two I recommend the stun gun. Do you know how a stun gun works?"

Nicola shook her head.

"Here's how it works; let me show you." Jer took a device from under the counter and placed it on the glass top. "That's a stun gun," he said.

Nicola picked it up and turned it around. "It looks like a yellow highlighter."

"It's supposed to," said Morgan.

It was so small. How could something so small possibly save her?

"Here's how it operates," Jer said. "Press this level and out pops—there. See those two metal prongs?"

"The stunners," said Morgan.

"Well that's what we call them. Those prongs carry, in this case they carry one hundred thousand volts and when you touch a would-be assailant with them—Morgan, do you want to be the would-be assailant?"

"Here I come," said Morgan, and he put his hands out toward Jer.

"Stop!" Jer said and touched Morgan on the arm with the gun.

"Can I try that?" Nicola said.

"It's not actually on," Jer said.

"What's this little orange light then?"

"Oh, I guess it is on. Did you feel that, Morgan?"

"Shit," Morgan said. "That was cool."

"Well, what happens if you do it right—I didn't really touch Morgan on the arm, or just for a second, but if you do it right, if you hold it for three or more seconds it causes the would-be assailant to experience temporary loss of balance and also some mental confusion. It does this by scrambling the nervous system. And it scrambles it by sending energy at a very high-pulse frequency making the muscles work quickly but not very efficiently. It also depletes blood sugar by converting it into lactic acid. Morg, are you all right? That's why the would-be assailant usually falls down. Morg, you okay?"

"Yeah. Shit," Morgan said. His speech was slightly slurred.

"So, anyway, the combined effect of energy loss and so on, the mental confusion and so on, all this makes it difficult for the attacker to move."

Nicola took the pen in her hand again. Amazing. Amazing, if it was true. There was a titillating combination of technology and basic human survival here that intrigued her. "And then what?" she asked.

"You run," Morgan said. He smiled a loopy smile.

"How long does the mental confusion last?"

"Long enough for you to get the hell out, ha!"

"Now this one looks like a little flashlight," Jer continued. He was holding a plastic package with a slender blue stun gun over a picture of an American bald eagle. "It can be carried on a key chain. It also comes with a key flail backup," he said.

"What's a key flail backup?"

"You flail your keys. Aaaa-aaa-ar!" he demonstrated, waving the package in her face.

On the other side of the San Bruno hills, back in the city, Scooter and Dave were standing in the middle of Golden Gate Park. They had had a small run of bad luck and were now taking a break.

"It's fucking freezing," Dave said. He was wearing a long flannel shirt as a jacket. "They must be hiding out in their pen."

They were looking for buffalo. Scooter peered over the fence. "I don't want to leave until I see one," he said. "Nicola and I used to come here and feed them."

"You can't feed the buffalo."

"Can't you?"

"You could never feed the buffalo."

An hour ago they decided to take a breather from customizing the dog racing database—a task that was taking much longer than either one anticipated and added to that it was almost unbearably boring. Plus they lost money on their last two races, too, and were beginning to snap at each other. Dave suggested a burrito from a burrito shop just outside the park, and Scooter came along even though he was trying to cut down on carbs because a) he was tired of sitting on a semi-broken lounge chair in Dave's parents' basement and b) he wanted to see the old neighborhood again.

What could he say, he was kind of sentimental. He wanted to look at the building where he and Nicola once lived, and say hello to the bicycle guys who ran the shop below them, and maybe get some raw organic food from the raw organic food store. But the bicycle shop was now a three-star Asian-fusion restaurant and the organic food store had been turned into a furniture shop selling mostly, as far as Scooter could tell, small trunks from southern Indonesia that could be used as end tables. So while Dave was at El Taco Scooter bought a raspberry banana wheat grass smoothie and then suggested they go into the park because at least the buffalo would still be there.

But he forgot about the pen, he forgot that the animals might not want to come out. Scooter moved the smoothie straw up and down in the lid making plastic music as he strained to see just one animal. But he couldn't see anything. A sign by the upper paddock read: American Bison (*bison bison*). But all Scooter could see were a couple of wheelbarrows with some hay sticking out of them. He stopped pulling the straw up and down and sucked on the smoothie, even though it was making him even colder and in addition to that he really had to pee.

"We named one once, a female one," he told Dave. "We called her Erna."

Dave snorted.

"After Nicola's grandmother," Scooter went on. He didn't want any more of his smoothie, which had some weird protein boost taste to it, but he took another sip of it anyway since it was in his hand. He and Dave were standing just off the road on the grass in front of a long, fenced-in field where, as Dave said, the buffalo so-called roamed. It was impossible to see inside the pen, which was a quarter mile back at the western edge of the field. Down the road, toward the ocean, stood the windmills and next to them was Queen Wilhelmena's tulip garden, where men met each other at night for a quick date in the long grass.

"A female buffalo—what would you call that? A sow?" Dave asked. He was holding onto the first wire fence, the one not electrified, with his fingers.

"Not a sow. Maybe a cow."

"You call female lobsters hens," Dave said. "I learned that at the Monterey Aquarium."

"School trip?"

"Kinda. My parents were Christians and they kinda Christian homeschooled me until I was twelve."

"Cool," Scooter said.

"Yeah. It was pretty lame though. We studied the rainforest, sign language, art—we water-colored—and the recorder for music, and what do you call it, health or gym or whatever you call it when you go to the Y."

Scooter pulled his straw up and down a few times, then walked down a few feet and looked through the fence again. "This is a better angle," he decided.

"We were living in Daly City then. My dad drove the church bus and we used to go on all these field trips. Mostly we went to other schools who were having some lame religious event, like a puppet show or a play based on the Bible. But once we went to the aquarium. I liked that trip best. We got to stay in a hotel with a Jacuzzi in the basement."

"Huh," Scooter said. He started making puckering noises with his lips.

"In Monterey, I mean. That was about the only non-school place we went to." Dave looked toward the animal pen. "I think they're pretty dumb," he said.

"Buffalo?"

"School events. They were mostly plays, like *Noah's Adventure in the Twentieth Century*. I remember that one. Or *Sodom meets Gomorrah in Downtown Los Angeles*."

"I detect themes."

Dave said, "Are you kidding?"

"Wait, I think I see movement," Scooter said. "Whoa, here they come."

Two heavy-shouldered beasts moved slowly out of the pen, looking neither left nor right. Their shoulders were so big that they appeared off-balanced and they walked slowly through the short grass as if they were ex-professional athletes with bad knees.

"They're not really that big," Dave said.

"Is that a joke?"

"I always think they'll be bigger."

"I really remember feeding one celery," Scooter mused.

"Anyway," Dave went on, "we stopped all that when my dad got into an accident with the church bus. He smashed up the kneecap; they had to reconstruct it all and they did this by splitting the bone. He got four rods put up there, some of them permanent. And that was the end of his faith."

Scooter was following the buffalo along the fence. They were walking at a diagonal away from him and he noticed again how their fur seemed to be in a continuous state of molting. "Doesn't sound like he had much to begin with if that's all it took."

"That's what I thought!" Dave agreed. "That's exactly what I said to him before he kicked my ass."

Scooter continued to walk along the wire fence, making puckering noises to the buffalo, which ignored him.

"There is something just not right about these animals," he said, walking closer to the fence.

"The transition to traditional school was really hard for me. I mean, think about it: junior high school. It was so noisy, that's what

I couldn't get over. No one looked at me, or if they did I didn't want them to. It was better in high school when I found Dave. She was really nice to me, and I liked how she dressed. We had the same lunch period, that's how we met. After that we always made sure we would have the same lunch period."

"We should probably go back," Scooter said, pulling on his straw.

"Now I don't know what I'll have," said Dave.

Neither one of them moved. Dave felt in his pocket for his mini-tool, then remembered that Davette still had her tool, too. He took it out and looked at it, then put it back in his front pocket. Scooter took another sip of the smoothie he did not want. After a few moments the buffalo stopped walking, but although Scooter and Dave waited and watched, the animals did nothing else—didn't eat, didn't move, didn't yawn; they just stared straight ahead at nothing.

"I don't know what I'll have now that Dave has defected," Dave said again after a minute. "And you know who I blame?"

"Hunh."

"Your wife."

"Ex-wife," Scooter corrected. He was still watching the animals. "It's weird," he said, "I remember that they were more interesting than this."

They walked back to the car past a group of Korean men wearing thick nylon jogging suits. The ground was sandy and peppered with mole holes, and on the road a few cars slowed as they drove past the buffalo. Scooter unlocked the car door, then sat for a moment with his hands on the wheel, drumming his thumbs.

"Back to the dog races, eh?" Dave asked.

Scooter stopped drumming and stared straight ahead. "God," he said.

Dave pulled his minitool out of his pocket again and looked at it. Wasn't there a little toothpick on it somewhere? "I can't believe we lost the four grand," he said.

"We'll make it back," Scooter said automatically. "We just need to plug up some holes."

"Well, anyway, the database is almost done. Or, like, halfway."

But Scooter didn't answer. The trees seemed heavy and full of some dense toxic gas and Scooter looked over at the two buffalo staring out into the middle of the field doing absolutely nothing. What were they doing? They both looked bored out of their minds.

Scooter sighed. "I had plans for a great shining life," he said.

Dave glanced over at him. He noticed Scooter's hands and feet were unusually still.

"Can I have a sip of your smoothie? If you're finished?"

Without turning his head Scooter handed him the oversized Styrofoam cup. Dave took a sip. "Your wife really fucked you over, didn't she," he said.

"Ex-wife."

"She always been like that?"

"I don't know what 'like that' means."

"You know, it occurs to me," Dave told him, "that we should be the ones in charge, not her. I mean we already did a crime, didn't we? You and me? We did a crime already."

"Yeah, but she foiled it."

"So what she foiled it, like so what. We did the hard part—we organized it, planned it, got it going, got it rolling. She messed it up, that's all. It's easy to mess things up; believe me, I should know."

"Yeah, well, it doesn't inspire much confidence," Scooter said.

"You still in love with her?"

Scooter started the motor. "For me love has always been a story of humiliation and despair," he said mildly. He put the car in gear and looked back into the rearview mirror.

"Listen," Dave said. He took a long suck at the smoothie, then began pulling the straw up and down in its lid, making plastic music. "I have an idea," he said.

Nineteen

Chorizo was looking for Nicola. He couldn't leave it any longer. Nicola had seen him at his motel, she had recognized him, and he couldn't shake the feeling that he needed to do something about that. Probably it meant nothing. Still, she was a link between the last girl—he hated the word victim—and his motel. He'd picked up the girl at the same café, the same day, after Nicola had turned him down. Melissa, her name was.

He decided at this point the direct approach was best, but although he sat in the West Portal Café for almost three hours drinking their overroasted coffee she never showed up. It was a risk, sitting there. As he got up to pay he saw the missing-girl poster Scotch-taped to the counter. He put on his sunglasses, but no one looked at him twice.

On the sidewalk he checked his watch. Just past three-thirty. The wind blew in sharp, sideways gusts and the waves were breaking at five stories high. Only that morning a young boy had been swept out to sea then saved by the Coast Guard. Chorizo thought of the ocean as an animal, something caged and fierce which occasionally escaped from its chains. Take that energy and use it, he thought, zippering his leather jacket. He knew that a warrior could advance in strength, or retreat with honor. Now was the time of strength.

But it was too early to go to her office. He wanted to wait until she was nearly through for the day and he could woo her away. When, with any luck, she might be alone. A pity she didn't come with him the last time. Or was it a pity? Chorizo crossed the street to look at the West Portal theater marquee. No, it was better this way.

"Film's been rolling for an hour," the clerk at the theater said. He had purple hair and trendy eyeglasses and was reading a magazine put out by the American Motion Picture Association.

"That's all right," Chorizo said.

"You missed the best dialogue already."

"I thought this was an action movie?"

"Exactly," said the clerk.

Chorizo took his time. He wasn't hungry but he bought popcorn and a fourteen-ounce bottle of water and a hot dog without meat. He should be careful about what he put into his body but at the same time he needed to load up on carbs. Tonight he would need all his energy.

But as he turned away from concessions he thought for a moment he could still hear the wind. Like a woman's cry. Ghostly. It wasn't often Chorizo thought of the ones he had killed, but that wind— there was something about it. He put the boxed popcorn on a counter and checked his front pocket for his passport. It would all be fine, he told himself. He was in the wings now, before the show. A little tense but okay.

Gathering strength.

Nicola's cell phone began to ring just as she was unlocking her car. She opened the door and set her bag of self-defense items down on the passenger's seat. Inside, the air was hot and stuffy.

"It's me," Davette said. Her voice sounded high and young with the vacuous tone of a teenager, and she told Nicola that Carmen and Lou were back; everything was okay. And Carmen had in fact found a few disks at the office.

"I'm looking at one now. There are a couple of new files. One of them is a sliced image, an image of a hand."

"Whose hand?"

"A man's hand. There are a few other files here but they're compressed and I don't have the right decompression program." Davette named a couple of applications that might work.

"I have both of those in my office," Nicola said. She shifted the phone to her other ear and began backing out of the parking space. "I'll stop by and get them."

"If you tell me your e-mail address I'll send you the hand image now," Davette said.

Nicola gave it to her, then turned out of the parking lot and followed the road alongside the highway, looking for the entrance ramp.

"Okay, done. But listen," Davette went on, "I wanted to say something else, too. It's just—well, I feel a little bad about Dave."

"About Dave?"

"I feel like I kind of just abandoned him."

Nicola passed another strip mall entrance, a Quickie Lube, and a motel with a marquee which read, WELCOME BACK MABEL MCKEYS.

"Listen to me. Is Dave on the boat?" she asked.

"What?" Davette asked.

"Is Dave on the boat or is he off the boat?"

"What boat?"

"It's a figure of speech, you know what that is?"

"Oh, a figure of speech, okay. Okay, well yeah, he's off the boat."

"It was his decision to get off."

"Yeah, I know, it was his decision."

"Then go on; let him be. Let him do what he wants."

"Okay."

"And you can do what you want."

"You're right."

"Because you know what? You're a strong woman. You make good decisions. You're intelligent. You pay attention. And anyone, any guy, can be with you or not. They can come along or not. Because you're the boat, Davette. Did you know that? You are the boat."

"Okay. Um, I don't really get that," Davette said.

Nicola smiled to herself. "I'm really glad you're doing this with me, Davette. You're really good at all this."

"Really?" Davette asked. She sounded pleased.

"So I'll stop by my office for those programs and then call you from there."

Nicola found the entrance ramp and as she merged with the oncoming traffic she began to accelerate but not too much because it was really windy now and she could feel it beneath her car moving the frame slightly back and forth. A power line was down next to the BART tracks and a couple of cars were stopped on the meridian, though maybe for reasons unrelated to the weather. Still, it must be really bad on the bridges, she was thinking. Once when she was going over the Golden Gate Bridge in a windstorm she had the brief sensation that she was floating on the pavement with no steering and no power—it was as if the car had been lifted slightly and taken from her control. Of course, the wheels were still touching the ground and she must have been in control no matter what it felt like. Or was she?

She glanced at the bag of goodies from the gun shop. What would her mother think if she saw them? Her mother, who often told Nicola to stick up for her principles. Nicola was fairly sure this wasn't what she meant.

The problem was she didn't know where the nearest police station was—or any police station, come to think of it. Did she have time to stop for a latte or something beforehand? She was nervous and it seemed fairly certain to her that her story would sound foolish.

There's a man who tried to pick me up . . . I saw this missing-girl poster and the same night she vanished a man tried to pick me up. . . . My landlord took an overdose of methadone and I believe this is connected to. . . . My landlord took an overdose of methadone yesterday. Although seemingly unrelated, a man tried to pick me up and I think he picked up this other girl who then vanished . . .

Nicola frowned. It sounded ridiculous—ridiculous, all of it. But what could she say? What would they pay attention to?

"A crime has been committed," she said aloud.

The car swayed in the wind then steadied itself. Nicola slowed down. It was becoming clear to her that in order to go to the police one has to agree to appear stupid. Could she agree to appear stupid?

Christ, Nicola thought—she hated this indecision. A gray hill rose up in front of her and the highway turned itself into a narrow, busy, city street. A flock of pigeons flew up from the roof of a Presbyterian church that doubled as a day care, and as Nicola watched one of the birds detached itself from the group and fell behind the building. A sick bird? A dead bird?

Oh my God. Nicola suddenly pulled over and stopped in a bus zone. She dialed Lou's cell phone number. Oh my God, I get it, she thought.

"Hello?"

"Lou, thank God you're there," Nicola said. "Listen, I just figured something out. Can you get to the library? There was this article in the *Chron* last Friday; Chorizo was reading it. It was about a rash of pigeon deaths near Civic Center. It's been going on for a few weeks now."

"Pigeons?" Lou asked.

"Chorizo was reading it at the café that day. They were all poisoned, and I bet you anything it was methadone."

"The same thing that killed Robert," Lou said.

"Exactly," Nicola said.

"Chorizo," Lou said.

"Right. A practice run."

They agreed they would meet at her office, or she would call him if she finished up early and went home. Her heart was pounding hard. How would she find the nearest station? On the other hand, going there was going to take a lot of time and she wanted to get the program disks to Davette as soon as possible so they could show the police something useful. Or did she mean believable? Her office was actually really close to where she was now. She sat with her hands on her lap, still parked at the bus stop, and a Volvo veered by erratically as if the driver was constructing a bomb from a kit while he drove.

Why was she thinking about bombs? She looked down and noticed her hands were shaking. Outside the moon was rising early like a lopsided grin and Nicola watched a row of palm trees pull back like slingshots in the wind. She compromised: she would go to her office and look up the nearest police station address, and just grab the disks quickly. Maybe she could give them to Audrey.

That's a good idea, Nicola thought. Maybe Audrey could drop them off at her house while she sat and said—what?—to the police.

There's this guy, he's running this Web site, it's hard to tell but I'm pretty sure the girls are dead. He runs it from a server from Finland . . .

Christ, Nicola thought again. Through the rearview mirror she could see a bus coming; its blinker was on, it was going to pull into the stop. Nicola turned the key, looked back at the lane of cars, and headed out toward her office.

Chorizo stepped out of the movie theater and began walking down the street to Nicola's office building. In the theater bathroom, just for fun, he had thrown a rune to see what he would get. It was Hagalaz: the rune of disruptive natural forces. Chorizo smiled to himself. Change, freedom, liberation—this is what Hagalaz represents. Expect a great disruption, says the rune. Expect something strong. Here comes change, here comes power, here comes the big boss and it is you.

Well, that was fine. That was good. Chorizo crossed over the muni tracks and the wind blew sideways at him with that sound, that sudden wail. Chorizo tried to close his mind to it. He knew that his own nature was creating what was happening. Sometimes he thought about karma, but more often he did not. Would his karma be favorable at this point, or not so much so? Two women carrying copies of *The Watchtower* stood on the street corner and as he walked by one of them noticed him looking.

"Like to take home a copy?" she asked.

Chorizo shook his head. "I'm not from around here."

"God doesn't care about that."

"Your God might not."

The light was red and he didn't mind talking to them a little. One was quite pretty, though a little too old for him—that is, around his age.

"All God is one," said the other woman, the one who was not so pretty—she had small eyes and lips that stretched unevenly over her teeth.

The light changed to green. He was a block away from Nicola's office.

"Is that right," Chorizo said, starting to step away.

"All God is one all-merciful being," the not-so-pretty one told him.

Chorizo looked back at her for a moment. "No," he said. "Your God is merciful. My God is just."

It took her a while to find parking, which was always the case around this time of day and made Nicola think again how good it was that she could take the muni to work without changing trains once and how she really wanted to stay in her home. But what would happen now that Robert was dead?

She took the side staircase up to her office, hoping Guy had gone home already, but when she got upstairs she remembered that he and Aria were at a Japanese management retreat for two days. Everyone else seemed to be gone too.

"Hey there," Audrey said. She was putting a sweater into her backpack. "I thought you were sick."

"Oops, I forgot," Nicola said. She smiled.

"They're all gone anyway. I was just about to leave myself."

"What's up? It's barely five o'clock."

"When the cat's away," Audrey explained.

Nicola went over to the bookcase and took out a couple of software packages. "Listen, could you do me a favor?" she asked. She looked around for a paper bag. "I have a couple of things I'd like you to drop off at my home for me."

"Sure, but why can't you do it?"

"That's a long story," Nicola said.

Chorizo heard the elevator coming down as he climbed the front staircase, holding onto the metal handrail and feeling something—what?

Almost like joy. The building was stucco, old-fashioned, and made him think of Los Angeles in the 1940s—an image he had from late-night television. He had never actually been to Los Angeles. So far he had only been to two places in America: San Francisco, and New York. He had made a lot of money in New York but he couldn't go back there anymore because of the extortion charges and whatever other petty crimes they had on file. It didn't matter. Of the two, he preferred San Francisco.

The building seemed quiet and he hesitated when he got to the second floor. Which office to try first? He chose the one to his left. A bell sounded as he pushed open the door and crossed the carpeted threshold. A woman sat behind a glass window partition reading a magazine. No one was in the waiting room.

The woman looked up at Chorizo and frowned. "Do you have an appointment?" she asked. "Dr. Mursky is just finishing up for the day."

"Actually, I'm looking for someone, a dental hygienist," Chorizo said. "And I'm not sure if she works here or not."

After Audrey left Nicola looked up police stations in the blue government pages in the front of the phone book. She was still wearing her coat. As she suspected, there was one right here in West Portal only a few blocks away. Should she call and make an appointment? Do police take appointments?

She decided to check her e-mail first.

When the woman told him none of their dental hygienists were named Nicola, Chorizo tried the next office. This one had no piped-in music and inferior wall-to-wall carpet. He could hear the faint sound of drilling from behind the interior door. In the waiting room, two men sat on opposite naugahyde chairs with computers on their laps. One wore a suit.

"Hello," he said to the receptionist. He looked through the open window and noticed her beautiful nails. "I'm looking for someone who works here," he said.

Nicola opened Davette's e-mail attachment and when the image came up on her screen she gasped. It was Chorizo's hand, no doubt about it. By enlarging the picture she could just make out his beautiful nails and a few silver chainlinks from his chainlink bracelet. She could not mistake that bracelet. She enlarged it some more, then fooled around with the contrast a little bit. The colors looked a bit washed out. Also, she wanted to see if she could get more of the hand, a thumbnail, the tip of a finger. Something more distinctive. She thought the image might have been snipped from something—one of the videos? She looked at the file on her desktop again. The icon was blank; the computer couldn't read what kind of file it was, and Nicola began to think that maybe the file was actually a video file and not a still image. Maybe the file name was deliberately misleading.

I bet this is the last frame of a video, Nicola thought. I need those decompression programs I gave Audrey. Damn.

She began to look around her office to see if any of the computers had one of the decompression programs installed. Audrey: no. Carlos: no. Then she looked at Christian's huge, souped-up computer.

Ah ha. Here we go.

Chorizo closed the dentist office door behind him and stood in the hallway, confused. The receptionist, like the other receptionist, had never heard of a hygienist named Nicola. But he had definitely seen Nicola walk into this building and there were only two dentists here. Wait, though; she had been with that other girl. Perhaps it was the other girl who worked here, not both of them? Perhaps she was just walking her friend back to work? Chorizo felt a tick of annoyance. He had assumed Nicola worked here, which was a mistake. Never assume, he scolded himself. A true warrior doesn't guess; he seeks the truth.

He pressed the elevator button. He didn't want to leave, but what could he do? He really needed to find this woman and he felt himself getting upset.

But what was that? Chorizo turned toward the front of the building. Again, for a moment, he thought he heard the wind. Like a woman's low voice asking why.

Ridiculous.

"Relax, remove," he told himself. "Distance yourself from the problem."

He wished he could sit still for a moment, have a minute of yoga. That always cleared his head. Chorizo closed his eyes and let himself run through the options one by one. Should he give up and try again tomorrow? Should he go to the café once more? Should he plant himself somewhere on the street and hope she walks by him on her way home?

How was he going to find her?

The large white downward arrow lit up and the elevator doors opened. Chorizo hesitated. Wait, he thought. What about the other girl—the friend? If Nicola was walking her back here, the friend might be here now. She might be able to help him. There was only one office left in the building, an Internet design firm up on the third floor. It was a long shot, but why not try? Chorizo pressed the up-arrow button this time. As he waited, his cell phone began to ring.

"Yes?" he answered. He listened. The elevator came and he got on. He put his phone to his other ear and frowned as the elevator ascended. When the doors opened onto the third floor he stepped out, but as they started to close behind him Chorizo suddenly turned and reached out to catch them.

"Where are you?" he asked, quickly stepping back inside.

Nicola heard the elevator ding and then a man's voice. After a moment she rolled her office chair back to look out the open doorway but all she saw was a man's trouser leg as whoever it was went back into the elevator. Probably looking for one of the dentists, she figured. It happened all the time.

She rolled back to Christian's computer and stared at the screen. The decompression program didn't have any apparent problem with the file, and the video was now loading all right. Still, she wouldn't know whether it had actually decompressed correctly until it began to play.

She'd done this before. She'd been burned before. Sometimes everything goes smoothly and you're so happy until you open the file and what you see is a big blank nothing.

Nicola turned the screen slightly to cut down on glare. The sun was low now, just about to dip under the horizon, and the last of its light streamed through the window. The video stopped loading and started to play, and, oh thank God, it was not blank—she could see the same bed she remembered from the snuff video. A poster on the wall. A metal side table. And then there he was—Chorizo. Not his face, but the side of his body and his hand as he reached up toward the camera. That was it. The video ended abruptly.

Quickly, she searched through the other files Davette had sent. There were ten of them. They were all videos, probably. She knew she shouldn't take the time to decompress them and then view each one individually—Davette was going to do that—but she couldn't stop herself. I'll make a file for the police, she told herself. Something to substantiate this ridiculous story.

An hour later she was almost done. It was after six. Lou called just as she was opening the last video; he had found the articles about the pigeons, and yes they were all killed by large doses of methadone, which the seeds had been coated with.

"He was practicing," he said. "I bet he has it in pill form. He crushed up the pills and coated the birdseed with it. Then, when he was sure it would work, he gave the girls a couple of pills and told them they were something else, like Ecstasy or something. You can swallow them with water or, if your stomach gets easily upset, with milk. Depending on the dosage and your tolerance for drugs, two can kill you."

"I didn't know you could overdose on methadone," Nicola said.

"If you take enough, sure. It's like morphine. It's morphine based. He probably gets it from a junkie who is trying to get clean, but to tell you the truth it's going out of fashion at detox programs. At least in New York."

"You've been to a detox in New York?"

"I followed around a junkie for a while. Now *that* was an easy job. Anyway, all I'm saying is there might be only one or two detoxes that dish methadone these days."

"So maybe he couldn't completely cover his tracks."

"Unless he got it on the street, third or fourth hand."

"Right." Nicola watched the end of the video clip. Again there was the bed, the poster, the girl, but nothing as incriminating as the first clip with the bracelet. "Do you have anything else?" she asked Lou.

"Whoever he gets it from can't be pregnant or have kidney problems or a biliary tract disease. No one would prescribe it for them. What is a biliary tract disease?"

"A disease in an organ that carries digestive bile," Nicola said. "Like your liver. What else?"

"Alcohol increases its effect. It's not all that hard to overdose on if you've been drinking too."

"And Carmen says Robert drinks," Nicola said. She stopped the video clip and looked at her watch. "Anything else?"

"One last thing, and this is kind of interesting—apparently there's a very quick and effective antidote if you do overdose," Lou said. "Of course, you have to get to the emergency room within a couple of hours. It's called Narcon."

"Narcon?"

"It reverses the effects."

"Even for pigeons?"

"I don't know about pigeons. It's probably never been tried on pigeons."

Nicola looked at the computer screen again, then renamed the last video and saved it to her police file. "This is probably enough," she said.

"What is?"

"I'm going to the police with what I have." She gave Lou the station address and told him to meet her there.

"And I'll bring these printouts, too," he told her.

But almost as soon as she hung up, her cell phone rang again.

"Did you forget the address already?" she said, answering.

"What address?" asked a low voice.

Nicola felt her jaw clench. She recognized that voice.

It was Chorizo.

Twenty

Nicola felt her heart give a sudden hard beat and she looked
back at the computer screen as though she was afraid Chorizo
could see through the phone to what she was doing. She carefully extracted the disk from the computer, then wrote on it "Police."

"I thought this was . . . was someone else," Nicola said. She swallowed. It was important to sound normal but at the same time her
mind seemed to be casting out in all directions. Why was he calling
her? Had she even given him this number?

Chorizo said, "This is Mehmet Pamuk." It was the name he had
used at the café. His real name? "You remember me," he said.

"Mehmet—but . . ." Nicola paused. This was awkward. She tried
to think what might be the normal thing to say, if she was just that
girl from the café who knew nothing more about him than whatever
it was she had known then. "How did you get this number?"

"A boy gave it to me. Said his name was Dave."

"Dave," Nicola repeated. Her face suddenly felt like wood.

"Yes, a total stranger to me," he continued in his low silky voice, "who seemed to think I would give him some money in exchange for, I don't know, information I guess. He wanted to meet me. Turns out he had some interesting . . . ideas about me."

Nicola didn't know what to say. How far had this gone? "All right," she said.

"He mentioned your name."

"You met with him?"

Chorizo laughed. "Listen," he said.

There was a pause then she could hear a couple of short, shallow breaths. "Hey, Nicola," said another voice.

"Oh my God, Dave."

"Yeah, WAL, right? I mean me." His voice sounded a little slurred.

"Dave, sit tight," Nicola started to say but Chorizo was back on the phone.

"Oh," he said, "he's sitting tight. Very tight. Listen, I want you to do something for me. Are you listening? I want you to bring me that disk you have. The copy you made of that video. In fact, bring me the whole laptop."

"That's ridiculous," Nicola said. "That's not going to stop anything. I might have copied the video onto twenty computers by now."

"Well, actually," Chorizo said, "it's you I want."

Nicola agreed to meet Dave and Chorizo at the Polo Fields in twenty-five minutes—fifteen minutes longer than he suggested because she claimed she was in San Bruno. She didn't know what else to do— she had to get Dave away from him. "But how do you know I won't bring the police?" she asked.

"Because I don't think you'll want to see the inside of Dave's head spread all over the pavement," he had answered.

She pressed the off button then dialed Lou's number again. "Lou.

Listen fast," she said when he answered. "Chorizo just called me. He's got Dave. And I'm pretty sure he's given him methadone."

"He's got *Dave*? How did that happen?"

"More bumbling and idiocy. Listen. You have ten minutes to call up your uncle the doctor and get a dose of Narcon, and you have ten more minutes to get yourself and it to the bookstore on Irving Street. I'll meet you there."

"Why the bookstore?"

"It's on the way for us both. Plus I want to see if they have anything that will tell me how to use it."

"Use the Narcon?"

"I don't know how much methadone he gave Dave."

"Nicola, I don't like this," Lou said.

"I know, but I was thinking. All the information he has he got from Dave. Dave doesn't know about Carmen, remember? She was hiding in the bathroom when he came. And he doesn't know we know about the Golden Gate Arms. If this man wants to get rid of me he's going to take me there. Not to his house or anywhere that can be easily traced back to him."

"You don't think he can be traced to his own hotel?"

"I don't have time to argue. It's the logical choice. Just get the police and go there."

"I don't like it, Nicola," Lou said again.

"Neither do I," she said.

After she hung up Nicola looked around for her bag from the gun shop and began ripping open the package for the strobe-light-and-screamer key ring. Then she pulled out the other self-defense weapons. Was there anything that wasn't wrapped in about four hundred yards of hard plastic? Pretty soon everything will come with its own tool to open it up with, she was thinking.

"Ow," she said, pulling her hand away. She had cut her finger on a plastic edge. "Shit." Nicola looked around her office for something—what?—some kind of inspiration. But it was just a room full of toys. Her brain felt locked. She didn't know what Chorizo was planning to do—kill her, probably.

I'm way out of my depth, she thought. Was it true that there was a moment of peace before even the most violent deaths? She was tired and it seemed to her she'd been running around forever doing the next vital thing like a small crazed ant.

But she didn't have time to question what she was doing. She didn't have time to think. Dave—bumbling, naive, high-school Dave—was loaded up on methadone and being held by a man who killed women on film.

Nicola grabbed her computer case then pulled on her coat. Just keep it moving, keep it moving, she told herself.

She got to the Polo Fields with about eighteen seconds to spare. Her purse was filled with self-defense weapons. The vial of Narcon was wedged into her bra. She felt skittish and at the same time unable to focus completely. Like she'd had too much coffee and not enough food.

Lou had met her at the bookstore with the Narcon, and before she left he kissed her—an amazing, I-will-see-you-soon kiss. As Nicola turned and parked she could still feel the pressure on her lips. Was she being incredibly stupid coming here? She was probably being incredibly stupid coming here.

But the police will be waiting at the motel, she told herself, when we show up.

She didn't know why this wasn't more comforting.

Nicola cut off the engine and sat for a moment looking for a car with someone waiting inside. The polo fields were below her, past a group of thick conifer trees with long two-story trunks and branches that spread out from the top. It was cold and windy and the park

seemed deserted. RESTRICTED, a sign read. And further on: NO PARK-
ING OR STOPPING.

Nicola got out of her car with her laptop, her heart pounding.
The wind hit her suddenly, like a fist through her hair. She stumbled
a little. The grass was long and brown and resembled the matted fur
of a dog. A man in army fatigues walked past her holding a black
and white toy collie on a leash. She wanted to say, Could you just
stay here a minute? Help me make a trade? The man lifted his head
in greeting, then pulled at the leash.

In twos and threes the street lamps began to come on, casting a
slight orange tint onto the road. At last a blue four-door Toyota
pulled up. Chorizo rolled down his window partway.

"Laptop?" he asked. She showed him the case. Chorizo unbuckled
his seat belt and got out, shutting the door carefully behind him. He
looked up and down the road. Nicola tried to swallow. She watched
the wind blow his hair up and to the side.

"Where's Dave?" she asked.

Chorizo motioned to the back, where Dave was slumped against
the window. But his eyes, Nicola noticed, were open.

"Do I get to negotiate?" she said.

"No."

She handed him her computer case and tried to keep her voice
steady. "This is completely ridiculous. My computer isn't going to
help you at all. Plus I have all my tax files in there."

"Give me your purse, too."

She handed him her black bag.

"Now," he said, "let's get out of this wind."

"Wait. You have to let Dave out first."

"I don't think so."

"That was the deal."

Chorizo said, "I don't think that was the deal, Nicola."

He smiled and put his hands on her. There was no one around

anywhere—where the hell was everyone when she was being forced into a car? As Chorizo pushed her inside she noticed that Dave was handcuffed to a chain soldered onto the door. Both doors had chains soldered to them, she saw. Were these for a girl? Someone who changed her mind?

"I see you're looking at my equipment," Chorizo said. He was pulling handcuffs out of his pocket. "They're just a precaution really. I did them myself."

"Use them much?"

Chorizo unlocked the cuffs and flipped one band open. "Actually, this is the first time. But a warrior keeps himself prepared."

"A warrior? You're a warrior?"

"I like to think of myself as a spiritual warrior."

Nicola raised her eyebrows. "You kill spirits?"

"Hah," Chorizo laughed. "I never thought of it like that." As he was cuffing Nicola to the car door, Dave looked over and smiled a gentle little bird-smile at her.

"Nicola," he said. "Hey." For once he spoke without sounding snide. He was really very high, Nicola saw. His face had a soft, vacant look to it and he seemed younger and, well, *nicer*.

"Hi, Dave," she answered. "How's Chorizo been treating you?"

Dave shrugged and moved the hand that was chained to the door as an answer. Chorizo went back to the front seat with Nicola's black bag where he began searching through it with both hands.

"I wish people would stop doing that," she said.

"Doing what?"

"You're messing with my organization."

He took out her driver's license. "Nice picture. The red was a good choice. Let's see now, 3584A Santiago. That's interesting, I didn't know there was a 3584A. That would be where, behind another house? Oh I have it, the Russians."

"You've done some homework. But why do you care?"

Chorizo didn't answer. He put the driver's license in his pocket then continued to rummage through her purse. He found the pepper spray and the can of mace.

"I see you also have The Cry For Help. But what's it programmed to—fire?"

"The recommended setting," she said.

"You don't have much faith in your fellow man, do you?"

"These days, no."

He threw the defense items onto the street, also the X-acto knife and bungee cord she had thrown in on impulse at her office. "Let's see your coat," he said. He leaned over and put his hand into each of her coat pockets and she could see the line of gray hairs on his head that seemed to start from the temple and work their way up. Chorizo pulled out a bobby pin from one pocket and a coupon for a free latte from the other, threw those out the window, then he sat back in the driver's seat and fastened his seat belt.

"Aren't you going to frisk me?" Nicola asked. She could feel the slight, hard edge of the Narcon needle next to her breast. It had a special plastic cap and was smaller than a pen.

"I'm hoping," Chorizo said.

He started the motor and made a U-turn then began driving back through the park. The car smelled strongly of aftershave lotion. Chorizo looked through the rearview mirror, then at the side mirror, then through the rearview mirror again.

"No one came with me," Nicola told him.

"Of course not," he said, though he did not sound entirely sure. "You're a smart girl."

Girl? Nicola fell forward as they turned, then righted herself without hands. I'm almost getting good at all this, she thought.

They were snaking back to the main road. Nicola felt herself breathe a little more slowly—Chorizo was right, it was good to get out of that wind. They would go to the motel, she told herself, and the police would be there. Just keep that thought.

"Do they really play polo?" Chorizo asked.

"What?"

"At the polo fields."

"Oh." Nicola stared out the window. "It's mostly used for soccer matches now."

There was nothing to see. Already people were beginning to leave the city and fly back east or fly to the mountains or fly across the water to Hawaii for the holidays. Chorizo checked the mirrors again then turned on the radio. There was news of a runaway train in Michigan, and a progress report on an international war crimes tribunal.

"I met that man once," Chorizo commented.

"The dictator?"

"He is thinner than he looks in the pictures. Some sort of colon problem, I believe."

Was he nervous too? He kept checking the mirrors, and this chit-chat. Maybe he's never done it this way before, Nicola thought. Maybe he's never picked up a woman who knows what he's done.

But was that better for her, or worse? She looked down at her chained wrist. One thing, she would definitely need to stay on her toes.

"Did he really murder his own brother?" she asked.

"I don't know all the politics."

"Well, I think it's appalling."

At that Chorizo laughed. "Oh you Americans. Do you know what America's motto is? If we don't like it, you can't do it."

"Hey," said Dave. "That's good."

"It's true that fratricide is generally frowned upon here," Nicola said.

Chorizo stopped for a red light. He looked down at his hands and after a moment began pushing back the cuticle on his thumb.

"So what did you do to this one?" Nicola asked.

"Dave? Oh just a little downer. Maybe two." Chorizo smoothed the skin around his thumbnail. "Listen to me, Nicola. I'll give you a tip."

"What's that?"

"Never cut your cuticles. They prevent bacteria from entering the lunula."

Nicola looked back out the window. "Tell me something I *don't* know," she said.

The light turned green and they drove up Seventh Avenue past the reservoir then continued up the hill toward Portola. So far they were heading in the direction of the Golden Gate Arms and Nicola felt a little bit smug, a little I'm so smart. It would be okay, she thought. They will go to the motel, the police will be there. She pulled the chain on the door because you never know, maybe she'd turn out to be really lucky and the handcuff would unlock by itself.

But instead of turning left on Portola Chorizo went over the hill and down the other side toward Glen Park and the highway. Nicola suddenly felt something wash over her, a clammy kind of sweaty feeling under her arms. This wasn't the way downtown. This wasn't the way to the motel. Where was he headed? She stared out the window in something like shock. She wanted to say: but the party's downtown!

"Where are we going?"

Chorizo didn't answer. She could see his profile, his dark birthmark, when he checked for oncoming traffic—he's definitely nervous, she thought. As for her, well at this point nervous wasn't the word. The wind was blowing even harder now; she could hear it through the windows. A wind from the north. This was bad. Nicola didn't know what to do. What should she do?

At last the car turned left onto a small side street, then turned left again. Nicola looked hard at the corner sign as they passed.

"This is Bliss Street," she said.

"That's right."

The car went to the end of the narrow, dreary block, and slowed in front of the last house. Nicola stared at the address spelled out in gold above the door: 12 Bliss.

She said, "But this is where Robert lives."

"Lived," Chorizo corrected.

Twenty-one

Twelve Bliss, Robert's home, was the last house on the block, built against a hill with cement steps leading—where? To the bus line, Nicola guessed. She had never been here before.

There was something slightly off about the place. It was turned away from the other houses on the street, not quite on the grid, and thick wires crossed over the roof in several places protecting it like a loosely made web.

The street itself was short and dark and empty. If this was bliss, then bliss was a kind of dry, secluded event, something solitary and enjoyed largely because of its furtive nature. Tall deciduous pines leaned dangerously near Robert's property and the front yard was covered with nasturtiums—flowers that grew in chokehold vines around the house.

In the garage the car's headlights shined on a couple of metal desks against the back wall. On the desks were two computers—the computers Lou had seen. Chorizo cut the headlights and all it once it was completely dark. As Nicola's eyes adjusted she could see two small points of lights like far-spaced eyes: the monitors' power lights.

"Robert left his computers running," Nicola said.

"Those are mine. I do a little of my work here sometimes."

"In Robert's garage?"

Chorizo didn't answer. He turned off the motor, got out, then, rolling down the window, he unlocked Dave from the door. Dave was still conscious and he seemed perfectly able to walk by himself; still, Chorizo held onto his shoulder and hip and guided him out of the car then through the doorway.

He came back for Nicola saying, "You're next." He unfastened her seat belt, unlocked her from the door, then locked her hands in front of her.

"Watch your head."

"Oh, I've had plenty of practice with this," she said, getting out.

He took a square, black gym bag out from under the passenger's seat, then with his other hand he held Nicola's arm. She asked about her purse.

He said, "We'll leave that in the car."

They walked through badly fitting French doors into the room behind the garage, which had a low ceiling and wood paneling and smelled faintly like mold.

"Robert had this room recently done over," Chorizo said in the semidarkness. He carefully twisted the window blinds closed before he turned and flicked on a light. "The contractor did a terrible job. Look at that floor. So uneven."

In the middle of the room there was a futon couch and a low table with an empty glass on it. Dave was sitting in a chair in the corner. Behind him were three small, square windows and a door leading, presumably, to the backyard.

But Nicola was staring at the opposite wall. A row of inflated rubber dolls were sitting, legs dangling, on a custom-built shelf. They wore wigs and their faces were painted in such a way that they appeared to have on makeup.

There must have been twenty of them; they took up the entire wall. But weirdest of all were their costumes—negligees, camisoles, bustiers, chemises, and all in ugly, vibrant colors. Nicola couldn't take her eyes away. In spite of the makeup there was something manly about the dolls, as if they were painted to look like guys in drag.

"I knew about this, this rubber doll business, but it's . . . it's different actually seeing them. It's sick," Nicola said.

"Isn't it," Chorizo agreed. He narrowed his eyes into a kind of smile.

He said, "Wait until you see what's next."

Her mouth went dry and Nicola felt herself washed of all feeling, preparing herself to take the worst. But Chorizo merely opened a cabinet. The cabinet was actually a tiny desk, she realized, a tiny workstation, with a computer and a pencil holder and several narrow black shelves. Inside, on a shelf, was a monitor.

"Watch this," Chorizo said.

He sat in the desk chair then felt for the button underneath the monitor. The screen blinked and came to life. It took Nicola a minute to understand what she was seeing: a room. Everything was gray and small. It was not a very good picture really, the resolution was terrible. She could make out a bed, not made, and something—a foam mattress—on the floor. Someone was lying down on the mattress, someone who looked familiar . . . she knew that hair. Nicola stared. It was Carmen.

And then she got it. She was looking at the bedroom in her own house. She was looking at a live monitor of the bedroom in her own house.

Chorizo was watching closely, the shadow of a smile on his face. "Surprised?" he asked.

I can't believe it, Nicola was thinking. Scooter was right.

"I was looking for Carmen and I was looking for you," Chorizo went on. "I came to Robert's house and here I found both of you. Isn't that lucky?"

"Unbelievable," she said. She was still thinking about Scooter. How unbelievably annoying! When was the last time he was right about anything? She hated thinking that she should have listened to him. Nicola looked back at the dolls.

"So he used me to dress his mannequins. He used my clothes. Clothes like mine."

"His model, so to speak."

"Creepy."

"He probably had an itch for you."

"Let's hope it was just the easy access."

Chorizo turned the monitor a bit. "Yes, well, my problem was, I didn't know where the camera was, what house he was videoing."

"You weren't doing this together?" Nicola asked.

Chorizo smiled. "We had our own separate hobbies. He showed me his Web site with the dolls and that's how I got my idea for . . . for my own enterprise. He let me set up a computer in his basement here, and he put a link to my site on his page. But I don't think he had any idea what I was really doing."

Nicola looked up again at the dolls. "You know, I thought some of those outfits seemed familiar. What, did he zoom in on my catalog covers as well?"

Chorizo grinned. "Do you read them in bed?"

She shuddered. "Thank God I haven't had sex in a year."

"You haven't had sex in a year?"

Nicola hesitated. "That sounded better before I said it."

In spite of herself she kept looking back and forth from the monitor to the dolls. Really, she was more annoyed than disgusted. She was annoyed with Robert for being such a sleaze, and she was annoyed with Scooter for being right, and she was annoyed with Chorizo for showing it to her with such obvious enjoyment.

Suddenly though Chorizo's smile faded and he stood still for a moment, listening to something. Or *for* something? He frowned. Then checked the window locks again.

"All right, well, I think we're set here," he said after a minute. He went over to a long wardrobe against one wall and opened the door. There were easily thirty pieces of lingerie hung neatly on hangers inside.

"Now here we have *my* stock. Of course, I never told Robert what I used them for. I wonder what he thought! But let's see, what would be a good one for you. Hmmm. I can see you in red," he said. He pulled a garment out and fingered the soft material.

"Red?"

"For the video. Feel this. It's hard to believe it's made out of tar."

Nicola said, "What is?"

"Nylon. It's made from tar byproducts. And do you know where the name nylon comes from?" he asked.

He was teasing her: cat and mouse. Nicola thought, okay I'll play your little power trivia game.

"From the World's Fair in New York," she said. "That's where it was first shown. They took the name from the city initials."

Chorizo lifted his eyebrows. "I forgot you were a clever girl."

"It caused the collapse of the Japanese silk market in 1940," she said.

"Is that so?"

"And I prefer black if you have it," she told him.

Chorizo smiled. "I like your courage," he said.

"I don't intend to let anything happen to me."

"Well, unless you have the key to those handcuffs you might be in for a surprise."

Nicola sat down on the floor with her handcuffed hands in her lap. The carpet was thin and smelled new. He knew she was bluffing. The dolls were creepy but the lingerie reminded her what she was here for. What *was* she here for? How far would this go? Her voice, at least, sounded steady, but her heart was racing like a bull.

She had to face it: she was alone. She was alone and no one had any idea where she was. How could they possibly guess in time? Or ever? Nicola rubbed the nubby carpet with her two hands, trying to think, trying not to panic. It was all up to her now. Dave was no use. She thought of her little epiphany back at the warehouse, when Scooter arrived and untied her at last—that she could get what she wanted if she believed in herself. She could be in charge of her life.

Well at this point, she thought, I pretty much have to be.

Chorizo took a bottle of water out of his gym bag and unscrewed the top, then suddenly stopped and tilted his head again.

"What *is* that?" he asked.

Nicola held her breath for a second to listen. "Just the wind," she told him.

"Does it sound . . . unusual to you?"

"It comes out of the north this time of year. December and January."

"I don't mean that," Chorizo said, but he didn't say what he did mean. Instead he quickly stepped across the room and locked the French doors that led back to the garage.

There was no doubt, he was also on uncharted ground. A little jittery. Here's a woman who knows what's going down, who might fight him. I can't just give up, Nicola thought. But she could feel the edge of panic like something clammy brushing against her skin. Her hands were shaking. She exhaled slowly and thought: what I want is to live.

When Chorizo came back he gave her a drink of water, holding the bottle to her lips. She felt the warmth of his hands under her chin and her chest seemed to tighten. He is not going to hurt me, she told herself. It was a resolution.

I can't be afraid.

She looked over at Dave, who was clearly in his own world. Meanwhile Chorizo began sorting through the rack of lingerie. Next to the wardrobe was a long mirror, and Chorizo held a garment up to his chest then looked at his reflection.

He had a beautiful straight back and beautiful gestures and he took hangers off the rod and lifted them out with a neat but showy gesture. He was really very handsome, Nicola thought again. For a freak.

"So, Chorizo," she began.

"Why do you call me that? You said that before, in the car."

"I don't know. It's how I thought of you before I knew your name. It's what you eat at that café."

"Americans with their nicknames." He held a sheer black negligee up to his neck.

"So, anyway, what's your story?" Nicola asked.

Chorizo selected two black chemises and lay them carefully across the back of the office chair. "I have no story."

"Everyone has a story."

"Everyone has a life," Chorizo corrected. "Not everyone has a story." He smoothed the fabric of a purple bustier. "Let's consider this one too," he said, and laid it on the chair with the others.

"People go from point A to point B," Nicola continued. "I just want to know how."

"Or why."

"Or why."

"And that's what I won't tell you," Chorizo said.

"You won't tell me why."

"I won't tell you why."

"Isn't it in the code of murderers to tell their victims why?"

"I hate that word."

"Murderer?"

"Victim," said Chorizo.

"Look at that boy," Nicola said, meaning Dave. His eyes were closed now, and his head had fallen back on the chair's headrest at an odd angle. Was he unconscious?

"He's so young," she went on. "How much time does he have?"

"Oh, maybe an hour."

"He's barely begun to live."

"The world won't miss him."

"Yes, but. . . ."

Chorizo was looking at another black garment. "Please don't start in about his mother."

"I was going to say yes but he'll miss the world," Nicola finished.

"You think after he dies he'll be sitting somewhere looking down at the rest of us?"

"Could be."

"So you believe in the afterlife."

Nicola shifted on the carpet. "At this point I would have to say yes."

"You're only saying that because you are about to die."

"According to you."

"If you're only saying that because you're about to die, then it's not a belief, it's a hope."

"What else could it be?"

"Faith," Chorizo said. He stopped looking through the rack for a moment, and looked down at his hands.

"Do you hold this faith?" she asked.

"No."

"Do you hold some hope then?"

Chorizo hesitated. "No."

"This life is it," Nicola said.

"This life is it," he agreed.

"Then why do you do it? Why kill people when this life is it for them? You don't seem like that kind of person to me."

"I don't go in for that sort of thinking," Chorizo said. He looked over at himself in the mirror again. "I do what I need to," he said.

Nicola watched him watch himself. There was more than just vanity there. "You must believe in something," she said.

Chorizo smiled. "You remind me of my wife."

"Ah ha."

"Yes, that's right, I have a wife."

"You're doing all this for her."

"Maybe."

"Is there a camera in this room somewhere?" Nicola looked around. "Is she watching this somewhere?"

"Not where she is."

Chorizo picked up the pile of clothes he had selected and brought them over to Nicola. She was still sitting on the floor. He held one up and Nicola looked at it and shook her head.

"Too small. So, is she dead?" she asked him. "Your wife?"

Chorizo's face changed.

"Not dead," Nicola said. "But inaccessible. In jail?"

She watched him closely. Chorizo didn't move.

"She's in jail," Nicola decided. "You're trying to get her out. But how can snuff films help?"

Chorizo put down the chemise he'd been holding up and picked up the next one.

"What about this?"

"No," she said. He put it down and picked up another. She shook her head again. "Too many poky things. So your wife is in jail; you want to get her out. . . . Okay, I get it, you need the money. You're charging, what, probably hundreds of dollars to view one show. Let's say five hundred dollars a hit."

Chorizo looked at her.

"My guess is bribery," she said. "You need money for bribes."

Chorizo shrugged his shoulders and held up the next piece of underwear and Nicola shook her head.

"So she's not in jail in the U.S.," she said.

Chorizo laughed. "You think United States officials will not take bribes?"

"I'm thinking how much you will make on the snuff films. Not enough for someone in the U.S. Enough for say, Turkey."

Chorizo's face didn't change.

"Or Greece."

She watched him carefully.

"Or, oh, I have it, Cyprus."

Nicola watched Chorizo and almost laughed. "That's it," she said. "Cyprus."

"You are very good," he said. "How do you do it?"

"I pay attention. I believe my instincts."

"Do you know what an instinct is?"

"It's information your brain receives but doesn't know how to process," she told him.

"That's good. That wasn't what I was going to say."

"So Cyprus, that makes sense," Nicola said. "You can practically see Cyprus from Kas."

"You *can* see Cyprus from Kas," Chorizo corrected. "From what I hear. Though I've never been to Kas myself."

"But it's your hometown, you said. You told me that last week."

"Oh, I just heard you talking about it one day to the waiter. I've never been there myself. Too many tourists."

Nicola thought for a moment. So he'd been listening to her conversations. Gathering information. "You mean I was a target all the time?"

"Potential target. I always let the universe make the first move."

He held up a sheer black chemise with a red ribbon running through the top.

"That's the one," she said, and he threw her the garment. It landed in her lap and she looked down at its shiny surface, a black that seemed to absorb everything and give nothing back.

"I'm going to enjoy this," he told her.

"What did your wife do to get herself in jail?" Nicola asked.

"Revolutionary work."

"For Greece or Turkey?"

"Try to guess."

She looked at him. "I can't tell," she said. He smiled. "That's probably because it does not matter," she said.

He shook his head. "You're very, very good. How long have you been doing this?"

"You're my first customer," Nicola told him.

"Well, I am impressed."

"Do you have enough money now? To get her out?"

"Close enough."

"And I assume a way back to Cyprus."

"That's all taken care of."

"A false passport, that sort of thing?"

"I'll say nothing more."

"So you don't really need to kill me. You can take my laptop and go."

"I guess I could. I could even go without the laptop since, as you say, you may have copied what you found on other disks that I don't know about. But extradition is very difficult these days, and who knows, even in that case I might even prevail."

"So why not just walk away? I'd give you a head start, I promise."

Chorizo laughed. "But I like happy endings," he said. He came very close to her and took her hand. For a moment she thought he was going to kiss it, but instead he began rolling up her sleeve. His touch is very gentle, Nicola found herself thinking. Her hands, still locked together, lifted slightly up toward him as if in the act of receiving communion. When her sleeve was rolled out of the way Chorizo pressed his thumbs gently near the crook of her elbow.

"Oh, you have a beautiful vein here."

"So the boys tell me."

He took a prepared needle out from his black gym bag.

"It only hurts if you look," he said, pushing the needle into her skin.

Chorizo told her that since they were injecting the meth it would work much faster and the dosage was—he didn't specify what, exactly. But he did say she would probably go before Dave. Those were his words, go before. She thought of it as a gesture, like someone opening the door for her in a restaurant. Dave was graciously allowing Nicola to die first. If Chorizo was telling the truth.

Meanwhile Chorizo turned up the heat then uncuffed Nicola so she could change into the black chemise.

"You don't need your brassière," Chorizo said.

"I do, it's a push-up," Nicola told him. She turned the chemise toward him. "See, this has no support."

"I don't need support."

"Oh you'd notice the difference." She was thinking about the Narcon. Before she undressed she turned slightly away, as if being modest. The boat-necked nylon top was tight across her middle and held up by two narrow silk straps over her shoulders. As far as chemises go this one was a fairly long one—reaching to her thighs—and the skirt flared a little, like a baby doll dress. Underneath the brassière the material opened up into two sections, exposing her belly.

Chorizo took her over to the mirror. "What do you think?"

She looked herself over. Her legs looked even longer, and her black hair just touched the tip of her shoulders, brushing the silk straps. The red ribbon bobbed up and down through the fabric, calling attention to her breasts.

"I look great," she decided.

Chorizo laughed. "You never stick to the script, do you? You say what's on your mind."

"Lately I've been trying."

"I don't even think you're frightened. I admire your approach to death."

She thought of her heart, which was no longer racing. Was that a bad sign?

"Oh, I'm frightened," she said. "But what will that get me?"

Chorizo laughed again. "I like you, I really do, little one. Listen. Let's stop all this. Run away with me instead. I could teach you some things."

"Just you and me and your renegade wife."

Chorizo began rummaging through his gym bag. He brought out his manicure case.

"Now. I hope you won't be bored, but I don't want to start all this too early," he said.

Nicola looked at her own nails, which were strong and unpolished.

"How did your wife get caught, anyway?" she asked.

Chorizo said, "It was an accident. Stupid." He stopped for a moment, then said, "She could have died, but luckily . . . it was only her hands." He looked down and continued pushing back the cuticle of his thumbnail.

"Only her hands?"

He was frowning, and Nicola wasn't sure for a moment if he would go on or not. But he said, "A stupid accident. She was assembling a bomb and it went off. She was an antinationalist. She wanted Cyprus to let go of its allegiance to both Turkey and Greece. Her mother was Turkish, her father was Greek, and she hated them both."

He put down his cuticle pusher. "And they hated me. Her father called me untrustworthy."

Nicola said, "I can't imagine."

"Oh, I wasn't like this then. All this came after. After the accident. After she lost her hands and went to jail—twenty years, they gave her! And no one even died!" He shook his head. "I knew someone in New York and I went there and that's when I was introduced to a Shambhala colony. I learned there what I needed to learn to survive. What I needed to get her out."

"And what was that?" Nicola asked.

"The principles of Shambhala," Chorizo said. "The principles of the spiritual warrior."

Nicola almost laughed. "You've got to be kidding."

"The tradition of fearlessness, the tradition of human bravery. This is the very heart of what it means to be human. Now where is my hand lotion?"

"Are you telling me that you killed those poor girls out of some misplaced spiritual sense of what, courage?"

"I killed those poor girls for the money the videos would bring. In life we each have to make a personal journey and that was part of my personal journey. Cowardice is trying to live our lives as though death does not exist."

"Okay, that makes no sense."

"True fearlessness is not avoiding fear, but rather moving beyond it."

"You're right," Nicola told him, "I don't understand any of this."

She was beginning to feel slightly warm, then a flush went through her, a kind of nausea. It *was* nausea, she decided, but somehow it didn't feel altogether normal—like it was happening without her, or in an unusual part of her body.

She was quiet for a while, and Chorizo looked up.

"Feeling better?" he asked.

"Actually I'd like to . . . lie down," Nicola said. In truth she wasn't at that point yet but she could feel it coming—a slow sensation like an oncoming tickle. She put her hands to her head because she figured it would help her case if she seemed worse than she was.

"The futon couch opens up," he told her. He put back his manicure case, then leaned over to pull the contraption into a bed. When it was flat she could smell the factory smell on the frame. She noticed there were no pillows or sheets.

"I better get the camera," Chorizo told her. "And I need to handcuff your hands behind you now. Otherwise they'll get in the way."

"In the way of what?"

Chorizo smiled. "I promise you'll like it."

"But that wasn't you on the video. I didn't think you went in for this kind of thing, yourself."

"Not usually. But something tells me I'll enjoy this one. Besides, I'm due for a treat."

Nicola pushed some hair off her face with the top of her arm. "What, are you going to wear some disguise or something? A false nose?"

"This one is not for the general public," he said.

"A private screening?"

"Exactly."

"Just you and your wife."

He looked at her. "You are so clever," he said again, but this time it didn't sound so complimentary.

Then he left the room, shutting the door behind him. When Nicola heard the sound of his shoes on the hard cement floor she stood up and ran to where Dave was sitting. Her mind was already beginning to feel a little looser, like something slipping away, and she felt a strange, almost itchy sensation on the palms of her hands.

Don't think, she told herself. Just stay on the task at hand.

Kneeling sideways in front of Dave Nicola checked his front pockets. He opened his eyes and smiled and his pupils were dilated and his skin was a mottled white mask.

Nicola said, "Shh."

It was awkward, what with her hands cuffed behind her and all, plus her fists were a bit too big to both fit into his pocket and too close to each other to keep one out of the way; nevertheless she managed to hold the pocket open with one hand and push her other hand in until she found what she was looking for: Dave's miniature multitool, which contained, among other things, a tiny lock pick. She remembered Dave saying, back when he kidnapped her a hundred years ago, that he carried it everywhere.

"Which one is the lock pick?" she asked Dave now.

Dave looked at her. "Um," he said. Then he closed his eyes.

All right, then, she would find it. As she was turning over the tool she heard Chorizo swing open the trunk of his car. He was whistling a little. Quickly, Nicola went over to the mirror and turned so she could see her hands. She pulled out the miniature tools one by one, pressing buttons on the handle that released them, including a couple of buttons that seemed to do nothing, until at last she found the pick. Still watching herself in the mirror she twisted her hands trying to work the pick into the tiny lock before Chorizo came back.

She couldn't do it.

When she heard his footsteps she went over to the futon and dropped the tool on the mattress then sat on it. Her head was pounding slightly. As Chorizo walked back into the room she was looking straight ahead of her at the dolls.

"This one looks like me," she said.

"They all have names," he told her.

For a few moments he struggled, setting up the camera. The power cord didn't quite reach and he wheeled the desk chair over to use as a camera stand. Then he had to adjust the chair so the camera would point up, then a little more down, then more to the right, and so on.

"Half the time I turn this on by mistake," he told her, fiddling with one of the buttons.

"Really," she said.

"But I'm getting better."

He knocked the camera to the floor.

"Do you need some help?" Nicola said. "I'm really good at technical things."

"Hah hah," Chorizo said.

"What does that mean?"

"You're a woman," he said.

"What does that mean?"

Finally Chorizo had the camera set up the way he wanted. Nicola watched him move around the room adjusting the lights. She could feel the drug coming on like something creeping inside of her—it seemed to thicken, like paste. She knew she had to work fast.

"Listen, before we begin, could you get me some aspirin?" she asked.

"Your head should feel better soon."

"Please," she said. "Don't I get a last request or something?"

"You're thinking of a last meal."

"I'd like my last meal to be aspirin."

Chorizo laughed. "All right. Well, give me your hands."

"Why?"

"I'm going to cuff you to the frame."

He started to take her arm to help her move but she said, "I can do it," and she slid over a few inches to the side of the bed, moving the mini-tool with her slightly—enough—as she went. She could feel it now under her right thigh as Chorizo unlocked her right hand then locked her left hand to the left side of the bed. Well at least now she had one hand free. Her right hand. That might make things easier.

"You'll probably be more comfortable lying down," Chorizo told her.

"What?"

"With your arm at that angle."

She lay down carefully, feeling exposed. The two folds of her chemise opened, exposing her stomach, and with her free hand Nicola pulled them closed again. Chorizo looked down at her and smiled.

"You look fantastic."

"I feel like shit."

"That will change."

He picked up her clothes and folded her shirt, put her clothes on the table near Dave, then he leaned over and felt Dave's forehead. He looked at his watch. "Nine o'clock," he said. He went out the French doors and locked them behind him.

Nicola quickly sat up and glanced at Dave, who was nodding a little.

"Dave, stay with me," she told him. "Dave."

He didn't answer. Couldn't. Nicola pulled out the minitool. Had she ever picked a lock before? She turned the tool, trying to get the pick angle right. Once she slid open a dead bolt with a credit card, but that probably didn't count.

She could hear Chorizo walking around upstairs, wearing those ridiculous shoes. One thing she liked in a man was good taste in footwear. Well, her taste was definitely slipping. People told her after thirty that she would stop being so picky. And here she was, attracted to a man who polished his own nails compulsively because his wife no longer had hands.

The pick twisted in her hand up and down, then back and forth. What was she trying to accomplish here? As best she could tell she should move the pick this way and that until things fell in place. But what? Nicola closed her eyes and imagined the miniature mechanism inside the cuff. A small curved bar, no longer than a pen point. Time was slowing down again—how long did she have? She was beginning to feel dreamy. She was falling into a dream.

But then, suddenly, she felt the ping of the lock releasing. Oh my God, she'd done it. Slowly Nicola extended her fingers against the metal ring. The cuff widened, letting her hand go. Her knuckles hurt, but she kept pulling it open notch by notch until at last she got the ring big enough to slip her hand in and out. Then, the cuff still nominally on, she slipped the multitool out and dropped it under the futon bed.

She wanted to look handcuffed still. She wanted to catch him off guard. The bed was positioned so he could see it through the glass doors as he came down the steps; if she wasn't there he'd see that and have time to prepare.

The vial of Narcon was still in her bra. She was going to need it soon.

But what if he cuffed her hands back together? Her plan was to strike when he was vulnerable, too.

If she could, that is. If she could. I'll keep him talking, she thought. But her mind slipped for a moment and when she came back he was already down the stairs, unlocking the doors. Where had she been? She hadn't heard him on the stairs. Keep it together, Nicola told herself. She tried to concentrate but it felt as though she was just squeezing an empty tube.

"See his color?" Chorizo said. He was looking at Dave, who was fully unconscious now. "It doesn't look good. You, though, with your dark hair—the paleness is striking."

He handed her the aspirin and watched her examine the tablets.

"Oh, it's aspirin all right," he said. She swallowed it down and he felt her forehead. Then he watched her for a moment. "You're going faster than I thought. You must not do any drugs?"

"A good little girl."

"Well, I think it's time now."

She didn't know if he meant time to do drugs or time to get on with the show. Chorizo looked through the camera lens and adjusted the angle and looked through it again. Then he took off his shirt. His back was hairy, and it looked like he shaved part of his neck. She hated that.

"Okay," he said when he was down to his briefs. He sat down beside her. His thigh was touching her thigh. "As a way of settling into things, I like to tell a story. Don't worry, it's very short. It's about a crocodile and a monkey."

Nicola shifted away from his leg. "A crocodile and a monkey? I think I know this one."

"I don't think you do."

"The crocodile tricks the monkey into taking a ride across some water? Because he wants to eat his heart? But when the monkey finds out he tells the crocodile he left his heart back in the tree?"

"Well, well," said Chorizo.

"Is that the one?"

"You are absolutely full of surprises."

"I've always liked that story."

"So have I," said Chorizo. He put his hand on her knee. "Because it shows what you need to survive. Spirit, intelligence, and strength of mind."

Behind her, Nicola extended her fingers slightly inside the handcuff, testing its parameters. She could still slip her hand in and out.

"I thought it had more to do with courage and cunning," she said.

"Now you, you have intelligence, that's clear. Like the monkey. But what about spirit? The spirit of adventure?"

Nicola closed her eyes for a moment. "You're thinking about last week at the café. When you asked me out and I ducked."

"That's right. I was hopeful at first, but it turns out there was no spirit there, just a . . . a playful girl wearing a mask. For a while you can pretend to take chances. For a while. But a taste for real adventure? No."

"You've known me for how long?"

"It doesn't matter, I know you. I know you. I've seen you all over the world. The competent woman. You're smart, you're good at your job, you're a careful manager. You keep track of all the details. And your fear of letting go is so great."

For a moment Nicola felt shrunken. Was that all she was? A manager? But she said, "Well, maybe the monkey was like that, too."

"The monkey?"

"He kept hold of the crocodile even under the water. He didn't let go."

Chorizo hesitated. "That's true."

"And, hey, it turned out to be good for me. Otherwise, I might have been the have-you-seen-me poster girl last Friday. But what was the other thing? Oh yeah, strength of mind . . ." Nicola mused. "Do I have that?"

Chorizo moved his hand up her knee and under the skirt of her lingerie. "No, little one. You do not."

Nicola shifted a little on the bed. "How do you know?"

"That is a warrior skill," he said. "You are beautiful, yes, and as I said you are smart, clever even, and I mean that as the greatest compliment, but as for perseverance—no, you are someone who backs down. Gives in. Yes? You give in at work, you give in to lovers, you always give in. Right? Well, and it is important for some to be flexible; society couldn't function otherwise. But a true warrior, someone with courage and cunning and strength of mind, he doesn't give in. He's not like the others. He stands out."

Chorizo's voice seemed to be getting smaller and smaller. He was saying things—what were they again?—that she really should argue about, but her mind felt half-borne away on some current of its own. It was all she could do to keep up.

"Your role is to be someone else," he said gently.

"The one who dies," Nicola said.

Chorizo smiled. "Don't worry, first we have a little fun. Now. Do you like this?"

"It feels a little cold," Nicola complained.

"My hand?"

"I mean, we haven't led up to it."

"Oh we've been leading up to it all night," he said. He began to smooth her hair away from her temple. "Don't you know why language was invented?"

"Why was language invented?"

"Women wanted some foreplay."

Nicola looked up at the shelf of rubber dolls, some with their legs crossed, others who looked like a eunuch's idea of Marilyn Monroe. For a moment their heads seemed to bob toward her, as if they were bowing in prayer.

"Oh God, are those dolls going to be watching?" she asked. Her voice seemed to be coming out of someplace other than her mouth but she tried not to be distracted by that. "I'm not doing anything if those dolls will be watching."

"I don't think you have much choice," Chorizo told her, and he pulled her down next to him on the bed. He held her down by her two shoulders and looked at her face.

"I won't hurt you," he said.

Nicola said, "Bring it on."

She wanted to sound tough but instead she felt herself slip further—a soft, sinking feeling as he began touching her hair, her face, her arms. She remembered her fantasy about him. Was it only a week ago? Not even a week. But it's all right, it's all right, Nicola said to herself. She tried to concentrate on plan B, the details of which were fading away.

Because she was finding herself feeling . . . what was it? Almost content. The room was warm. The chemise was soft. Even the futon felt comfortable beneath her back. And, oh my God, he was good at this. She opened her eyes and found she was right: the dolls were all watching.

It was important to fight, but at the same time the thought came to her that maybe she wouldn't. How long had she felt the need to control every little thing? And yet, Nicola thought, I'm essentially powerless.

But it doesn't matter. I don't have to care. She could hear the wind outside, and the heated air coming in through a wall vent. Even the factory smell on the futon frame didn't bother her. What was it he called her? The competent woman. But I don't have to be that way, Nicola thought. She let Chorizo touch her and it felt so easy, it felt really good.

All she had to do was nothing.

"Are you worried?" Chorizo asked, his mouth close to her ear. "Do you know what is happening?"

Nicola thought for a moment.

"I care but I'm unattached to the outcome."

Chorizo laughed.

"Run away with me, Nicola," he said again. "My wife would love it if I showed up with a girl."

Nicola was looking at his face. "You know who you look like? Omar Sharif."

"Come here," he said.

She started to close her eyes again but a flash of silver caught her attention. Chorizo had something in his hand. Scissors.

"What's that?" she asked.

"Part of the game."

He leaned over and snipped off one of the straps to her chemise.

"What are you doing?" she said. Suddenly her voice sounded shrewish and her mind pulled a little, trying to snap awake.

"You know the game," he said. He cut a strip along one of the sheer front panels. "You saw the video. We do a little cutting first."

Nicola was appalled. "Wait! Do you know how much this cost?"

Chorizo laughed. "You really are funny. Listen to the sound." He cut another strip. "Isn't that marvelous? The clothes get cut away. Destroyed. Think of it as a symbol. Soon they will be in pieces around you."

He cut loosely, not bothering to keep straight lines. She could feel the side of the cold steel scissors touch her belly once, then again. The blades moved up and down like two pistons. The beautiful black chemise would soon be a rag and she couldn't help herself: the waste-fulness of it annoyed her.

"Let's move on!" Nicola said. "I don't like this part."

"Don't fight me on this," Chorizo said smoothly, and Nicola suddenly felt fully awake. Where had she heard that before? Then she remembered: Guy.

"Women should not fight," Chorizo told her.

"What?"

"According to a study I read about. It's not in their nature. They don't fight or flee, they . . . what was the phrase?" He stopped cutting and let the scissors dangle for a moment.

"They tend and befriend," Nicola said bitterly.

"Yes, that's it. Tend and befriend."

"You think I'm being friendly?"

He seemed to consider this. "Well, you could smile more," he said jokingly. Oh my God, thought Nicola. Something rushed through her: a sharp slice of anger. Was he just Guy in a Turkish suit? Chorizo opened the scissor blades and began to cut through the middle of her garment.

"I'm not going to hurt you," he said again. Then he stopped cutting for a moment and bent down. Nicola closed her eyes. She felt his lips on the side of her mouth. She felt stronger, as though that last spurt of anger kick-started her adrenaline. How could she listen to any more of this? It was time to take over.

"It's not me I'm worried about," she said and, pulling back, she lifted her knee and kicked her foot squarely into his groin.

"Aaaah! Ah ah!" Chorizo shouted, bending over double by the side of the bed.

"It's Dave I'm worried about," she told him.

Quickly, she pulled her hand out of the handcuff and threw the ring around Chorizo's hand, locking him to the futon frame. Then she threw the scissors across the room and grabbed Chorizo's pants, which had the handcuff keys in them.

She wrapped Chorizo's pants around her elbow, picked up Dave's minitool, and ran to the back door. The glass window above it looked thin and old.

The minitool had GPS software in it but she had to get the tool out of the building so it could send out its mapping signal.

Nicola pressed the GPS pager, took a breath, then drove her elbow into the middle of the pane. Glass shattered everywhere. Please, Nicola thought, please let Davette have her minitool turned on. She threw the minitool out into the yard, catching a few shards on her hand as she did so. For a moment she stopped to put her wrist to her mouth.

But Chorizo was up already, moving toward her with one hand cupped over his groin and dragging the futon frame with him. Nicola stared at him for a second. Jesus, he was strong. She took a few steps toward him, then kicked him at his sternum.

"Dave, get up," she shouted, as Chorizo struggled to stand again. But Dave was way beyond getting up. Nicola grabbed him and started to fall because her body was getting woozier and woozier from the drug and for the first time in her life she really felt like she was seventy-five percent water, like the scientists said.

"You broke my nail!" Chorizo shouted.

Nicola got behind Dave and grabbed hold of him in the lifesaving position then she began to drag him, chair and all, to the door.

"You'll never recover," Chorizo said. "I gave you too much."

"Oh shut up, Chorizo."

"Stop calling me that! It makes me sound fat."

She was trying, but she couldn't get Dave out the door. The chair stuck in the doorframe and Dave was on the wrong side, facing Chorizo. In a moment Chorizo had gotten hold of Dave's leg with his free hand. Nicola was on the other side.

"I don't really care which one of you dies first," Chorizo said, and he put his free hand around Dave's neck.

Nicola ran to the car and, oh my God, thank God, it was unlocked. Her purse was in the front seat. She grabbed it and dumped everything out on the garage floor and found her last remaining option—the stun gun disguised as a highlighter. It had fooled Chorizo at least. But this was the floor model, the one Morgan used, and she prayed that the batteries were still good. Was the orange light on, or off? It was hard to tell in this light. Staring at it, her eyes felt crossed at the back.

Well she didn't have time. What was it Chorizo had said about faith, or hope? But he wasn't talking about battery power, which at this point was the only thing Nicola cared about.

It would have to work: after he got through with her, and Dave, he would go after Carmen. Now that he had seen Nicola's address on her driver's license, he knew where Carmen was. And, like herself, Carmen knew everything.

But Nicola didn't know that going back through the garage would be so hard; she felt she was moving through sludge, she was running in a dream. She had to get back but it would take a couple of months at least at the rate she was going. Help, she thought. Then: I've got to do this.

Her adrenaline burst was fading and meanwhile Chorizo was choking Dave; she could hear Dave gurgle and gasp as she came up behind him with the stun gun in her hand. She willed herself to focus, but it was getting harder. Before Chorizo had time to do anything she thrust the stunner in his face then kept it there as he squirmed. Stick to the task, stick to the task, she thought. She held the stun gun hard to his cheek.

He didn't make a noise, just fell away onto the floor. But how creepy—his eyes were still open. She could see how he was struggling even now, a second later, to regain control of his body. How long do I have, she had asked Morgan? Long enough to get the hell out, ha ha. Nicola saw the deep yellow bruises on Dave's poor soft neck and his bluing lips and she was angry now, really angry.

"Don't be afraid," she said. But was she speaking to Dave, or herself?

Nicola rolled Dave's chair into Chorizo, who was still struggling on the floor, then she pushed Dave around the side of the chair and off of it and pulled him through the doorway. Her arms felt like noodles. I will not let the drug take over, she thought. I will not let it. I have to stay conscious.

Everything now was in absolutes.

Chorizo began thrashing around under the chair and got it moved aside, then he pulled the futon frame with him to the door and the futon turned sideways a little as he did so. When he saw that he tried rolling it all the way over to fit it lengthwise through but that didn't work either.

"You don't have the time," he said.

He pulled on the handcuff then looked around for something, a tool. "I'll find a way to break the frame. Meanwhile, you'll be dead. Do you know how much I gave you? You should be dead now."

Nicola knew she couldn't waste energy talking to him anymore. Her mind was fighting to fade, she could feel herself going. The adrenaline was gone. Soon she'd have no more control. Was she dying or just passing out? It felt as though she was dying.

Strength of mind, she thought. She wanted to close her eyes just for a second but she was afraid she would never open them again. She was afraid even to blink too slowly. With an effort she pulled out the Narcon from her bra and uncapped it.

"What's that?" Chorizo said.

Her mind let go for a moment. She struggled. She wasn't thinking so much as groping around looking for a handhold. I am here. I am here. She opened her mouth to speak; she wanted to say it aloud, I am here; she wanted to tell herself this in a way she would really believe it.

"I am," Nicola said. It was all she could manage.

Chorizo was watching her. It didn't matter what she had. Timing was everything. He smiled.

"It's too late, little one," he said.

"No," she said, and she turned and took Dave's arm and plunged the needle into, she hoped, one of his veins.

Twenty-two

The kitchen featured a Viking stove, there was a full Jacuzzi in the master bath, but the living room had nothing except stained wall-to-wall carpeting and a cassette player the size of a microwave oven.

Nicola had brought the cassette player herself. Grandmaster Flash was singing with a voice like asphalt pouring out through the speakers: "It's like a jungle sometimes, it makes me wonder how I keep from going under."

Nicola knelt on the stained carpet to lower the volume.

"You have to picture it with furniture," she told Audrey.

But Audrey wasn't looking at the room; she was standing in front of the picture window next to Lou. "I can't believe this view," she said.

Lou said, "Isn't it amazing?"

"Chairs, couches, lamps," Nicola continued. She stepped up to the doorframe to examine a curl of peeling paint. "Maybe a couple of bookcases flanking the fireplace."

"This view is better than mine," Audrey complained. "That can't be fair."

"It's not better, it's just closer."

"It's not fair," Audrey repeated. She was still wearing her coat, and she looked down at Lester, whom she held by a leash. "Your new home," she told her.

"Well, not for a couple of weeks yet," Nicola corrected.

"By the way, Carmen called this morning. She found another camera in the closet. She said it was never installed properly, though."

For the past few months Nicola had been living with Audrey and Declan while she looked for a place of her own. Carmen was living in the house behind the Russians. Nicola couldn't wait to start using dressers again instead of cardboard boxes and milk crates. I'll need a dining room table, she suddenly realized.

"Oh and here, I have something for you, too," Audrey said to Lou. She handed him a newspaper.

"What, my review?"

"Congratulations."

"Your review made it in?" Nicola asked, coming over to look.

"I found it this morning," Audrey said.

Lou looked at the cover. "They said next week."

"Good thing I checked."

He began turning the pages, dropping the sections he didn't want on the floor. He was wearing his standard uniform, the white shirt and the clean blue jeans, and when he found the review he folded the paper carefully in half.

"Do you want to hear it?"

"Absolutely," Nicola said.

"I'll skip the boring intro."

Audrey sat down on the carpet and threw the leash over to Nicola, who unclipped it from Lester's collar then sat down, too. They were leaning against the wall, their backs to the view. The room was large and square and seemed even larger to Nicola without furniture. How will I fill this up, she wondered?

Lou cleared his throat then tilted his chin. "Blah blah blah, okay. 'Nicosia is the first truly upscale Cypriot-inspired restaurant in San Francisco,' " he read, " 'And well worth the problems with parking. After you make your way through the strangely organized menu, you'll find the food, especially the starters, lusty and bucolic.' "

"What does that mean, lusty and bucolic?" Audrey asked.

Lou was still standing. "I was thinking in terms of hearty and country," he said. "I was trying to do some hearty and country combination."

"I think it works," Nicola told him.

" 'Their house salad,' " he continued, " 'has an interesting ingredient: pickled caper thorns, which are native to the island of Cyprus. The antipasto sampler ($6.95) is another tongue-pleaser, with its assortment of grilled and marinated vegetables—notably the kappari, which is somewhat like a turnip.' "

He described a few entrees—the slow-cooked lamb, a spicy smoked sausage called loukanika. Nicola listened to his slow, even voice—like the voice of a poet, she thought—while she looked around the room. She realized that her furniture would fill up exactly one-fourth of the space. When she had first seen the house, before she made her offer, this room was filled with low couches and faux jade statues and circular stone tables with little buddhas and framed pictures of students wearing tasseled caps. It was filled with someone else's life.

But now that was over. Now every room was empty, waiting to start again.

Lou moved his fingers over the newspaper. "Okay, I'll skip the dis on Cypriot wine, skip the lesser entrees, and get on to the desserts."

"Those were good," Nicola said.

" 'The desserts were good to fantastic,' " Lou read. " 'For my money, I'd go back to the fruit mousse with mango and lime, or the savory vanilla crème brûlée.' "

"That *was* good," Nicola agreed.

" 'Not all the desserts seemed particularly Mediterranean, but they all come with nuts and a delicious hard cheese called Kefalotiri'— I'm not sure if I'm pronouncing that right—'along with a pitcher of sweet Cyprus honey.' " Lou moved his thumb to the bottom of the column. "And then there's just parking information, restaurant times, and prices."

He looked up. "The end," he said.

"Wow," Audrey said.

"That was great!" Nicola told him.

"One hundred and fifty dollars," Lou stated. He looked over the paper again, then folded it carefully and put it in his back pocket. "Plus two free meals."

"They pay for your meals?" Audrey asked.

"Well, I can write them off."

Nicola stood up and turned to look out the window. The previous owners had left the blinds, thank God, so she didn't have to worry about *that*. The house was about ten blocks from the ocean, and from here the waves looked like a line of snow on the shore. Half a dozen sailboats stood huddled to the north, waiting for the start of a race.

"The fog is still holding back. There's going to be a nice sunset tonight."

Lou looked up. "It's great to be able to see the weather."

"This house is wonderful," Nicola agreed. She watched the sailboats disperse like tiny flags on the water; the race had begun. "Who knew Chorizo would be wanted in New York *and* California?"

"Reward money. I love it. You could say your home was federally funded," Audrey said.

"No more landlords." Nicola smiled. "And I'll have my Lester

Pearl with me again." Lester moved closer to Nicola, who began scratching her chin. After a moment Lester turned her head slightly to get just the right scratch angle.

"Will you miss the baby girl?" Nicola asked Audrey.

"I'm afraid to answer that," Audrey said.

"Well, you have Declan. And of course Scooter now."

"Always your cast-offs."

The doorbell rang. When Nicola answered it she found Davette on the doorstep with the minitool in one hand and a mobile phone in the other. Her hair was dyed a very yellowy blonde.

"*Now* where am I?" Davette said into the phone. She listened for a second, then stepped into the house.

"What are you doing?" Nicola asked her.

Davette put the phone to her chest, covering the mouthpiece. "I'm messing with Dave," she whispered. She asked about the bathroom.

Nicola showed her where it was, then went back into the living room saying, "A constant source of fun."

"What's that?" Audrey asked.

"The minitool companion." She rolled her eyes.

"You know, you should be grateful for the minitool companion," Lou reminded her. "Since it saved your life."

"Oh, I am. I am. Believe me," Nicola said. She sat down next to Audrey again and pulled Lester onto her lap. "I'm also still amazed that Davette actually had hers on that night."

Lou was still standing by the window. "We were in the motel office with four police officers and a medic team," he told Audrey, "and Davette kept going, What's that beeping noise? Then she realized it was coming from her purse."

"Yeah, I heard that part," Audrey said.

Nicola began scratching Lester's short puggy nose. Her memory of that night was like something underwater; everything was further away than it looked. "Apparently by the time they got to Robert's house I was passed out in the garage," she said, "and Chorizo was trying to unscrew the door hinges with a pen cap."

"I heard that part, too."

"Dave couldn't work the garage door. He said the Narcon gave him a vicious headache."

Audrey began doing stretching exercises on the floor. She said, "You know, you've pretty much told me the story every day since it happened."

"It's a cool device, that mapping system thing," Lou said. "What do you call it again?"

"GPS."

"Maybe even twice a day," said Audrey.

"GPS," Lou repeated. "Amazing. We knew right where to go."

"Dave has certainly made some interesting purchases in his young life," Audrey commented, bending over her leg. "My favorite so far is the camouflage pants with hidden food-storage units."

Nicola stopped scratching Lester for a moment. "Yeah, but look where it got him! All that survival preparation made him over-confident. I mean, I can't believe he actually *called* Chorizo. Called him. On the telephone. Then agreed to meet him. Jesus."

"The good news is we never learn from our mistakes," Lou told her. He knelt down and began stroking Lester's back. "You know what the Buddhists say."

"What do the Buddhists say?"

"The past is merely preparation."

"The Buddhists don't say that," Nicola said.

"Really? Then maybe it's the NBA."

Nicola laughed.

"But you know, Dave is even more insane now," she said, teasing Lester's fur up a little with a hairdressing motion. "He's making Davette wear a beeper around her wrist. He's like some frantic mother."

Audrey said, "Listen, you should be glad Dave is insane."

"I am glad Dave is insane. It's just, he gave me my own gas mask for saving his life. This is his idea of a present. It has a left side filter mount and adjustable cinch straps."

"What's a filter mount?" Audrey asked.

"A mount for a filter?" Nicola suggested.

"Ha ha."

Davette came out of the bathroom and handed Nicola the phone. "Dave wants to tell you something. Whoa, nice view," she said.

"Hi, Dave," Nicola said.

"The GPS so does work inside a building," Dave told her.

"Really?"

"We've been testing it out," he said.

"So where am I now?"

"Like I told Davette, you're all at Audrey's house. And I am inside my mom's garage as we speak."

Nicola shook her head at Davette. "Are you now."

"Totally and completely inside a building."

"Well, why don't you come over to Audrey's house and we'll feed you some dinner?"

"What're you having?"

"What are we having for dinner?" Nicola asked Lou.

"Fettuccine with pancetta."

"Fettuccine with pancetta," she told Dave.

"Cool," said Dave.

Nicola gave Davette back the phone and began rolling down the window blinds. "We'll meet you at your house," she told Audrey.

"Okay. By the way: great house," Audrey said. "Aside from the better view I completely approve."

"Yeah, TFO," Davette agreed.

Nicola looked at her. "TFO?"

"Totally far out."

When the other two were gone, Lou helped Nicola lock up. "Well, you have your house now," he said. "Bigger, better, and almost twenty percent your own."

Nicola smiled.

"So what's next? Retirement perhaps?"

"I didn't get *that* much money," Nicola said. "But I do see a future where I fire Guy and take over the company."

"Or we could live on my reviews."

"Those won't keep me in lingerie, I'm afraid."

"We'd have to eat out a lot," Lou said. "We'd have to go to a new restaurant every night."

"Can we make that sacrifice?"

"I think we can."

They stood by the front door in the semidarkness. Lester was sniffing something on the floorboards. Again Nicola felt the emptiness of the house. In two weeks she would begin to fill it with her chairs, her stereo components, her choice of rugs and photos and kitchen equipment. A new life. Her new life. She needed more pictures for the walls; the toilet had a rusty flusher; some tile was cracked in the kitchen. There was so much to do. But she had begun to make lists, and that always made her happy.

"You would have to move here, you know," she said to Lou. "You can't commute from New Jersey just for dinner."

He took her in his arms. "Well, it looks like we're working in that direction anyway," he said.

"Yes, it does."

"I'm here a lot."

"Every weekend at least."

"And your new place will be big enough now."

"Two people and a dog," Nicola said. "We can definitely do that."

"Besides, I like California."

"You do?"

Lou kissed her forehead. "The food is very, very good," he said.